"How do you

I looked up

tioned that rig

"Yes," he ge~~~~~~~~~ a tapestry as he walked around the base of the altar. "Princess Lucille, King Alfred's only child, has been taken by an evil dragon."

"What? Hold on a minute." I looked up at the tapestry and the giant lizard embroidered there. If I squinted, it appeared that the dragon was picking pieces of knight out of its teeth. I looked from that to Elhared. The wizard didn't *look* insane. Then again, he was a wizard, and they were not renowned for mental stability. "You just said 'dragon.'"

"A small one."

"You're asking me to rescue a princess from a *small* dragon?"

"King Alfred the Strident has pledged a great reward for whoever saves his daughter from the dragon's clutches, and returns with her and the dragon's head."

"And I'm sure that will make some warrior knight very happy."

"Frank, you can't tell me you are uninterested in a reward from the king?"

"I'm more interested in living to spend it."

Dragon • Princess

S. Andrew Swann

DAW BOOKS, INC.

DONALD A. WOLLHEIM, FOUNDER

375 Hudson Street, New York, NY 10014

**ELIZABETH R. WOLLHEIM
SHEILA E. GILBERT
PUBLISHERS**

www.dawbooks.com

First Printing, May 2014
1 2 3 4 5 6 7 8 9

For Princess Lilli.

CHAPTER 1

My name is Frank Blackthorne, and I'm going to tell you a story.

While it is customary to delegate such duties to historians, scribes, poets, minstrels, and such, there are two primary reasons I'm taking on this duty myself. First, I'm not a person of historical note. My deeds have not been particularly heroic, and, generally speaking, epic ballads are not composed to honor mediocre thieves whose primary claim to fame is a run of particularly bad luck.

Second, those drunken bastards always get everything wrong.

So I will tell my tale myself, even if doing so may infringe on the rights of some storyteller's guild. After what I've been through, the thought of an angry army of mandolin-wielding bards coming after my hide holds no terror for me. Besides which, it gives me the opportunity to skip the boring prologue where I'm supposed to tell you of the ten-thousand-year history of the world leading up to your less-than-noble hero's birth.

I *hate* that.

So if you don't know anything about the regional politics across my part of the world, the geography, or the local religions, you'll just have to hang on and catch up.

The important part of this story begins in the Kingdom of Lendowyn. On any reasonable map it's a tiny smudge on an unattractive stretch of southern coastline. It's a boiled potato of a country; soft, bland, cheap, with a distinct absence of anything to recommend it beyond the minimum requirements of its own existence. Very few people choose to make a destination of Lendowyn. The majority of those within its borders are there only on their way to someplace else.

Myself included.

I had ventured within Lendowyn simply because it intersected the straight-line course I had taken south, away from the lost Ziggurat of the Dark Lord Nâtlac. Now, after staring at the water for an hour or so in frustration, I realized my month-long retreat from that fiasco had simultaneously run out of both land and money, and the far end of Lendowyn wasn't nearly far enough from Grünwald for my comfort.

It really wasn't fair that they put an ocean in my way.

The unfortunate geography didn't give me many choices. I could follow the coast, which cost me little but time, but would painfully slow my retreat from the royal court of Grünwald. I could attempt to escape on an outbound ship, but I didn't have the resources to buy passage. That left the unpleasant prospect of being pressed into service aboard one of those scows, and terminating such employment was a bit more difficult than obtaining it. I'll not discuss the fate of stowaways. I wasn't yet quite *that* desperate.

The day was still young.

My last option was to blow what was left of my funds getting drunk, and worry about my problems later. I polled myself, and that choice won by unanimous vote.

At midday, I wandered into a nameless dockside tavern to drown what sorrows I could manage with the copper I had left. Unfortunately, with two coppers to my name, drowning them wasn't really an option. I had to settle for taking one sorrow out for a quick dip in rather shallow waters.

The cheapest drink in the place was called Mermaid's Milk. Perhaps in the wider universe there is a beverage more misnamed, but I have yet to hear tell of it. Two coppers bought me a large flagon of the stuff. The liquid was gray-green with an opalescent sheen that did not seem natural. It smelled vile, and I asked the barkeep what was in it.

"Seaweed, goat's milk, and fermented herring," he said without looking up from wiping down the bar.

"Of course."

I turned and noticed glances and raised eyebrows from the scruffier denizens of this scruffy establishment. Their reaction told me that I was about to punish myself with something that was usually only consumed upon losing a bet.

I walked back to an empty corner table with my purchase. I could smell the fish now, and the sheen seemed to be oils floating on the grayish milk. *Lactating mermaid my ass*, I thought. *This looks more like something from an ogre's backside.*

My eyes watered, and I wasn't sure if it was the fish smell or the alcohol.

I chalked it up to the latest in a long line of bad decisions. Put in those terms, it was barely even perceptible when aligned against my last epic failure of judgment. In hindsight, the hideous concoction I was seriously contemplating drinking was only the penultimate consequence of my last bad idea . . .

I raised my flagon to the other patrons and said, "A toast to the Royal Court of Grünwald. May all their prayers be answered, at length and in person."

No one paid attention to me. I slammed back as much of the Mermaid's Milk as quickly as I could before I started tasting the stuff.

Now, the aforesaid bad idea—the one that led to me being broke, on the run, and toasting my enemies with the vilest beverage that could be consumed by a man who wished to continue breathing—had, like most bad ideas, seemed perfectly reasonable at the time.

I had accumulated a debt to the Thieves' Guild of Grünwald in the amount of six months' worth of dues. Not that I hadn't paid them, you understand. But when the rat-faced individual to whom I had been giving a cut of my take disappeared to parts unknown along with a substantial amount of the guild's money, it became my responsibility to make up my portion of the shortfall.

That's what's known as honor among thieves.

When presented the choice of doing some contract work, or losing the middle two fingers on my right hand. . . . Well, like I said, it seemed reasonable to me.

A gentleman with far more money than good sense had hired the guild's services to retrieve a sacred scroll from an abandoned temple. The guild gave the job to me as a means to even up my sudden debt. I suspected that they had taken an advance payment considerably more than what they said I owed, but I didn't argue. Fingers are rather important in my line of work.

Besides, it should have been a rather simple job for a thief such as myself.

As long as I ignored the fact that the temple was dedicated to the Dark Lord Nâtlac. That's the kind of name you don't bring up too often unless you want to risk earthquakes, crop failures, or livestock birthing young with one head too many. That was probably the primary reason the guild elders decided to ship the job my way.

I told myself, a little foolishly, that it wasn't that big a deal. I'd just wear gloves, and try to not look at the scroll too closely.

It'll be fine, I had thought, *in, out, no problem.*

Which brings me to the *other* serious problem with the job. Everyone had overstated the abandonment of the temple. "Overstated," as in, bald-faced lied.

Turns out there are worse people to have after you than the Thieves' Guild of Grünwald.

I discovered the hard way that the whole Royal Court of the Kingdom of Grünwald had taken up the worship of the Dark Lord Nâtlac. And, as with all courtly fads, they all took it *way* too seriously.

They didn't take kindly to me falling from the shadows above and disrupting their sacrifice. I really shouldn't have done it, but there are few enough virgins in the world and I really couldn't stand by and watch them waste one. So I grabbed the naked young woman, kicked urns of goat entrails onto the queen and prince regent—at least, I really hope they had been goat entrails—and escaped in the ensuing confusion.

I managed to deliver her safely to her father's farm. Unfortunately, while *she* was very grateful, her dad took issue with me assisting her in the avoidance of any virgin-hunting cultists in the future. So I retreated, leaving one less virgin in the world, but at least one who was still around to enjoy it.

I'd been on the run from Grünwald ever since.

I set the half-empty flagon on the table in front of me. The other half of my beverage sat in my gut like a large rotten fish that had been soaked in oil and set on fire. When I let go of the flagon to cover my mouth, I felt somewhat surprised when the flagon did not slide back on the table toward me, since everything seemed canted at a rather steep angle.

I tried to sit up and my chair started tilting backward.

That shouldn't happen.

The back of the chair and the back of my head hit the wall behind me simultaneously. I heard the thud about three seconds before it registered on me that it was my skull that had bounced off of the timber framing. By then I was leaning up against the wall, as if that had been my plan all along.

"Ouch," I said quietly.

This was a record drunk for me. The Mermaid's Milk had slammed what was left of my good sense so hard that I didn't even care about my throbbing head or the fact that my mouth tasted like I'd chewed out the lining from a fishmonger's boots. My stomach screamed in rebellion, but my brain wasn't really listening.

Somewhere, back in the land of the sober, someone called my name.

I heard the words, "Are you Frank Blackthorne?" and it took a few more seconds to realize that the speaker was referring to me.

Normally it would be axiomatic that a stranger calling my name in an unfamiliar location spelled no uncertain trouble. The Thieves' Guild and the Court of Grünwald were just the latest in a long series of people who wanted to physically arbitrate some disagreement with me. Sober me would have already noted possible exits and be a half step toward them. The current me, post Mermaid's Milk, narrowed his eyes at the approaching stranger and folded his arms across his chest.

The intent of the pose might have seemed intimidating, but really I was just afraid of accidentally rolling off the chair, and the daylight from outside had just become unaccountably more intense. I swallowed a belch that was equal parts bile and swamp gas and asked, "Who wants to know?"

At first I thought the old man approaching me was swaying, but I think that was just a side effect of the whole tavern rocking. He was of that indeterminate age between threescore and dead, and wore rich robes that were so out of place in the tavern that even in my impaired state they made me wonder what was keeping the less savory denizens of the tavern from liberating this man of his purse. I mean, I knew *my* excuse; it sat on the table smelling of fish oil, seaweed, and sour goat's milk.

He slid into a chair across from me, his back to a dozen lowly thugs more sober than I, and I realized that the locals knew this guy.

Great.

My visitor lowered his hood, wrinkled his nose at my beverage, and told me, "My name is Elhared," as if that should mean something.

It probably should have, and I fumbled with a dangling thread of familiarity in my booze-sodden memories.

When in doubt, or drunk, stall.

"And?" I said quietly, somewhat impressed at my sudden eloquence.

"And I am the court wizard of Lendowyn, here on behalf of the crown."

Had I been drinking at that moment, Wizard Elhared would have been the recipient of an instant shower of fermented herring. Instead, I leaned forward, and the front of my chair was reintroduced to the floor with a bone-jarring impact. I splayed my arms before me to prevent myself from flopping face first into the table. I said, again drawing on unplumbed depths of erudite reserve, "You're Elhared the Unwise?"

That was the point I realized that the other denizens of the bar had been slowly and quietly taking their leave of the establishment. At my outburst, the remaining population dispensed with the "slowly and quietly" part.

Elhared frowned slightly at me. The way the skin on his face wrinkled, it seemed a habitual expression. His skin had that corpselike pallor associated with wizards, goblins, and other underground denizens. He had a close-trimmed beard that was so translucent that it seemed to blend seamlessly into his skin. "Few people have the temerity to use that name to my face."

"Yes, but I'm drunk," I responded. So drunk, in fact, that I was only at that moment connecting the evacuation of the bar with Elhared's arrival and my big mouth.

"You certainly are," Elhared said. His mouth twitched into a smile that seemed so alien on his face I briefly feared that I was beginning to hallucinate. "But I still need to talk to you."

"Of course you do." In my head I had finally managed to dig up a belated paranoia. Here was an official of the Royal Court of Lendowyn, and I was forced to consider what kind of relationship Lendowyn might have with Grünwald. Any official contact by someone at that level could not bode well. I tried pushing myself to my feet and surprised myself by succeeding. However, I still had a death grip on the table holding myself upright, spoiling my chance at stalking out of the tavern. "I don't have to talk to you."

"No," Elhared said. "You don't *have* to. But I have a proposition."

"A proposition?" After a slight hesitation, I slid back into my chair, never letting go of the table.

"Yes. How would you feel about saving a princess?"

CHAPTER 2

I stared at him for a good fifteen seconds before my drunken eloquence kicked in. "What?"

Elhared sighed, reached in his robes, and pulled out a small silver flask. The scrollwork engraving on it glinted in the sunlight from the open door, stinging my eyes. He unscrewed the top and held it out to me. "Do us both a favor, Francis, and take this."

"Don't call me Francis, I hate that." I grabbed the flask and looked at it. "What is this?"

"A medicinal preparation, to help restore your wits."

"My wits are fine."

"Perhaps. I suppose I should I leave you to the cultists of Nâtlac then?" He reached for his flask back, but I didn't let go.

"What do you know about that?"

"How did you think I knew who you are?"

I waved my free hand and wiggled my fingers. "Magic," I intoned.

"Much more prosaic. Disrupting the main feast day of one of the Seven Dark Lords of the Underworld tends to be talked about in arcane circles. Especially the part about the entrails."

"That *was* amusing."

"Your swashbuckling rescue of the fair maiden made me think you were the man for this job. Perhaps I was wrong." He tugged at the flask, and I pulled it away.

"Hold on a minute there." I sniffed the flask. "What did you say was in this?"

"Don't concern yourself."

I never claimed that my judgment improved with intoxication. But the smell curling up from the open flask was more wretched than the Mermaid's Milk; it cut through my sinuses like an angry troll with a dull axe. I set the flask down on the table and said, "I don't think I'm drinking *that*."

"Oh, *drinking* it isn't necessary."

I looked up at Elhared, who seemed to be suddenly glowing as everything around us became painfully bright. I felt woozy, and clutched my stomach. "I don't feel so good."

I pitched forward, but I don't remember ever hitting the floor.

Cheap as it was, Mermaid's Milk did not skimp on the hangover. The axe-wielding troll inhabiting my skull had disposed of his weapon and contented himself with gnawing on the backs of my eyeballs. I groaned myself awake and cautiously opened my eyelids slightly.

I saw flickering candlelight and my skull-troll started kicking my temples in time to my pulse.

Given my profession, I have awakened in places far worse than I found myself now. The surface I'd been sprawled upon seemed to have been designed for the purpose, there was a roof above me, and the general character of the chamber suggested that it was meant for human habitation despite how disorganized it might seem at the moment.

I slowly pushed myself upright, and my fingers sank into several layers of brocade fabric that buried the chaise I'd been lying on. The fabric was rich and showed some glints of golden thread, but my motion pushed out a small cloud of dust that made me sneeze.

The skull-troll *loved* that.

After the pain receded and I could focus through my watering eyes again, I tried to figure out where exactly I was. The chamber was stone and windowless, lit by thick candles in iron sconces entombed in what seemed several decades' worth of wax deposits. Shelves climbed up three of four walls in a chaotic ascent toward a vaulted ceiling. The shelves held a variety of objects: books, jars of herbs, powders and liquids, yellowing skulls of human and other origin, loose sheets of parchment, wood carvings and small metal tools.

Frankly, my present location wouldn't have

been much clearer if Elhared had written "Wizard's Lair" across the ceiling in glowing mystical runes.

The hangover left me in a foul mood, especially after such an abbreviated bender. There was a copper's worth of fermented herring and seaweed-flavored goat's milk sitting abandoned in a tavern somewhere. I felt cheated.

I rubbed my temples and called out, "Your 'medicinal preparation' leaves something to be desired."

From beyond a doorless entry into an adjoining chamber, I heard Elhared's voice say, "Nonsense." He strode into the room and looked me up and down. "You're awake. You're sober. Why don't you get to your feet?" An air of impatience infused the man, and I almost expected him to say, "Time is of the essence," or some other nonsense. Instead, he just stood there, allowing me to realize that I was making a wizard wait, one powerful enough to wrangle a cushy job from a royal court. It might only be the *Lendowyn* royal court, but at some point I needed to break my streak of pissing off people who could do me serious harm. I pushed myself up off the chaise with a groan and another cloud of dust.

"Good man," he said with another surreal smile, and slapped me on the back, guiding me into the chamber he'd just come from. If the room I had awakened in had said "Wizard" in no uncertain terms, the room Elhared led me to sang a wizardly aria. Torches joined the candlelight, along with smoldering brass braziers that gave the room the scent of a burning herb garden. Glyphs, runes, and circles had been drawn on the flagstone floor in dense chaotic patterns made of chalk, salt, paint, and some other materials I didn't examine too closely. I made sure to follow Elhared's steps exactly across the unmarked portions of the floor. He led me across to a stone altar too reminiscent of the one I'd seen in the ceremony honoring the Dark Lord Nâtlac.

That was probably paranoia. After all, most sacrificial altars do share some basic similarities: waist-high stone, generally coffin-size, anchors for restraints, depressions in the upper surface that tended to bear rust-colored stains. No reason to think this one had anything to do with Nâtlac.

That thought wasn't as reassuring as it should have been.

Fortunately, the only thing on the altar at the moment was a small cache of military gear: helmet, armor, a broadsword, that sort of thing. On the wall behind the altar, a tapestry hung, the brocade showing an unnerving portrait of a dragon sitting on a huge pile of gold and gems mixed with human bones.

"So, Francis—"

I sighed and rubbed my temples.

"Sorry, *Frank*. How do you feel about saving a princess?"

I looked up at him. "Yeah, I think you mentioned that right before the floor hit me."

"Yes," he gestured at the tapestry as he walked around the base of the altar. "Princess Lucille, King Alfred's only child, has been taken by an evil dragon."

"What? Hold on a minute." I looked up at the tapestry and the giant lizard embroidered there. If I squinted, it appeared that the dragon was picking pieces of knight out of its teeth. I looked from that to Elhared. The wizard didn't *look* insane. Then again, he was a wizard, and they were not renowned for mental stability. "You just said 'dragon.'"

"A small one."

"You're asking me to rescue a princess from a *small* dragon?"

"King Alfred the Strident has pledged a great reward for whoever saves his daughter from the dragon's clutches, and returns with her and the dragon's head."

"And I'm sure that will make some warrior knight very happy."

"Frank, you can't tell me you are uninterested in a reward from the king?"

"I'm more interested in living to spend it."

"Oh, the king is offering something much better than material wealth." Elhared reached up and took hold of one side of the tapestry and walked across behind the altar, drawing it aside. Hanging on the wall behind the tapestry was a life-size portrait of a stunning young woman, statuesque without being arrogant, youthful curves filling out her gown in dangerous places, amber-blond hair framing an expression that was half amusement and half seductive pout. "The Princess Lucille," he said unnecessarily.

Being a royal portrait, it had to be false advertising. But it served Elhared's purpose by making me picture myself saving her from some distress. Hell, it made me picture a lot of things.

I decided not to ask the old wizard why he kept a picture of his boss's beautiful young daughter down here hidden behind an altar.

"The king," Elhared said, "is offering his daughter's hand in marriage."

Of course he is. "You know, hypothetically speaking, I'd prefer gold."

"This reward is preferable to any material compensation, a peerage—"

"I can be quite creative with gold."

"—and a spot in the Royal Court of Lendowyn. I doubt that Grünwald would care to disturb the peaceful relations between our kingdoms for something as petty as a few misplaced entrails."

He had me there. A spot in the royal court would put me out of reach of most of the people who wanted my hide. Even in a court that couldn't afford to pay out actual rewards to mercenary princess saviors. And, believe me, offering the princess as a reward might make for a good ballad, but it was a sign of financial desperation.

I looked away from the princess's portrait and to Elhared. I decided that his smile was rather creepy, especially since I didn't know if the grin went with the mention of a hypothetical marriage to the young princess, or to the entrails reference. "Let's continue with the hypothetical," I said. "Your princess was abducted by a giant flying carnivorous fire-breathing lizard—"

"A small one."

"—A *small* flying carnivorous fire-breathing lizard." I tilted my head at the tapestry bunched up next to him, where the embroidered dragon was still visible. "Sounds like lunch to me. How do you know there's any princess left to rescue?"

"Do you know anything about dragons?"

"Almost as much as I know about princesses."

"You must know of their avarice."

I shrugged. "I know, nesting in piles of treasure and suchlike."

"Well it should be obvious that a dragon that can fly off with a hundred stone's worth of bull on the hoof—"

"I thought this was a small one?"

"—isn't after its next meal in our royal waif. She'd barely be an appetizer."

"Then why snatch her?"

"The same reason anyone abducts a royal personage."

I sighed. "Ransom."

"Of course."

"And the reason King Alfred doesn't pay up?"

"It's the principle of the thing, dear boy."

"And an empty treasury?"

"Sometimes it is necessary to be frugal."

I rubbed my temples trying to push back the hangover-troll who felt on the verge of chewing his way out of my skull. "Aren't a bunch of other wannabe dragon-slayers on this job, or is this invite only?"

"No the king made a public announcement a fortnight ago, and I've seen a dozen hopeful young men ride out the city gates in their quest for glory."

"Sounds like you got it handled. Why do you need me?"

Elhared slid the tapestry back, covering the portrait. "You might guess my motives aren't completely altruistic." *The wizard has an agenda? Color me shocked.* "You understand Lendowyn is not a particularly rich country." *Sort of like how Mermaid's Milk is not a particularly pleasant beverage.* "Well, a court wizard is something of an extravagance. Since there is a poverty of heirs as well as finances, and I do require a significant fraction of the kingdom's wealth to support my work, it behooves me to do what I can to ensure that the next-in-line to Alfred's throne is well aware of how much return the crown gets from that investment." *Translation, I'm skimming the treasury under the king's nose and the next monarch better be indebted to me.*

"I see."

"I'm sure you do. You seem reasonably intelligent."

"Uh huh."

"You still seem unsure."

"Of course I am. You want me to go slay a dragon! I'm a thief. I don't slay things."

"Then think of it as stealing the princess back."

"I don't think that helps."

"Ah. But I have something that *will* help. Something those dozen fools of King Alfred's do not have." He stepped behind the altar, facing me, and picked up a broadsword with an ornate golden handle in a somewhat worn leather scabbard. He held the hilt with one hand and with the other drew the scabbard so the blade was revealed.

The black blade burned with an unearthly light that infuriated hangover-troll who began trying to kick his way out of my head through the bridge of my nose. I gripped the troll's point of attack and squinted to see a somewhat blurry image of black iron engraved with blood-red runes that glowed as if the metal beneath were molten. I could even feel heat rising from the blade.

"Okay, magic sword, I get it. But you realize I'm not a swordsman, right?"

Elhared sheathed the blade. "This is *Dracheslayer*. Forged by blind dwarves in the diabolical heat found at the bottom of the Earth's Wound in the darkest land of Grundar. When it senses the blood of its adversary it will practically wield itself. You'll handle it as easily as that dagger on your belt."

He tossed it at me and I staggered back with the sudden weight as I caught it. "You have magical armor as well?"

"Afraid not, one priceless anti-dragon artifact pretty much maxes out the budget." He reached down and lifted an armor chest piece from where it rested on the altar. "This should be sufficient."

"You want me to go into battle with a dragon in used leather?"

"It's quite serviceable scale mail. Barely used. Only two squires have died in it."

"Don't people generally ride to the rescue of a princess in full plate?"

"Oh, you don't want that kind of hassle. All the fittings involved, you need two assistants just to get it on you—this is much more convenient—"

"And cheaper."

"—and you won't need to ride anywhere, the dragon's lair is less than a day's walk."

"You know where the dragon and the princess are?"

"Of course I do."

"And these dozen knights?"

"Oh, I'm sure one or two must have run into the dragon at some point." He set down the armor. "But they didn't have *Dracheslayer*."

I hefted the sword in my hands, every instinct screaming "bad idea." I think even the hangover-troll joined in the chorus, bellowing his objection. I hadn't seen such an obvious setup since the Thieves' Guild of Grünwald told me, "No problem, abandoned temple."

How do you gracefully tell a powerful wizard to shove off? To all appearances, Elhared could give the priests of Nâtlac a run for their money in the ancient mystical darkness department. Also, turning down a request to aid the king's daughter? Let's just say it seemed less than wise to have another house of royals after my head.

Not good.

Elhared cleared his throat.

"Yes?" I asked.

"I should mention, in addition to the princess you will also get first pick of the dragon's hoard before it's repatriated to replenish the Lendowyn treasury."

I had to wonder, did I *look* like a rube who would get drawn into any questionable enterprise just on the promise of some treasure?

To hell with it.

"Fine," I told him. "I'm in."

CHAPTER 3

I was still recovering from my hangover when Elhared the Unwise threw a bearskin cloak over my
shoulders and dragged me in front of King Alfred. I tried to protest. I wasn't in any state to meet
royalty. I still had a month's worth of back roads
to wash off me, I hadn't shaved in days, and for
some reason I expected that I looked like a drunk
someone had peeled off the floor of a dockside
tavern.

Elhared told me I looked the part of a barbarian
prince.

The wizard dragged me into the throne room
where the king was receiving envoys from some
kingdom of even less note than Lendowyn. When
the envoys were done, and the herald waved us
on, Elhared shoved me forward and presented me
as Sir Francis Blackthorne of the Northern Wastes,
here to serve the kingdom and rescue the princess.

The king eyed me with a sigh and muttered
something about scraping barrels. He was a very
large man, intimidating in a way that made me

suspect he had been absolutely terrifying in his prime. He looked at me with steely gray eyes in a way that made me suspect that he wanted to go out and deal with his daughter's kidnapper himself. "The Northern Wastes, eh?" he asked.

At this point, I really couldn't contradict El-hared without causing myself even more problems. "Yes, Sir."

"Then why do you have a Delharwyn accent?"

"I travel a lot."

"That is quite a distance."

"Well, you see, uh, my parents were traveling merchants from Delharwyn." I paused, and steeled myself. "Mordain, actually, before the Duke's war. They had a shop, but they heard rumors of the coming annexation and fled with their goods. Of course, having their shop nationalized in a proxy war left them with no love for the southern nations—"

I kept going in that vein. While I normally prefer stealth, there have been enough times I've had to ply my trade face-to-face that I've gotten reasonably good at crafting tales extemporaneously. It's a useful skill to be able to plausibly explain your presence in places where you otherwise shouldn't be.

It helped my case that my story was mostly true—not that it had anything to do with me. The life story I told the king belonged to an angry red-headed barbarian with whom I'd had the misfortune of sharing a cell in the city of Delmark about two years ago. I suspected he had embellished some of his tale—I left out the bear wrestling—but it provided a convenient superstructure on which to hang the story of Blackthorne of the Northern Wastes.

I measured my success by the king's eyes glazing over and the envoys and herald staring off into the middle distance, all apparently wishing they were somewhere else.

That was my cue to wrap up.

"—and that's how I ended up in your fine country, Your Highness."

"Yes, yes." I heard what sounded like relief in the king's voice. "Well, good fortune and gods' speed, Sir Blackthorne."

All in all, that had gone about as well as could be expected.

The way Elhared had been pushing for "Sir Blackthorne's" quest, I'd expected him to toss me out the gate to face the dragon as soon as we'd left the throne room. But some glimmer of sanity still shone on the wizard, albeit dimly and occasionally. I got board for the night, a decent meal, and a chance to wash up and get some real sleep before going out at dawn.

Morning had me walking a wooded path northwest of the city, dressed in a dead squire's scale mail and carrying *Dracheslayer*.

Elhared had given distressingly precise directions to find the dragon's lair, and I probably would have found it rather suspicious if it wasn't for the fact that *I was being sent to slay a damned dragon!* That tended to preoccupy my thoughts.

Of course, I'd be a rather poor thief if I didn't consider a Plan B, which involved me slipping away westbound, along the coast and out of Lendowyn, and finding a proper place to sell the priceless magical dragon-slaying artifact. The sword could probably fetch enough in the black market to get me passage on a ship halfway across the world from dragons, crazy wizards, and Nâtlac-worshiping royals, and leave me with enough of a stake to get myself somewhat established on the other side of the ocean.

Of course, as Elhared pointed out to drunken me back in the tavern, the world of wizards is a small gossipy one. There'd be little question that wherever I sold this sword, word would get back to Elhared and I'd have a pissed-off wizard after me. And after the last debacle with the Grünwald court, I had promised myself that I would make a serious effort to *reduce* the number of powerful people who wanted me dead.

Besides, there was a possibly innocent princess involved. Even if I'd half-convinced myself that she'd been either eaten, or saved already by one of the dozen knightly rescuers that preceded me, walking away from this would not help me sleep nights. Much as I might try, I wasn't that much of a bastard.

So I told myself about the dragon's hoard and kept on the path as Elhared had instructed me.

The day went quickly, and I came to a clearing in front of a rocky cliff face before I was ready for it. The sun had barely passed midday and shone down across the south-facing cliffs, letting massive overhangs cast deep shadows on crevasses into the hillside beneath them. The face of the hillside shrugged up above the trees in a rocky dome that probably rose five or six hundred feet. Not nearly a mountain, but as lairs go, it was probably as impressive as a dragon could find within the bounds of Lendowyn.

If there was any doubt where the dragon might have been holing up, a couple of skulls glinting whitely on a ledge about halfway up provided a rather significant clue to what resided here. I stared up at the cliff face and froze in place where I stood at the wooded edge of the clearing. I kept my hand on the pommel of *Dracheslayer*, momentarily convinced that the dragon would descend upon me any moment.

I waited.

And waited.

And waited some more.

No attack came my way, and as I stood there, every nerve stretched taut, I thought I could hear a sound coming from somewhere above, up the rocky hillside.

Snoring.

The ascent was nerve-racking but uneventful. Climbing up to inaccessible locations was part of my job description, even though I usually did so without a bunch of armor and a massive sword strapped to my ass. The climb was exhausting and I decided that Elhared had been right. Plate mail probably would have been a bad idea.

After what seemed like hours, I had made my way to the opening by the skulls. I eased my weight on to the ledge, the rumbling snore so close now that it resonated in my chest.

Before me, the crevasse into the hillside was much wider than it had appeared on the ground. The sun was now low enough in the sky that I could see about thirty feet in, across a slowly sloping floor, before the depths were cloaked in ink-black shadow. I didn't see the dragon, but what I did see was enough to make me reconsider my Plan B and deal with the wrath of the Wizard Elhared.

The skulls I had seen from the ground were not the only remains. The entrance to the lair was carpeted with them. Bones had been scattered across the floor, some polished white, some charred black, and some with gnaw marks and bits of flesh attached. I saw remains from cattle and horses for the most part, but I counted six human skulls, some next to piles of armor much nicer than what I wore.

What did the wizard say?

"You know where the dragon and the princess are?"

"Of course I do."

"And these dozen knights?"

"Oh, I'm sure one or two must have run into the dragon at some point. But they didn't have Dracheslayer."

The sword wasn't reassuring me.

Think of the hoard, I thought. I'd taken bigger risks for smaller reward before.

No I haven't, went my contrary internal monologue.

The cave resonated with the snoring from Elhared's "small" dragon. I could feel sulfur-tainted breath brush my cheek as it exhaled. I couldn't see it in the darkness within the cave, but I already knew that "small" would not be the word I'd use to describe this thing.

Run, I thought, *or do what you came to do.*

Standing around waiting for the lizard to wake up wasn't really an option. I also thought it'd be a waste of my efforts if I ran away without actually seeing what I was running from, so I grabbed the pommel of *Dracheslayer* and slowly drew it from its scabbard as quietly as I could manage and eased forward into the lair of the beast.

I trod carefully, watching so each step came

down on stone rather than animal or human remains. And once I stepped out of the light, I stopped so my eyes could readjust to the dimness within the shadows. Now that I was out of the sun, and the light was all behind me, the shapes within the cave began to resolve themselves.

As I began to see, I edged to the wall of the cave so my silhouette did not form such an obvious target against the daylight. Even as I did so, I realized that strategy was rendered moot because of the glowing sword in my hand. I silently sighed at the magical glowing target in my hand, but I wasn't going into the dragon's den without having *Dracheslayer* ready for action.

I followed the wall farther in, leaning against it as it curved deeper into the cave, holding the glowing sword down so my body was between the glowing red runes and the rest of the cave. Even so, as the daylight lost itself behind me, *Dracheslayer*'s hellish glow gave enough light to see immediately around me. Fortunately not so much that it woke the slumbering dragon sprawled in front of me.

The dragon snored and I was blasted with the smell of sulfur and devil farts.

Small dragon my ass.

Its head alone was as long as I was, half of that mouth, and three-quarters of *that*, teeth. The muscular jaws looked like they could bite a warhorse in half. It rested its head on its forelimbs, and its serpentine neck curved around to a huge body that merged into the darkness where *Dracheslayer*'s glow did not reach. I saw hints of vast demonic wings before I realized I had gone from assessing the situation to freezing in panic.

It's asleep, there's its neck, here's a dragon-slaying sword. . . .

It was going about as well as it could possibly go, which meant I shouldn't have been at all surprised when I took a step forward and heard a sharp intake of breath from above. A glance told me that Princess Lucille was alive, unhurt, and a bit shorter than her portrait would lead you to believe. She gaped at me in shock from a niche in the rock wall above me, bound hand and foot but, unfortunately, not gagged.

I turned back toward the dragon before she said, "Look out!"

I hoped she was talking to me.

In front of me the snore had come to a choked conclusion, and a lid slowly drew up from a golden eye the size of my head. I was already committed. My slow stealthy advance had drawn me in too close for any quick withdrawal.

When you can't go back, go forward.

I rushed, swinging *Dracheslayer* above my head, and brought the magic runesword down on the beast's unprotected neck with a visceral scream of premature triumph.

Every second thought I had been having, every suspicion, every sense that all was not right with

Elhared's proposal, all of that was confirmed as *Dracheslayer*, magic dragon-slaying sword forged by the blind dwarves of Grundar, hit the dragon's neck with a bone-wrenching impact and crumbled like week-old cheese.

Yeah, I was right, bad idea.

The loss of the magic blade plunged the cavern back into darkness, and for a few moments I stood in shock, cradling in my hands the ornate hilt that was all that remained of the priceless magic sword *Dracheslayer.* The shock lasted until the darkness was obliterated by a gout of flame to my right. It provided enough light to show that I now faced a vertical wall of dragon-scale and muscle.

I did the sane thing and ran off in the opposite direction. My retreat lasted all of three steps before a scaled hand with foot-long talons scooped me up to hold me ten feet off the cavern floor in front of an annoyed lizard. Steam curled from its nostrils as it stared at me with slitted golden eyes, and I braced myself for the inevitable.

For a few moments I wondered what was preferable, being burned alive, or being chomped in half. By the time I realized my vote was for chomping, I also realized that neither was happening.

The light hadn't faded, and I realized that the dragon hadn't aimed its breath at me, but at a no-longer dormant campfire in the center of the chamber. The dragon held me up next to the fire, as if using the light to examine me.

Above me, I heard the princess shout down at me, "What kind of rescue is this?"

The kind your father can afford. I sighed, shook my head, and muttered to myself, "That could have gone better."

The dragon spoke in a voice that made my chest ache, **"In fact, your attack was rather pathetic."**

Great, they were both heckling me. I shook the remains of *Dracheslayer*. "I was cheated on this sword."

"That's the least of it. You have no form, a weak swing, and you left yourself wide open for any counterattack. Are you sure you're a knight?"

"I . . ."

I trailed off because the dragon had turned its massive head away from me, not waiting for an answer. It looked deeper into the cavern and called out, **"Is this a joke, Elhared?"**

Both Lucille and I had the simultaneous reaction, *"What?!"*

Emerging from the deeper shadows in the cave, Elhared the Unwise strode out, carrying a large book wrapped in tooled leather of unfortunate origin; the kind of evil tome of wizardry that makes the death rolls of the Dark Lord Nâtlac look like a compilation of love poetry.

He looked up at the dragon and said, "I chose the thieving sot for his looks, not his fighting prowess. Now don't mess up his face."

CHAPTER 4

I don't think I can adequately convey the rush of conflicting emotions I felt at that moment. The fear goes without saying, the kind of bladder-freezing fear I don't think anyone can understand who hasn't been restrained four feet away from something with both the inclination and the capability of eating you. Then we have the embarrassment at being so obviously conned, worse for someone like myself who often prides himself on being the one doing the conning.

I blame the Mermaid's Milk.

Then there was the dull shock from the fact that in all the scenarios I had seen this particular bad idea get the best of me, I hadn't seen it go awry in quite this way. And, I am ashamed to say, underneath everything else, I felt a small surge of self-congratulatory vanity as the wizard complimented my looks. Though I wondered what my appearance had to do with facing down a dragon.

Elhared gestured to the dragon, and it moved to hold me before the wizard, who gave me an appraising look that would have been more appropriate on someone haggling over pumpkins with a street vendor.

Above us, I heard Princess Lucille call down, "Elhared? You old coot, what are you doing here?"

Elhared chuckled to himself as he opened the evil tome he carried. "I'm saving you from the dragon, my princess." From where the dragon held me suspended I could see more of the pages than I cared to. The sight of the written language in that book had something of the same effect as looking very closely at a worm-infested wound on a none-too fresh corpse. It didn't help that Elhared had marked his place in the tome with a pixie that had been flattened and dried in the midst of some obscene act.

I looked up from that unpleasant display and tried to look the wizard in the eye, but his head was bowed to pore over the open pages. Still, I cleared my throat and said, "So, Elhared, isn't this where you amaze us with the description of your intricately crafted plans?"

He just grunted in response.

"Seriously, if you wanted to win her hand in marriage yourself, why recruit me?" Even as I said it, I got an uneasy feeling about his comment about my looks.

Above us I heard the princess say something about how she appreciated Elhared's efforts, she really did. And she liked him well enough, just not *that* way.

I tried again. "No boasts? No gloating? No regaling us with your genius?"

By now I think he was just making a point of ignoring both me and the princess. I turned my head until I could just catch sight of the dragon holding me. It cradled its head with its other forelimb, and while its face wasn't particularly expressive, its body language radiated boredom.

"What about you?"

"What about me?"

"Shouldn't you be rampaging across the countryside? Why are you hooked up with this guy?"

"He agreed to cover my marker."

"What?"

"I didn't beat the spread on the last three-kingdom jousting tournament."

"You're working with a diabolical wizard because of a *gambling debt*?"

"I'm temporarily short of funds at the moment."

"But dragons . . ." I trailed off as I realized that, now that it was well lit, I could see a distinct lack of a dragon's hoard in this cave. "You're broke? You're really broke?"

"Just a dry spell. I'm due for a big payoff any day now."

Elhared finally looked up. "Will you all stop babbling!" he snapped at us. "This spell requires perfect concentration!"

"What spell?" I asked.

Elhared leveled a bony finger at the dragon. "You, cover his mouth! Just don't mess up the face."

I sucked in a breath to say something more, but one of the dragon's fingers wrapped around my face and it was suddenly all I could do to tilt my head back enough to breathe. I could just barely see Elhared over the dragon's knuckle. He bent his head down to return to his spell, and winced as above us Lucille said, "Honestly, Elhared, you're older than my father."

"Should I cover her mouth as well?"

"Everybody shut up!"

"Can't you just let the young knight save me?"

He looked up at her and shouted. "Damn it woman! He *is* going to save you!" He returned to peruse his tome, muttering under his breath, "Just after a little soul transference spell."

That did *not* sound good.

The princess didn't quit while she was ahead. "Well, he is—"

The wizard slammed the book on the flattened pixie and told the dragon, "Yes, cover her mouth too!"

Elhared stood impatiently as the dragon stretched to reach the struggling princess with its free forelimb. She started screaming and kicking, both of which came to a halt as the dragon wrapped its fingers around her. All that remained visible of her was her head above the bridge of her nose, dominated by a pair of blue eyes glaring icy murder at the wizard.

The dragon held us both up in front of Elhared and the wizard stood a moment in contemplation, as if waiting for another interruption. I might have heard something muffled and very un-princesslike coming from my left, but then it might have been the dragon suppressing a belch. Without any more interruptions, Elhared opened his book again and resumed reading.

After a moment, I saw his lips start moving. It could have been a symptom of advancing senility, but that was a little too much to hope for. Especially when the text on the page he read began to glow with a light ominously akin to what I'd seen on the doomed *Dracheslayer*.

My right arm, hand still gripping the heavy hilt of that bogus sword, jutted out between two of the dragon's fingers. I had just enough freedom of movement to throw the hilt at Elhared.

I put all the effort I could manage into the swing, and I imagined the hilt striking the wizard square in the forehead and knocking him cold, if not killing him outright. Unfortunately, my aim wasn't quite that good, and given my restricted movement and my clumsy underhand toss, the force of the missile wasn't anywhere near disabling. The hilt tumbled lazily through the air to bounce harmlessly off of Elhared's chest, landing on the open book, knocking the flattened pixie off to flutter slowly to the ground.

Elhared's reaction was a startled glance toward me and a puzzled, "Huh?"

Someone, I am sure, has written a standard primer for those with an interest in pursuing the wizardly arts. Somewhere in there, in with the recommended beard length and the best materials to use for one's robe, I am certain there exists the following sentence: "When casting complicated spells of nefarious origin, uttering a random monosyllable three-quarters of the way in does not yield optimal results."

In response to the interruption, the glow from the text exploded into a burst of light fountaining up from the pages of the book. Elhared fell back as if the expanding light dealt him a physical blow, and I lost sight of him in the glare. The book fell to the floor of the cave and rolling smoke began filling the cavern. I felt a prickly heat from the pillar of red-blue light that made the hair on the back of my neck stand up. To all appearances, Elhared had vaporized in a flash of light and smoke.

The expanding light still grew toward us, and the dragon jerked backward. The pillar of light curved and rippled toward the dragon, as if attracted to it. The dragon made a startled sound that was almost a yelp, and threw me at the pillar of magic fire as if my flailing body could beat it into submission.

I hit the light, felt a burning tingle, and blacked out.

* * *

And I had thought the hangover from the Mermaid's Milk had been bad.

My first conscious thought after hitting that light was that I had been so very wrong. I would have embraced the return of the eyeball-gnawing skull-troll if it meant the eviction of the goblin army that had now taken up residence. Thoughts of more than one syllable caused me physical pain, so when I inhaled and started coughing up wizard soot I almost blacked out again.

The coughing fit subsided. I dropped my head back with an agonized moan. My head hit a tree root, and I gasped. I tried to reach to push myself upright, and I realized my wrists were bound.

Not good.

More troublesome sensations began filtering through the pain of the goblin orgy doing violence to my brain. I tried to move my legs, and they were bound as well. And things just didn't feel right, beyond the throbbing in my head. My body felt wrong, arms and legs shorter, my hair catching in ways it shouldn't underneath my neck, my torso—

"What the hell?" I whispered.

Even roughened by inhaling more than my share of carbonized Elhared, I could tell *that* was not my voice. I've never uttered a single word in what could be described as a husky contralto.

My eyes shot open to look down at myself, the glare making my vision blur. I told myself that it was the painful light making my eyes water, or maybe the stinging ash. After all, the sight of a woman's bosom had never before moved me to tears.

"Soul transference spell," I whispered to myself in the Princess Lucille's voice.

I stared at myself, at Lucille, and couldn't decide if I was more disturbed by sitting here in her body, or by the thought of her running around somewhere in mine. I didn't spend long feeling sorry for myself. It seemed that Fate had decided to take every impulse of self-pity on my part as a cue to show me exactly how much worse things could be.

As I stared, still disbelieving, down Lucille's dress, my thoughts were interrupted by the sounds of arguing. I glanced up and saw three men just a few steps away from my feet. They did not look the type to be rescuing princesses. Rescuing anyone, really. In fact, the trio of unsavory gentlemen had more the look of people princesses were rescued *from*.

Actually, princesses were probably out of their league. They were the type you would need to rescue a tavern wench from.

Then, as I listened to them arguing among themselves, I had to re-revise my revised sentiment. I seemed to be princess-by-proxy, and as Princess Lucille's stand-in, it sounded as if she— I—needed some rescuing from these unpleasant characters.

The smallest one, a nervous mousy sort barely taller than Lucille, had his back to me and stood facing the other two. He was engaged in an animated discussion, waving his arms and causing his stringy ponytail to dance about. He had captured the others' attention, explaining why they hadn't noticed me wake up yet.

"I's the one found her, right?" Mouse said. "I's the one says what we do with her." He said it with a force and intensity that would have been intimidating if he didn't have the voice of an asthmatic teenage boy.

The man to Mouse's left made up for him in the intimidation department. He was grossly fat, half as wide as he was tall, all wild hair and beard so dense and tangled that the only visible parts of his face were small strips of eyes, brow, and nose. "Listen to you. Sounds like your marbles finally dropped." If a bear could speak, that would be the voice it would use.

"You recognize the woman?" asked the last man, to Mouse's right. He was mid-height between Mouse and Bear, as hairless as Bear was hirsute, and wore an eye patch over his left eye socket that wasn't quite as large as the scars it covered.

"I's told you, a princess. Lucille of Lendowyn. We bring her back and should be some reward."

Bear laughed like he had some idea of the state of the Lendowyn treasury. Or he just imagined

Mouse being the recipient of Lucille's hand in marriage and found the image amusing. I might have shared his mirth if I wasn't in Lucille's place at the moment. However, his suggestion as to the proper use of their found princess was considerably less amusing.

By then I had recovered enough of my senses to use the trio's distraction to make an attempt to escape my bonds. You might think that a career as a thief meant I was adept at such things. Sadly you would be mistaken. While a daring last-minute escape from impossible bonds makes an exciting tale, in reality, a good thief spends much more time learning how not to get caught in the first place.

At least Princess Lucille's stature helped make things easier for me. Her small hands and additional flexibility allowed me to work her hands free without drawing the undue attention of the forest brigand debate society in front of me. I'd just started working free the knot binding my ankles when I heard Eyepatch make the sage announcement that he was going to split the difference between Bear and Mouse. They would all have their way with the princess, *then* they'd bring her back to Lendowyn for whatever award might be offered.

And that, my friends, is why they made him the leader.

I barely had time to undo the knot and resume

my post-unconscious posture on the ground, against the roots of a tree, hands behind my back, before they shoved Mouse down at me. He fell down, face against my stomach, to the sound of Bear's laughter. "You found her, right? You get the first taste."

Mouse pushed himself upright, so he was on all fours above me. He was trembling, and didn't look me in the eye. "S-sorry, Princess." The guy was almost making me sympathetic for a potential rapist.

But not enough to keep me from slamming my knee into his crotch, sending his marbles back where they came from.

"Apology accepted," I told him, slamming my fist into the side of his head. I don't think he noticed the punch. I'd never been a brawler, and Lucille didn't have any significant upper body strength. It did direct his collapse so he didn't fall on top of me as he clutched his groin.

Bear had stopped laughing, and I suddenly had an angry, hairy wall descending toward me. One look at his face and I knew that this bastard would probably take a kick to the testicles as a form of foreplay. I pushed myself up and bolted for deeper in the woods.

What Princess Lucille's body lacked in upper body strength, it made up for in speed and dexterity. I felt as if I practically flew to my feet, and I was racing for the cover of the woods before Bear had made it a couple of steps.

All of which meant I wasn't aware of the abnormal pain pitching me forward into the forest mulch until my face planted into a pile of dead leaves.

When I rolled onto my back and looked down at my feet, I expected to see a pair of bloody stumps. Instead, I saw what must have been the most ornate implements of torture ever devised by man. I knew the princess was short, but compensating for that with the heels on the jeweled monstrosities imprisoning her feet was a cost far too high. They were more effective restraints than the ropes I'd slipped out of.

I spat leaves and mulch and managed to remove one offending shoe before Eyepatch caught up with me. The guy was not much bigger than I had been before I found myself filling in for the princess. Currently, however, he had close to a foot in height and probably sixty pounds on me. He hooked one hand under my armpit and yanked me to my feet without showing a bit of strain.

And I'd been worried about Bear.

He sneered at me and grabbed my throat with his free hand. "Now, don't give me any more trouble, you little bitch. I have no problem cutting—"

His threat was cut short with a gasp as I brought the princess's shoe up and slammed it heel-first into his good eye. Eyepatch screamed and let me go, clutching his face in a way that showed that the shoe was at least as painful for him as it had been for me. He lunged at me in a literal blind fury, and I scrambled backward, kicking off the remaining shoe of death.

Bear caught up with us, and he made the mistake of touching Eyepatch's shoulder. Bear didn't get out so much as a grunt before Eyepatch lunged for him. He probably should have realized that Bear's throat was both higher and furrier than the one I wore at the moment. Then again, Eyepatch seemed *really* angry. Bear tried to peel the guy off of him, but that only made Eyepatch attack harder, and they both fell to the forest floor.

I took the opportunity to run out of there as fast as I could.

CHAPTER 5

I ran for a long time before I realized that I wasn't anywhere near the hillside where Elhared's dragon had been stashing the princess. I wasn't familiar with the landscape of Lendowyn, but the wizard had given me a pretty good briefing on the landscape near the lair, and what I ran through right now wasn't it.

For all I knew, I wasn't even *in* Lendowyn anymore.

I stopped once I was certain that I had made it clear of Eyepatch and his crew. I leaned up against a tree to catch my breath. I had just run a mile or two in bare feet. Now that I'd stopped, I realized how badly torn up the princess's feet were. They hurt almost as bad as they had with the shoes of doom on.

I slid down the side of the tree to sit on a large root. I groaned with relief as I took the weight off the princess's injured feet. I lifted one foot and looked at the sole. It was a mess. Despite wearing footwear that should have toughened them up, the skin of her feet was as delicate and soft as her own backside. At least as delicate and soft as I presumed her backside was. Since I was using it at the moment I didn't feel an urge to test the hypothesis.

The effect of the forest floor on the princess's unprotected feet resulted in a bloody mess that looked like her shoes had made them feel. I winced as I started pulling out splinters, pine needles, and pieces of pinecones.

"Whatever happened, Elhared, you twisted bastard," I whispered to a passing squirrel, "I hope it *hurt*." The squirrel sat up on its hind legs and chattered at me. I flicked a bloody piece of gravel at it and it ran away.

It was clear that I had disrupted Elhared's spell a few incantations later than I should have. The soul-transference bit happened, but it looked like it had been me and the princess who had swapped rather than me and the wizard. That was probably for the best, since last I remembered, Elhared's body had vanished in a pillar of magical fire. I didn't know why the princess ended up in the middle of the forest an indeterminate distance from Elhared's self-immolation, but I'm not a wizard. It probably had something to do with the dragon throwing me into the spell.

Now that I had a moment to think, I started coming up with a plan. The plan was simple enough, but the objective was pretty obvious. I needed three things. I needed to recover the lexicon of nastiness Elhared had been cribbing notes from. Books like that tended not to run into multiple editions, and if someone were to undo what Elhared had done, they would probably need a copy of the exact spell that Elhared had muffed. Of course, for that to be of any use, I needed to find the princess and, presumably, my body along with her. Lastly, I needed to find a slightly less corrupt wizard who could make sense of the whole mess and fix things.

Simple, really.

I shredded strips off the bottom of the princess's dress, grumbling because the rest of her outfit seemed as inappropriate to the situation I found myself in as the shoes had. I fostered that resentment because it was the only thing keeping me from staring at my—her—legs and thinking about exactly how it felt when I bent over to wrap my feet. The pain also helped distract me from paying too much attention to where the princess's clothing tugged at me—or the one important place it wasn't tugging at me.

Three things, that's all I needed. Of the three, looking for a sane wizard was pointless until I took care of the other two. Looking for the princess/myself was also going to be difficult if we were both randomly teleported to parts unknown.

Since I knew where the dragon's lair was, that left me with finding Elhared's evil tome of maleficence as my immediate logical first step.

Sometimes I hate logic.

But, besides fixing one third of my problem, if I had some luck, Princess Lucille would come to the same conclusions and go to recover the book herself and I'd take care of another third of the list at the same time. Then it would just be a matter of traveling back to the king, who would most likely help us find a wizard for step three. Even if the treasury was bare, there was a position for a court wizard that had just opened up.

My plan was a thing of beauty, simple, elegant, and flawless. Except for the state of my feet, and the issue that I had no idea where in the wide world I happened to be.

I pushed myself to stand on my bandaged feet and whispered, "One thing at a time, Frank."

Step one-half, find a village, a farm, or a traveler a bit more civilized than the brigands I'd left behind that could tell me where I was and point me in the right direction.

The simplest plans always prove to be the most difficult to execute. Finding a road or a village shouldn't have been this hard. I began to suspect that Eyepatch and company had not chosen their campsite for its accessibility.

The sky was edging toward dusk before I found a mud track that had seen use by more than the local wildlife. As the light faded, it began to sink in how bad my situation was. Hobbling through the woods in daylight, it was easy enough to avoid thinking of anything but my pained feet and finding signs of human civilization. Now that I had found those signs, and night was coming, it sank in that I'd be walking along an empty road in the body of a young, injured, unarmed woman.

The non-human predators that would soon be waking up in these woods would probably be a bit easier to reason with than the human predators that traveled this road at night. I had no desire to run into another group like Eyepatch's crew, if for no other reason than that I'd like to return the princess's body in a state close to how I'd found it.

I picked up a fallen branch that could double as a staff and a walking stick, and began looking for a safe hole where I could hide myself through the night.

But, before night fell, and before I could find a good hidey-hole, I heard the sound of approaching hoofbeats.

Oh, crap.

In one sense, it was exactly what I was looking for, a traveler who could tell me how best to get back to the areas of Lendowyn that I was somewhat familiar with. But I wasn't in a position to defend myself against anyone whose interest in wayward princesses was less than savory. I had an urge to run into the woods and find cover, but between my initial indecision, the lack of good cover on this stretch of road, and my tired, bandaged feet, there wasn't any way for me to get out of sight before the galloping horse was in view of me.

So I stood my ground and gripped my branch as if it might do some good. If I had been the princess, I might have been a little reassured by the appearance of the lone rider approaching me. The man rode a black charger, and wore mail that almost gleamed underneath a tabard bearing a device that marked this guy as a member of the nobility, a knight at least.

That might have reassured the princess, but it didn't reassure *me*. In a long career on the outside of the law, I had gotten to know plenty of people in the shiny armor of noble birth. The differences between such men and the dregs hanging out with Eyepatch were more teeth, better weapons, and nicer clothes. Honestly, most nobles I'd met didn't even edge out Eyepatch in the cleanliness department.

The knight drew his horse to a stop next to me on the road, and somehow he managed to keep his mount from kicking up a soup of mud and horse crap on me. He had long blond hair tied behind his head, and a long mustache whose ends curved down below a chin so broad and stonelike that it seemed as if he could sharpen his sword on the cleft. He called down to me as if he were performing an oration for the benefit of an unseen audience. "Ho! What evil has left a maiden alone to wander this dismal wood?"

I gripped my makeshift staff and, even though my present appearance had been the foremost worry in my mind for the past few hours, I still found myself glancing around for the maiden he was referring to. I sighed, returned my gaze to the knight, and said, "It's a long story."

The knight's eyes widened and he exclaimed, "My lady! Are those the arms of Lendowyn upon that ill-treated frock?"

"I suppose they are—" I hadn't really paid much attention to the princess's clothes, aside from trying to tear them into something slightly more appropriate to hiking in the woods. Though, strictly speaking, complete nudity would have been more appropriate.

The knight vaulted off his horse and landed in the road in front of me. Again, he somehow managed to keep from splattering mud over either of us. His tabard rustled in a slight breeze, along with his hair, as if he had been granted special favor by the gods of high drama. He bowed down to one knee, effortlessly finding the single patch of road that was not a sloppy mess in which to genuflect. "It is an honor. I am Sir Forsythe the Good, slayer of monsters and savior of fair maidens. As fate would have it, I was on my way to Lendowyn to offer your father my service in rescuing you."

Of course you were.

Somehow, my perfectly simple plan had overlooked the fact that there was an outstanding bounty on return of the princess. Just because the princess was no longer in the clutches of an evil dragon didn't mean there weren't still all manner of freelancers out to save her.

That complicated things.

"Well, uh, Sir Forsythe? I think I've managed to rescue myself, thank you." I bit my lip because I wasn't used to talking to people bowing at me. It was a little disconcerting. "You can get up."

He stood, slowly enough that it gave me a really good sense of how much he towered over me, how much he would have towered over me even before I had been princessified. I was suddenly very grateful for the privileges of rank. I straightened up, looked Sir Forsythe in the eye, and tried to muster up all the royal arrogance I could manage. "I appreciate your effort, Sir Knight, but all I require right now is proper directions toward . . ." I hesitated. Despite steeling myself and trying for a tone of royal command, the sounds that came out of my mouth were more of the frightened teenager variety. But I couldn't very well turn back from the attempt now. "T-the nearest inn where I can get my bearings."

"Your Highness," he said in a way that made clear exactly what was coming. "I cannot in good conscience leave you alone in these woods. You have no retainers present to protect you." Of course he wouldn't. I'm a thief with no respect for authority, chivalry, or noble blood, and *I* wouldn't. "However," he bowed his head to me, "I would be honored to personally escort you to such an inn, and at daybreak take you to the castle gates themselves."

I opened my mouth to object, but the sane part of my brain kicked some sense into me. I was alone, unarmed. This guy was loaded for bear, and had transportation. Even if I didn't want to confront Princess Lucille's dad without the princess available, I couldn't see any logical objection to Sir Forsythe's offer.

Did I mention that sometimes I hated logic?

"That isn't necessary."

"Your Highness, to do otherwise would besmirch my honor, and I doubt the king would look kindly upon any knight that abandoned you in such a state."

I opened my mouth, but nothing came out as I realized that I could be counted in that princess-abandoning group. It may have been due to no fault of my own, but kings, as a general rule, were not known to be the most reasonable class of people. The power to have people decapitated whenever you were irritated was not conducive to the growth of emotional restraint.

I really needed to find Lucille before I was presented to the king, unless I wanted to push this princess masquerade a lot further than I wanted—which would result in the betrothal to the blond pretty-boy knight who walked me up to the gate.

Despite the temptation to explain everything, I held back. The only leverage I had with this guy was the fact he thought I was royalty. "Sir Forsythe, you may escort me to an inn. But before I return to my father we must—*oof*."

My royal pronouncement was cut short by Sir Forsythe scooping me up with one arm, and lifting me like a doll as he mounted his warhorse. We were galloping down the path before I had regained my breath.

It took a minute or two before I could regain my composure enough to speak. I was astride the horse in a terrifyingly unstable sidesaddle position in front of Sir Forsythe. The only thing preventing my slide under the beast's galloping hooves was Sir Forsythe's mailed arm clamped around my midsection.

"There are things I need to do before I meet the king," I half-yelled and half-gasped. Sir Forsythe gave no sign of hearing me. I didn't repeat myself, because screams of terror didn't seem to fit with the persona I was attempting to project.

I'll deal with it when we get to the inn.

CHAPTER 6

The *idea* of a kingdom, a geographic area under the rule of one particular sovereign, is pretty much a complete fraud. The authority of a king is a fiction beyond the sword point of his retainers, and no kingdom—especially one as poor as Lendowyn—can afford enough armed men to impose the king's rule beyond a tight little circle around each village. Beyond that circle of influence, the land was wild with monsters both human and otherwise, and the so-called kingdom might as well not exist.

But the kingdom was never the *only* source of order. Any time a large enough group congregated, for a long enough time, a form of "law" would develop, even if it wasn't the king's law. Everything from covens to monasteries, if not under direct protection of the king, would enforce its own sub-kingdom in its immediate area.

Long experience in extra-legal travel had given me an instinct for such things, and that instinct told me that the inn we approached, The Headless Earl, was the heart of one such sub-realm outside the command of King Alfred the Strident. It was obvious to anyone who was familiar with what to look for; the lack of fortifications despite its complete isolation, the horses stabled without so much as a guard present, the fact that dusk had fallen and travelers freely entered and left the wide-open entrance into a well-lit interior. The place was obviously protected, and flew no colors but its own.

Sir Forsythe drew his mount to a halt and said, "Here, Your Highness." He took his arm away from my midsection, and I found myself involuntarily sliding to the ground. Before I slid all the way, he released the reins and slipped both hands under my armpits to turn my uncontrolled descent into a gentle landing.

I still winced when my feet hit the ground.

He bounded off to land next to me. "We shall find you appropriate lodging here for the night."

We had become the focus of attention of a group of men gathered by the doorway. The trio reminded me uncomfortably of Eyepatch and his crew, all scars and leather and more knives than any reasonable person would need outside a juggling demonstration. One of them had a long facial scar that bisected his beard and made his gap-toothed smile all the more ominous.

There are two types of outlaw in the world. There were people like me, who traded on skill and stealth and subtlety. The kind of thief who, if things go right, you'd never know had been there until you found your purse or jewelry missing. Then there were those men who walked up to you, clobbered you in the side of the head, and took the boots off your corpse.

I was pretty sure these were the latter.

"Sir Forsythe," I whispered, "I think this may not be the best place—"

"Nonsense," he said. "You need shelter, and I will make sure that you have their best room."

"—it appears to be a haven for outlaws."

"No harm will come to you. You are under my protection."

Did I mention stealth and subtlety? I am afraid I have sinned against the gods of language by mentioning those words in the same breath that named Sir Forsythe the Good. The man was as stealthy as a thunderstorm and as subtle as an incontinent ogre. He strode into the common room of The Headless Earl, drawing the kind of stares you'd expect if I—meaning the princess—walked naked up the gangway onto a prison ship that had just completed an eight-month voyage.

He might have believed he was talking in hushed tones after calling the innkeeper over, but given the sudden silence falling over the ragged clientele, he might as well have been screaming at the man how they needed to provide the best room for the princess, expense no object.

"Of course my good knight." The innkeeper told him with a voice that made me want to wash my hands. The fact that he kept glancing in my direction and rubbing his own hands didn't help the impression. "Our best room, guaranteed luxury and proof against any brigands. Follow me."

The innkeeper waved us upstairs. I followed closely behind Sir Forsythe. If nothing else, I could put his chivalrous bulk between me and any of the disreputable patrons of the inn downstairs.

Paranoia is normal for someone in my profession. But the fact that I currently wore the skin of a nubile young princess had amplified that normal trait into a full-bore panic. And the patrons of this establishment were probably sniffing out that panic like a pack of hungry dogs.

By the time our smarmy innkeeper presented my room, I had decided that I had to make a run for it just for the sake of my own—borrowed—skin. I could slip out of a window once I was alone.

I could . . . if the room wasn't the innkeep's "best room" and "proof against any brigands." I took a step inside and saw immediately that the windows were barred. That was just sinking in as money changed hands behind me and the innkeeper told Sir Forsythe, "The door is solid oak with an unbreakable iron lock, with only one key."

I turned around to see the innkeeper leaving, hefting a small bag of coins. I could have probably found better use for that money.

Looking at that purse, I realized that I'd missed the perfect opportunity to lighten the knight's purse. With me pressed against him, and all the galloping on the way here, he never would have known.

"*I'm slipping*," I muttered to myself.

"Your Highness?"

"Nothing."

"I will stand watch outside your door."

It would have been nice if that had made me feel better.

Sir Forsythe hefted a heavy iron key and walked outside closing the door behind him. I hesitated a moment too long before I said, "Hey, shouldn't I—"

The door shut and the key turned in the lock.

"—have the key?" I finished. I raised my fist to pound on the door to get my gallant protector to unlock the door and return the key to me, but I had second thoughts. All I would be doing was drawing attention, and while having the door locked on me was irritating, it wasn't as if I were trapped. I had no doubt that I could pick the lock from this side if need be. Besides, if I was going to slip away from Sir Forsythe and this tavern of ruffians, doing so through the front door wasn't my first choice, especially with the knight doing guard duty.

I let it go, and tried to relax. The room did appear to be secure, and it was appointed fairly well for an inn in the middle of the woods. There were several tapestries along with a bed with clean linens a lot larger than I was used to. There was also a washstand with a fresh pitcher of water . . .

. . . and a mirror.

"Oh, hell," I whispered, very conscious that I was not speaking in my voice.

It wasn't that I had forgotten what had happened to me. My body was giving me dozens of alien signals every passing minute. My drop in stature had inflated the world around me so everything seemed half again larger than it ought to be. When I licked my lips, the skin around them felt freakishly smooth. I couldn't take a breath without reminding myself I had a pair of breasts.

Somehow, my brain had done a valiant rearguard action, preventing any of those sensations from coming to the forefront of my perceptions. Even the increase in paranoia on my part was more me intellectualizing the fact that I was in a situation where a young woman should be nervous than it was any visceral reaction.

So, even though seeing Lucille looking back at me in the mirror shouldn't have surprised me, the sight was a punch to the gut. I wasn't *me* anymore. I stared at the woman in the mirror, and watched her expression go blank, and the color drain from her face until the streaks of dirt looked like gouges in marble. I watched her mouth press into a thin, bloodless line. I watched her small fists clench, and her arms tremble.

I whispered to her, "Stop it."

I saw tears leaking from her wide staring eyes. I watched them trail across her cheeks and felt them burning my skin.

"Stop it!" I told my reflection. I was in no position to start losing my cool now. I forced my fists open, and my hands shook. I looked away from the mirror and stared at my hands, willing them still. "Stop it. Just stop it."

I took several deep breaths and told myself to calm down. Things could be *so* much worse; bad alternatives ranged from being bisected by a set of dragon jaws, becoming a smear of soot like the unlamented Elhared the Unwise, or even failing to awake before Eyepatch and crew had finished their debate.

"All things considered, I'm doing pretty well."

I looked back into the mirror and the ironic half-smile I saw there just felt weird. It took all the creepy sense of wrongness and added a level of seductiveness that felt even more wrong. I pushed the feelings aside and tried to concentrate on practical matters. I needed to clean myself off, and it started to dawn on me that I hadn't answered a call of nature since I had awakened. I looked at the mirror, then down at myself.

I bit my lip. I felt my face get hot, and glancing at Lucille's pensive, embarrassed expression in the mirror didn't help things.

"Oh, come on," I berated myself. It wasn't as if

I could avoid disrobing at some point. Besides, it was only fair. I was sure that the princess faced the same issues with my own body . . . Besides, there were several intimate spots that, between dirt and sweat, had begun to itch uncomfortably.

Cleaning up and relieving myself. These were things that needed to happen if I was going to be a conscientious tenant of someone else's body, right? I sighed and disrobed.

And I don't think it is possible for me to properly convey exactly how disturbing that whole process was.

Lucille, despite her height, was very attractive, and that attractiveness was not just a product of an elaborate infrastructure of clothing, jewelry, and makeup as it was in a lot of pampered nobility. And, of course, I was a healthy male—in my head, anyway—so seeing her body in such an intimate fashion should have an effect, right?

It did.

But it was the *wrong* effect.

There are physical consequences for that kind of attraction, but those are the province of the body, not the mind, and the body I wore responded in a way that was completely alien to me. Much more . . . internal.

Then there was the fact that the things I had to do were not attractive at all, and I still felt . . .

Suffice to say I ended the whole process cleaner, but very uneasy.

I dressed again, focusing on the den of thieves below me to avoid thinking about other things. If I was lucky, the bulk of them knew the state of the Lendowyn treasury and realized that theft or kidnapping wouldn't be very profitable. Then again, I couldn't help but think a lot of the patrons downstairs didn't seem particularly bright.

I massed the covers on the oversize bed to resemble someone sleeping, and folded myself into a dark corner of the room farthest from the door and the window. Sitting on the floor, knees drawn to my chin, I felt smaller than I ever had, even as a child.

I told myself it was probably just the princess's stature.

I didn't sleep well.

Between the raging paranoia, and the fact that every time I shifted my weight I felt something that reignited my uneasy unfamiliarity with this body, I kept jerking awake.

About the dozenth time I opened my eyes to the darkened moonlit room, I glimpsed a shadow passing across the wall opposite the window. I glanced at the window, and saw only a clear starry sky. Then I started looking back toward the shadow on the wall, and stopped my gaze when I faced the bed.

The shadow was cast by a person, dressed in black, descending from a hole in the ceiling that had not been there earlier. The intruder moved silently, dangling from a thin rope, sliding down a fraction of an inch, then freezing, all attention on the covered mass on the bed.

I didn't even have my stick.

As the intruder descended, I mimicked his cautious, halting motion, moving when he did, pushing myself to my feet. I reached for something to use as a weapon, and my hands found the handle of the chamber pot.

The figure pulled out a small vial of something, uncorked it with a thumb, and poured the contents over where the princess's head should have been. That was my cue to act. With one hand unleashing a potion, the other holding on to the rope, the intruder didn't have a free arm for defense.

My quarry didn't realize anything was wrong until I'd jumped up on the bed and was bringing the chamber pot up against the back of his skull. The ceramic bowl shattered, and the contents sprayed against my victim and the wall.

He fell facedown on the bed, still conscious and trying to push himself upright. I dropped the handle and brought both my hands down on the back of his head, forcing his face down into the pillows. The pillows were spattered with filth, but more importantly, they were soaked with the vial of whatever potion this guy had intended to dose the princess with.

I heard the key rattle in the lock. "Your Highness! Are you all right?"

The struggles increased underneath me and I dropped on my knees between the guy's shoulder blades. "I—" I glanced up at the hole above me, a perfect escape route, "I-I'm using the chamber pot."

The rattling of the lock ceased immediately. "Oh. Forgive the interruption, Your Highness." I almost felt guilty at the note of embarrassment I heard in the well-meaning Sir Forsythe's voice.

But not guilty enough to reconsider my rapidly developing escape plans.

CHAPTER 7

Beneath me, the intruder's struggles slowed to a stop. I found a dagger on his belt and drew it while still straddling his neck. Then I waited.

I thought there was about a fifty-fifty chance that my would-be thief/kidnapper/assassin had a partner or three, and I didn't want to be caught by surprise. I waited for a long time in silence, until my friend started to snore. When no one appeared from the hole above, I relaxed a little and finished disarming my visitor, removing two full-size daggers from his belt, a weighted sap, a garrote, and a hideaway throwing knife from the top of his right boot.

Once assured I was better armed than he was, I began to liberate him from his clothing. Despite being somewhat befouled around the collar and shoulders from my attack, he was still dressed better than I was for the situation I found myself in.

The process took some time. Snoring or not, I wasn't about to trust that he would stay unconscious indefinitely. I kept a dagger in one hand while I peeled layers of leather and linen from his upper body. After that unnerving process was done, I sliced strips from the sheets and bound his sprawled arms to the bedposts. Only when he was restrained did I feel safe putting down the weapon and using both hands to pull off his boots and breaches before tying his legs to the bed as well.

My timing was impeccable; I heard his snores stutter to a stop as he sucked in a breath and tried to pull one of his legs free. He began to say something, a drowsy, "Wha?" and I darted over and shoved the remaining strip of torn bedding into his open mouth.

His eyes went wide and he started thrashing and moaning until I grabbed a dagger and placed the blade next to his jaw.

I whispered at him, "Stay quiet or I take more than your clothing."

The kind of day I'd been having must have leaked into my voice, because my would-be thief/rapist/assassin froze on the spot. I held my knife to his neck while I waited for any response from Sir Forsythe or this guy's hypothetical partners. No reaction came, and I slowly pulled the knife away.

"Good," I whispered. "Now behave or I'll relieve you of the only pouch you have left." I moved the knife to press the flat against the most sensitive bit of his exposed anatomy. There was a slight gasp and a shudder, but the guy didn't tempt fate. I was still angry enough to be almost disappointed.

I threw the blanket over his head and proceeded to swap the ragged remnants of my princessly ensemble for his oversize thiefly uniform. All I kept from Lucille's wardrobe were the undergarments—because my victim's underwear had been foul even before he'd been clobbered with a chamber pot.

Small as he was, I still had to work to get things to fit me. I doubled up the belt, rolled up sleeves on the linen shirt, did some quick violence on the leather outerwear with a dagger, abandoned the gloves, and doubled up on the bandage thickness on my feet so the boots wouldn't slide off. Not really optimal, but the weaponry and half-full purse made up for any other shortcomings.

I grabbed the rope that still dangled from the ceiling and hauled myself up. My estimation of the dubious nature of the place was confirmed by the fact that the scoundrel tied up in the princess's bed had come from a hidden passage designed for just such a purpose. Not only was the passage above roomy enough to accommodate someone three times my current size, but the walls had been padded with several layers of fabric and cork to keep noise to a minimum.

"'Proof against any brigands,' my dainty princess arse," I whispered.

I pulled the rope up and closed the entry after myself, and let my eyes adjust to the dark. Light came from several vent holes above, letting in moonlight. Unfortunately, none were large enough to present any opportunity for escape.

After a short wait, I could see that the passage dead-ended about ten feet from my room. I turned around and ventured back in the direction my would-be assailant had come.

I passed several hidden peepholes that looked down into other "brigand proof" rooms below.

Where was this place a year ago? If I had been able to hit travelers' purses this easily, I might never have ended up attempting the theft of dangerous artifacts from allegedly abandoned temples.

At the moment, though, that was not at the top of my agenda. I needed a way out, and I hesitated over slipping into even the unoccupied rooms as a means of escape. I'd have to pick a lock to get out, and it would place a hallway, Sir Forsythe, and a common room full of unsavory patrons between me and the exit.

I was hoping for less drama upon my departure.

The passage ended in a ladder that descended into what appeared to be a pantry. At this hour, the kitchen would offer a chance to remove myself out the rear of the inn unnoticed.

I hoped.

I slowly climbed down the ladder, being cautious with my too-loose boots, and dropped into the pantry. I edged up to the door flanked by shelves bearing baskets of root vegetables, wheels of cheese, and bags of beans and grain.

As I slowly pushed the door open, I made the mistake of telling myself that my exit seemed a bit too easy.

I peeked out the door into the kitchen, and I froze.

The center of the space was dominated by a large block of a table. Between the rust-colored stains, blood gutters, and the knives and cleavers dangling from the edges, it would have been equally at home in the ritual space of the Ziggurat of the Dark Lord Nâtlac as it was in the kitchens of The Headless Earl.

However, that wasn't the problem.

The problem was the five men seated around that altar to butchery, playing cards. None had yet noticed me.

The one facing most in my direction played a card and asked, "Isn't Diego going to be slightly pissed when he discovers Lendowyn royalty isn't in the habit of carting around fabulous jewels and such?"

The question was apparently directed at the inn-keep, who was seated across from him, his back to me. The innkeep chuckled. "Of course. But he paid for a way in, not a guarantee that he'd make back his gold. But I'm sure he'll make the best of it."

The other players laughed appreciatively at the innkeep's innuendo. It made me feel dirty just for sharing a profession with these goons.

But, as much as I suddenly wanted to carve

some respect for the fairer sex into these guys, I was outnumbered. I decided to slide quietly back and escape out one of the empty rooms upstairs.

I decided too late. One of the players turned in my direction and said, "Why don't we ask him?"

Another stared at me and said, "That ain't Diego."

I slammed the door shut as the quintet shot to their feet, knocking five chairs back to the ground. I cursed. The brief glance into the well-lit kitchen had killed my night vision, and I was left in pitch black, leaning back against the door handle, realizing there was no proper latch to the thing.

Someone started tugging from the other side, almost yanking the door out of my hands. I braced my foot on the doorframe to give me leverage, but it'd only be moments before the five men on the other side pulled it out of the princess's less than manly grip.

Thinking as quickly as I could manage, I pulled a dagger out of a sheath in my appropriated boots and shoved it through the door handle and into the wood of the frame. That held it well enough to give me a free hand. I drew another one of Diego's daggers, and shoved it into the gap between the door and frame opposite the handle, wedging the thing shut.

I let go, backing quickly away from the door. I was still nearly blind, stumbling over something in the dark. I only knew it was a barrel of pickles from the sudden vinegar smell sloshing over my boots. I heard wood splintering, and a sliver of light illuminated the pantry.

Last resort time.

I screamed.

"Help! Fraud! Rape! Regicide!" I started pulling down shelves between myself and the door.

I might have imagined it, but I think I actually heard Sir Forsythe spring to his feet from halfway across the inn.

More immediately, I watched as one plank of the door was torn free, revealing the innkeep's snarling face. I wondered for the briefest moment, *Why is he angry? He got his money.*

There was now enough light for me to see the shelves again, and I grabbed the nearest cheese wheel and threw it at his face, making him duck out of the way. I screamed, "Murder! Duplicity! Evil!" as I hurled a jar of preserves out the gap in the doorway. It thudded into the forehead of one of men back in the kitchen.

The door splintered apart as I backed into the ladder. I threw a sack of beans into their advance, causing the lead guy to slip and fall face first into the pile of spilled pickles. A dagger sprouted from a wood timber next to my head and I flattened myself against the wall, using the remaining shelves for cover. "Crime! Deceit! Thuggery!" I called out.

In response, I heard another door splinter behind the men advancing upon me. I glanced to see the men turning away from me, toward a flash of knightly armor deeper in the kitchen.

I took my opportunity to scramble back up the ladder.

I dropped into one of the empty rooms upstairs, abandoning any pretense at stealth. Below me, the sounds of an incipient war were more than enough cover for any noise I might have made. I made quick work of the lock and ran over to peek down the stairs into the common room. Using a wall for cover, I poked my head out low, below eye level.

My caution was superfluous at this point.

It seemed as if every thief, thug, brigand, and cutpurse in the area, aside from myself, had invaded The Headless Earl to converge on the kitchen. Enough people that I suspected this establishment rated its own Thieves' Guild to rival the ones in Grünwald. Everyone had some sort of weapon at hand, daggers mostly, but I caught glimpses of a sword or two, a few chairs, and one scary-looking specimen hefting one of the smaller tables.

I was probably a bad person for leaving Sir Forsythe to this riot, but by Lord Nâtlac's black twisted soul, he was the genius that chose this place.

I went downstairs, and as long as I faced the direction everyone was going, and yelled a few hoarse curses here and there, no one paid me any mind as I sidestepped along the rear of the crowd toward the entrance.

Once outside, I ran around the inn, toward the stables. While I had always been somewhat adept at disguise and mimicry, I was certain that any moment someone else might notice that the petite thief in the loose clothing was just a little too cute to be one of their number.

Once I made the turn toward the stables I stopped short as I almost tripped over the innkeep and one of his fellow card players. Fortunately for me, they were both unconscious and facedown in the slop behind the stables. As I stood there, staring, a third and fourth body sailed through the remains of the rear door of the kitchens. Inside, I caught a brief glimpse of metal-clad blond fury. I heard Sir Forsythe's voice cut through the sounds of the mob inside.

"No petty brigand may stand fast before the righteous annoyance of Sir Forsythe the Good. Tremble before my aggravation!"

I guess the guy can take care of himself.

I still felt somewhat guilty, but now it was more for my fellow tradesmen. However unrefined they might be, at least some of them probably didn't deserve to be trapped inside with that loon.

But that didn't stop me from liberating a horse and getting the hell out of there.

CHAPTER 8

Under the stars, an hour's ride from The Headless Earl, I tied my mount to a tree, climbed up into the branches, and slept much better than I had a right to.

Slept well. Woke poorly.

The sun filtered through the forest canopy to warm my face, and in waking I had a few moments of blessed amnesia where I remembered nothing of wizards and dragons and missing man parts. Then I stretched to untie some of the knots that my makeshift bed had tied in my muscles, and I felt my too-loose clothing tug against my body. I gasped in the princess's voice and grabbed myself in places where I shouldn't have had places. In my sudden recollection of everything, I lost my balance and started tumbling from my perch. I grabbed the branch as I fell, bark tearing at my ungloved hands. I fell on the princess's derriere, uttering a stream of profanity that sounded somewhat incongruous coming from her mouth.

The horse looked at me lazily, unimpressed.

I looked up and saw one of my ill-fitting boots

dangling from a branch above and decided that one of my first priorities, after finding out where I was, was to get some properly fitted clothing for my travels.

I found a good-size town within a few hours' ride. While I regretted the decision, I set my stolen mount free in some farmer's pasture as soon as I saw the signs that I was within a mile of a town named Doylen. I'd never heard of the place, but the horse had a rather prominent brand on its hindquarters that, given my luck recently, would spell trouble. Either one of the thieves' company back at the Earl had stolen the beast from some important family native to this town, or it was marked as property of some gang making its home here.

Neither option boded well for any stranger riding it into Doylen.

So the horse joined some farmer's draft animals to graze and become someone else's problem— without the less-obviously marked saddlebags and bridle.

I had never been in Doylen before, but there are some things that are common to all towns of a certain size, as long as you know where to look. In my specific case, after crossing a few unsavory palms with coin courtesy of Diego, I found myself facing a dark storefront. The only sign advertising its purpose were a few wooden posts supporting a saddle, bridle, and a set of leather armor. Given that I had wandered into one of the inadvisable parts of Doylen, the fact that the samples were unmolested strongly suggested that the occupant had the favor of the local Thieves' Guild.

In this case, it was exactly what I wanted. A reputable leatherworker might ask questions.

I walked into the shop, through a narrow aisle hung with all manner of goods, from gauntlets to bullwhips. The air in here was hot, stagnant, and smelled like the inside of a boot. In the rear, where it opened up into a workshop, a bald old man sat on a stool in front of a long heavy table running along the rear wall. The man was weathered enough that he wouldn't have looked out of place hanging on the wall with the rest of his wares.

He was working with a wicked sickle-shaped knife, doing violence to some sort of skin, his back to me. The skin was uncomfortably humanoid in outline, and I hoped that it belonged to an ogre or something similar.

I cleared my throat.

The knife stopped moving, and his head turned slowly toward me. He was bald on top, but a bushy white beard spilled out over his leather apron. He arched an eyebrow and asked, "Do I know you?"

"Gray sent me," I said, naming one of the disreputable characters who had directed me to this place.

The old man smiled, showing teeth with uncomfortably wide gaps between them. "Well what can I do for you . . ." his eyes widened a bit and his voice took on a syrupy tone that I did not like at all. "Miss?"

I hefted the saddlebags and dropped them on the floor and threw the bridle down on top. "Selling these," I said in what should have been an authoritative tone. Unfortunately, adding more husky overtones to the princess's voice did not make it more intimidating. "And I need to replace these boots, and this—"

The old man did not allow me to finish. "Yes!" he hissed, all too enthusiastically, slithering out of his seat to invade my personal space. He picked up the dangling end of my doubled-up belt and massaged the material between his fingers. "You need an entire ensemble." He placed his hands on my hips and pulled the loose ends of Diego's jacket so one end slipped off of my shoulder. "This will not do at all. Loose here." His hands traveled up my sides. "Tight here."

I backed up a step, leaving his hands clutching a phantom bosom. "Hey—"

His hands found his own hips, and he cocked his head. "And those breeches." He made a disgusted noise. "That inseam is all wrong, and where the crotch sits—chafes, doesn't it?"

I was mildly uncomfortable agreeing with him, so I just stared.

"Boots," he said. "Off with them."

"Can you—"

He clapped his hands sharply. "Please. The sooner we can dispose of this wretched outfit, the sooner we can equip you with something of value."

As I removed the boots, I asked, "How much?"

"Let us not be mercenary for a moment." He picked up my left boot and regarded it with a wrinkling of his nose. "Ghastly workmanship." He tossed it over his shoulder. It landed on a pile of leather scraps. My heart sank, since I had been hoping to trade Diego's outfit for one that actually fit.

With a deft sleight of hand, he had removed my belt before I understood what he was doing. "Hmm, salvageable," he muttered, dropping it with the saddlebags and the bridle.

This was going a bit too far. I renewed my effort at speaking authoritatively. "Before we start—" My words began as royal pronouncement, and ended with an embarrassing squeak as the man took the collar of my jacket and yanked it over my head. Too easy considering how loose it was. With my hands over my head, nothing was left to support the too-large breeches, which fell to my ankles.

The old man paid little mind to me. He tsked at Diego's jacket, saving special derision for my makeshift alterations. For a moment I was at a loss for what to do, then I bent and drew Diego's knife from where it hid inside the boot the old leatherworker had not tossed aside. Then I stepped out of the breeches, which would only be a hindrance at this point.

He tossed the jacket onto the scrap pile and turned toward me. He smiled in a way that made me very uncomfortable. "Now why don't you—" His eyes widened a bit as I brandished the knife, but he was looking off to my left.

"Oh, good," he said as he bent down to pick up Diego's breeches. There was a jingle and he rummaged in one leg and withdrew Diego's purse.

Oh, damn.

He hefted it, then tossed it back at me. I almost dropped the knife catching it. "Unless that's all copper," he said, "You can afford better than this." He tossed the breeches on the scrap pile. He walked over to his workbench and pushed the ogre skin aside and pulled out a length of rope with hash marks evenly spaced along its length. "It's been a long time since I was able to cater to a woman." He turned around, pulling his rope taut. "Now spread your arms."

I spent the better part of half an hour being exhaustively measured by the old leatherworker. While his closeness and the placement of his hands made me extremely uncomfortable, I had to admit his attentions—while not precisely innocent—were not quite the violation I had been worried about. He spoke nonstop, telling me of the years when he was the premier supplier for the women not just in Doylen, but for all of Lendowyn.

For a time I wondered at the thought that there were that many female adventurers in Lendowyn. Except for the occasional warrior princess, I hadn't ever heard of much demand for armoring the fairer sex. Then he said that a few items from his "special collection" would fit me without much alteration, and I understood.

My definition of adventure had just been too limited.

The outfit the old man produced was designed for a different form of combat than I'd been thinking of.

"Ah," I said.

"Gorgeous, is it not?"

"Uh—yes—the workmanship is excellent. But I was hoping for a little more protection."

He frowned a moment, then rolled his eyes. "Of course, you're going to wear this *outside*, aren't you?" He shook his head and disappeared deeper into his shop to rummage back in his "special collection."

In the end he came up with something that offered protection to more than my breasts and crotch, and boots whose heels were a sane height for hiking. I left the premises in an outfit that fit a little *too* well. I was a bullwhip shy of becoming a dominatrix, but at least I made an old man happy and got a good deal on the ensemble.

The downside of replacing Diego's armor was the fact that now no one could ignore my current body, including myself. Every downward glance showed me the princess's curves emphasized in well-tooled black leather. Even if I avoided glancing at my own—no, at the *princess's*—body, I could still *feel* it, every step I took.

But at least the old man's outfit finally allowed me to make the princess somewhat intimidating. As I worked my way through the underside of Doylen, I got more than my share of propositions, but I was able to deter the more aggressive ones by drawing my knife and offering free discipline from Mistress Blackthorne.

Even so, I bought a full cloak at the first opportunity, allowing the princess's assets to blend into the crowds a little better.

Unfortunately, the rest of my day, and the rest of Diego's money, were much less productive. I slid through a number of pubs, inns, and marketplaces ranging from the disreputable to the dangerous, attempting to find any information the rumor mill could give me about a dashing rogue called Frank Blackthorne, a shady wizard named Elhared the Unwise, and anything regarding dragons. I didn't mention princesses or the Lendowyn court. I was spending half my time dissuading unwanted advances, and questions about the woman whose body I wore seemed to be asking for trouble.

It always started out promising, with some version of the "dragon taking princess hostage" story. Then I'd get colorful anecdotes of Elhared's checkered past that I really wish I had known before the old bastard had hired me. Even Frank Blackthorne had gained some measure of infamy for his exploits in embarrassing the royal court of Grünwald.

And, each time, that's where the well went dry. No one seemed to have heard anything more about dragon, thief, or wizard. As I bought rounds for some of my more talkative contacts with my diminishing supply of funds, I began to develop an ugly suspicion that the ersatz Frank Blackthorne might have been captured by the Nâtlac groupies of Grünwald.

I started hoping that my body would end up on the far side of Lendowyn, away from Grünwald. I admit that, in the abstract, there was some appeal to having the Grünwald court take out their frustrations on my body while I wasn't resident. However, I doubted it would leave my body in a usable condition, and I wanted it back.

Besides, Princess Lucille didn't deserve that sort of treatment, even if she was royalty.

I had been through the stories enough by now to know when I'd reached a dead end, so I was ready to leave one particular dark hole of a tavern, when one of the newer arrivals interjected a comment into a pause in the conversation.

"Any you all hear of Ravensgate?"

A chorus of "no," rippled through the crowd around me. I certainly hadn't heard about it. I made the mistake of holding out some hope that this newcomer's story might be helpful to my mission in finding the displaced owner of my current body.

No such luck.

Not to say that his tale wasn't dramatic. According to the story he'd heard, yesterday morning at around the time a trio of thugs were debating what to do with a tied-up princess they'd found in the woods, a giant black dragon had appeared in the middle of the border town of Ravensgate. Our storyteller gave a loving description of the carnage, paying such special attention to the immolation of the city watch that I was left with the impression that he had some particular issue with official law enforcement.

Even if the story had been embellished, and Ravensgate hadn't been left a smoldering crater, I still asked for clear directions as to where Ravensgate was on the Lendowyn border—specifically in order to help me avoid it. Elhared's dragon seemed rightly pissed, and after the debacle with *Dracheslayer* I didn't want to come within four leagues of it.

Fortunately for me, the alleged massacre at Ravensgate was miles out of my way anyway, in the opposite direction from the capital from Doylen. More importantly, it was miles from the dragon's lair—which meant I would be able to find it sans dragon, and that made me feel immeasurably better. I would be free to search for signs of what had happened to Elhared's evil tome without fear of immolation.

After that, I could work on hunting down the princess and my body.

CHAPTER 9

The next day I found the dragon's lair right where I had left it. From the outside there was no sign of the wizardly apocalypse that had happened within. I loosely tied the skinny nag that the last of Diego's gold had bought me so she could graze the clearing while I was occupied, then I pulled myself back up to the scene of the crime.

Boobs aside, I practically flew up the side of the hillside in the princess's body. She might not be blessed with great upper body strength, but in comparison to my old body, she was tiny and lightweight, so I found myself pulling her body upward with almost disturbing ease.

That marked the high point of my expedition.

I lit a makeshift torch and examined every inch of the cavern, and I came up with nothing. There was little sign of any hoard aside from a few items glittering forgotten, fallen into inaccessible crevasses, and an occasional goblet or necklace on the ground that looked shiny until closer examination showed base metal and glass rather than gold and jewels. Elhared had found a dragon more broke than the Lendowyn government.

More prevalent than the remains of an ex-hoard were piles of bones from sheep, cattle, and a few wayward knights less lucky than I had been. Without the dragon's presence it all seemed sort of sad, and much less intimidating than the last time I'd been here.

Most importantly though, I found no malevolent book of wizardly nastiness. To all appearances it had been consumed in the misfire along with the unmourned wizard Elhared.

I stood over the splotch of wizard soot on the cavern floor, staring at a sharp rectangular outline within it—right about the place where Elhared must have dropped his compendium of darkness.

I uttered a very unprincesslike word.

Then I squinted and lowered the torch to examine the Elhared smudge a little closer.

Footprints.

"Well, what do you know?"

A set of footprints had scuffed the black soot on the floor of the cavern and had tracked carbonized Elhared out toward the cavern entrance. The tracks were feet larger than the ones I wore now, but about the right size for my lost body.

I let out a little victory whoop. Apparently the princess and I had had the same thoughts. And if the dislocated Princess Lucille had come back here in my skin to retrieve Elhared's evil volume of evilness, then the most sensible thing she could do would be to return to the Lendowyn court. She was probably there already, waiting for me—or at least her body—to show up. With me, the princess, and the book all in the same place, someone should be able to find a more reputable wizard to put everything right.

"Yes!" This was the first really positive sign I had seen since *Dracheslayer* had crumbled in my hands.

So, in retrospect, there was no possible way it could have lasted.

I scrambled down the hillside, impatient to get back to the castle and Princess Lucille. I had more than enough daylight left to get there even on my cheap broken-down mount. I was halfway across the clearing when the horse looked up and decided to prove there was still some life left in her. She reared at me and I took a step back.

"Calm down, girl. It's just—"

I had to scramble back to avoid being trampled. Swaybacked and half-lame she might have been, but she bucked like an unbroken colt.

"What's the matter?"

Her answer was to snap her lead from where I'd tied her and gallop into the forest. "Great," I muttered as the sky darkened to match the sudden change in my mood. It took me half a second— still way too long—for me to connect my horse's sudden spooking, my proximity to an abandoned dragon's lair, and a sudden darkening of the sky above into a coherent picture of what was happening.

I've said before, a sudden surge in optimism on my part is invariably a sign things are about to get worse. My head shot up, and I watched as my day obliged that particular rule of thumb.

Plummeting out of the sky above the clearing was a very angry-looking lizard with a fifty-foot wingspan. My horse seemed to have had the right idea. I bolted for the woods, and some cover, as the monstrous black dragon swooped dangerously low over the treetops. Branches and pine needles showered me from a near miss and the air suddenly carried a taint of brimstone.

The dragon's voice reverberated through the woods around me. **"You evil bastard! Give it back!"**

I had to stop short as a black shadow fell across the game trail in front of me, knocking smaller trees aside. A massive head dropped down, snaking in front of me on a serpentine neck.

Not quite *enough* cover, apparently.

"Bastard!" It screamed again, the force of its breath enough to knock me over. Good thing too, since the dragon's claws swept past where I had just been to splinter an unfortunate tree. It kept screaming at me, and all I could do was keep dodging as it grabbed for me. Each of its swings gouged craters into the forest floor and took out more lumber. It took a few moments of pure panic for me to realize a couple of things.

First, it wasn't trying to kill me; otherwise I'd be Princess Flambé right now. Second, it wasn't just screaming inarticulate curses at me.

It was sobbing.

My bad feeling about this got worse as I started listening to what it was saying between the sobs. **"It's mine . . . Give it back . . . You nasty old man . . .** *You're dressing me like a slut!"*

That will teach me to make unwarranted assumptions. Just because I ended up in her body didn't mean that she ended up in *mine*. Undoing Elhared's failed spell had just gotten a lot more complicated.

I tried to get to my feet to run out of her reach, but I had to duck again as the dragon's forearm took out another tree next to me. She might not be trying to kill me, or hurt her own body, but she obviously didn't know her own strength, and her hysterics were making things worse. Her mad grabs to catch me could probably snap a few bones without her even realizing it.

"Princess Lucille! I'm not Elhared!"

"Liar!" I rolled as a clawed hand came down, digging into the soil where I'd crouched, sending up showers of dirt to rain down on me.

"No, really! I'm Frank Blackthorne, the guy who tried to save you."

I winced as her claws came down in my direction, but she stopped with her hand about two feet over my head. **"Frank?"**

"Remember? I was the one who attacked the dragon—"

"Badly."

"I tried to stop Elhared—"

Her draconic hand curled into a fist above my head, and I realized that my attempt to prevent the wizard's invocations had arguably gone less optimally than my attack on the dragon.

"You screwed up his spell! It's your fault I'm like this!"

Oh, crap!

It wasn't as if I had a decent counterargument. She was right. If I hadn't interfered, there was a good chance that she would still be in the same skin—married to the old coot Elhared, but still a princess and arguably better off.

"W-We can get you out of this," I said, trying to salvage the situation. "We have your body, if we just find Elhared's book we can get someone—"

"Don't patronize me! Why do you think I'm here?"

Score one for the princess.

"Do you have the book?"

"Uh—"

"Where is it?" There was a rising note of hysteria in her voice that would have been deeply disturbing in a human speaker. From a dragon it was bowel-voidingly terrifying. **"You have it. You have to have it!"**

"It wasn't there."

The dragon raised her head to the sky and let out a scream of frustration that erupted into a shower of smoke and fire. I got to my feet and started running, because it looked as if Lucille was about to forget whose body I wore. I felt heat on the back of my neck, and heard splintering lumber behind me. **"No! You can't leave!"**

Then, as I crossed another game trail, I heard an all-too-familiar voice. "Fear not, fair maiden! Your salvation has arrived!"

I looked to my left and saw a white charger bearing down upon me, Sir Forsythe the Good astride it, sun glinting off his armor. Before I could react, his arm came down and scooped me up and across the saddle in front of him.

As we rode deeper into the forest, I heard the dragon shrieking and sobbing behind us. I didn't want to leave her in that state, but I didn't have many options at the moment.

The sounds diminished as we escaped. The last thing I heard was a quiet, heart-wrenching plea, **"Come back. Please. It's not fair."**

She was right about that much. As we galloped away, I shouted for Sir Forsythe's attention, "Hold on, stop!"

"Apologies, My Lady, but there is a dragon back there."

"I know," I shouted to make myself heard over galloping hooves. "You don't have the whole story!"

"No?"

"No! That dragon is the *real* Princess Lucille. There was an evil wizard—"

"If the dragon is the princess, who are you?"

"My name's Frank Blackthorne."

"Is it now?"

"Yes and—" I never finished that statement, because the gauntlet of Sir Forsythe the Good came down on the back of my skull and the world went black.

The sky was dark when I awoke next to a small campfire. I groaned, and Sir Forsythe responded. "Good, you are awake. I didn't get to tell you how gratified I was you survived that den of thieves, even if you were not who you purported to be."

"You hit me!"

"Well, that couldn't be helped."

I tried to place a hand to the still-aching side of my head, and my arms wouldn't listen to me. "You arrogant twit. I'm paralyzed."

Sir Forsythe clicked his tongue at me and said, "Don't be so dramatic. I simply placed a binding charm on you. Can't have you running away again."

I looked down at myself and saw that I now wore a necklace. A heavy chain suspended a glowing black stone set in a gold mounting inscribed with magical glyphs that wouldn't have been out of place in Elhared's book. Staring at that thing resting on the leather armor between the princess's breasts made my skin crawl.

That did not look like something a "Good" knight would be carrying around.

"Is that really necessary? You got to do your rescue bit. I'm sorry I'm not the princess—"

"Actually, it is a fine thing you aren't the princess. My liege will be quite happy that I've found Francis Blackthorne."

I opened my mouth. Then I closed it again. My luck couldn't possibly be that bad, could it? It took several moments for me to work up the nerve to ask who his liege might actually be.

I can't say I was surprised at his answer.

"Queen Fiona the Unyielding, monarch of the Kingdom of Grünwald."

"Of course she is." I sighed. "Doesn't this seem a little contradictory to you?"

"What do you mean?" He tossed another log on the campfire. Annoyingly, he still looked like a hero out of some popular ballad, all golden hair and shiny mail. His tabard still appeared spotless, and he had the nerve to still be smiling.

"Come on," I said. "You're supposed to be Sir Forsythe the Good, slayer of monsters and savior of helpless maidens—and you serve the Royal Court of *Grünwald*?"

"That's correct."

He doesn't know. That had to be it. It was easy to believe that this guy could be that naïve. "Sir Forsythe, the Grünwald court is in service to the Dark Lord Nâtlac."

"I'm a seventh-level acolyte myself. What is your point?"

"M-my point? *My point*? My point is that Nâtlac is one of the Seven Dark Lords of the Underworld, and generally agreed to be one of the top three nastiest. Nâtlac worship is just a little at odds with a heroic persona, don't you think?"

"I don't let that define me."

"W-what?"

"In fact, the powers granted by the Dark Lord are quite helpful in monster slaying. Strength, endurance, immunity to demon fire, the ability to inspire bowel-watering fear in one's enemies—"

"What about the ritual cannibalism?"

"Of course I find it personally distasteful, but what kind of knight would I be if I let such things stand in the way of my duties?"

"The Dark Lord Nâtlac is the personification of evil!"

Sir Forsythe shrugged. "Sometimes you need to take the bad with the good."

I opened my mouth, but my brain had had enough and refused to form any more words.

After the way the past few days had gone, it really wasn't that surprising. I wish I could have honestly said I didn't believe what he was saying, but I had long experience in the human ability to rationalize. It was a skill that those of noble birth were particularly adept at.

Silence settled around the campfire for a long time before I found my voice again, "Now what?"

I found it somewhat embarrassing that I sounded like a frightened little girl.

"We wait until dawn, and then we ride to the site of the offering."

I didn't ask what he meant. I had the strong suspicion that I did not want to know.

Instead, through the night, I tried to get Sir Forsythe to have a moral epiphany. I told him my story, how I got onto Grünwald's wanted list by saving a young innocent maiden myself, something he should empathize with. I explained Elhared's spell, and how we needed to save the princess's body intact so that the soul-transference could be reversed.

I don't know at what point in my tale the snoring started, but I kept going out of narrative inertia until I fell asleep myself.

CHAPTER 10

I didn't sleep well. My body grew increasingly uncomfortable being unable to move, and I woke periodically to the sensation of pins and needles across my left side. I spent my wakeful hours discovering that, despite my ability to move my head and neck, it just wasn't enough to grab hold of the evil necklace holding me in place.

Dawn came too soon.

Sir Forsythe the Allegedly Good threw me across his saddlebags, securing my body with some rope in addition to the binding charm. As he did, I felt twinges of nostalgia for the annoying chivalry he had shown me when he thought I was a princess.

"Is this any way to treat an innocent maiden?" I asked him as he climbed on his mount.

"You are Francis Blackthorne, are you not?"

"Yes."

"Then you are neither innocent, nor a maiden."

"And don't call me Francis," I muttered as my captor galloped off into the woods.

Slung over the horse's rear as I was, I couldn't see where we were going without craning my neck.

Even so, even though dawn was breaking, I could feel the forest growing darker around us. I lifted my head up periodically, and managed to see a bad sign.

Literally.

Next to the path Sir Forsythe followed was a large wooden sign nailed to a tree. For the benefit of the illiterate, the upper half of the sign showed a grossly obese ogre whose body was half mouth chewing off the head of some unfortunate traveler. Next to the ogre was an arrow pointing helpfully down the path in the direction we were going.

Below the disturbing image was text that I only glimpsed as we galloped by. I saw enough to get the gist. More or less it said, "Entering the Black Woods. Bad things ahead. The Kingdom of Lendowyn takes no responsibility for anything that might happen to anyone stupid enough to enter."

I suspect we passed more signs, but I only looked up in time to see one other, featuring an overly endowed demon abusing another unfortunate traveler. I decided that, if this was multiple choice, I would opt for the ogre.

Every glimpse I got of the woods when I lifted my head was becoming worse. It had to be full morning now, but where we rode the world was trapped in a gray misty twilight. Eventually the woods actually did turn black, the trees leafless and twisted, darkened as if they had recently burned. The road below us became a mix of ash, gravel, and bone.

"Let me guess, there's an altar to Nâtlac around here. Looks like his sort of place."

Beneath us, the proportion of bone in the composition of the road became higher and higher until we were traveling on a highway paved with half-buried skulls. Sir Forsythe brought our advance to a halt and I looked up.

I immediately wished I hadn't.

We had stopped in front of a twelve-foot-tall, bat-winged demon. The thing was a slavering potbellied horror, shaggy goat legs, rotting flesh crawling with worms, with the skeletal head of a stag whose massive spread of horns were decorated by a garland of someone's intestines.

I think the only reason I didn't start screaming was because I was simultaneously trying to gag and the mixed signals paralyzed my diaphragm.

The thing looked down at us with empty eye sockets and belched.

"Whatcha got there, Forsythe?" the horror asked in a tone of lower-class familiarity that would not have sounded out of place at The Headless Earl.

Sir Forsythe responded, showing no sign of being disturbed either at the demon's appearance or its overly chummy tone. "I have uncovered the thief Francis Blackthorne."

"Don't call me Francis," I said. Not that anyone paid attention.

Sir Forsythe's voice took on an air of annoyance, but it did not seem directed at either me or the demon. "What are you doing here? Is there actually a ritual going on? Now?"

"Sure enough. Prince Dudley is honoring the feast of St. Haggard of the Maggots, or some-such silliness."

The demon took a step toward us, and the breath left my lungs as one fetid clawed hand lifted my chin to face it. It stared at me with those empty eye sockets, and now I was close enough that I could just barely sense something unpleasant moving within them. "This don't look like the guy."

If you took a dead muskrat and threw it in a bucket of piss, left it a week until the body turned black and swelled to twice its size, then boiled the fluid until the stomach burst, the resulting odor would be preferable to the abattoir stench of the demon's breath.

"There was a soul-transference spell involved," Sir Forsythe told it.

The demon mercifully let my head go and stepped back, leaving my head and stomach in slow uneasy tumbles.

"Well, that explains the last one, doesn't it?" it said as it waved us onward.

It took several moments before I managed to gather myself to ask, "What 'last one?'"

Neither the knight nor the demon chose to enlighten me.

I redoubled my effort to strain my neck to see where we were going. Past Sir Forsythe's leg, I saw a rise in the middle of a clearing formed of cracked black earth. Dominating everything was a large obsidian obelisk covered in carved runes that would have probably made Elhared uncomfortable. About twenty black-robed figures surrounded the obelisk, their backs to us.

As Sir Forsythe rode to a stop and dismounted, I got a better view as one of the shorter figures broke from the circle and walked toward us.

"Well," the figure addressed him. "The legendary Sir Forsythe. Are you finally taking time out of your busy schedule for us?" The figure lowered his hood revealing a pudgy face that looked somewhat childlike, despite the graying at the temples in his disheveled mud-brown hair. The weak attempt at a mustache and goatee didn't help.

Worst of all, I recognized him. Even if he hadn't been in the front row at my one successful attempt at maiden rescue, right next to his mother the queen, it still wouldn't have been hard to place him. Crown Prince Dudley was a rather infamous bastard back in Grünwald, even for royalty. Being part of a dark circle devoted to the Dark Lord Nâtlac probably wouldn't even break the top ten in his personal list of iniquities.

I heard Sir Forsythe sigh before he addressed Prince Dudley in appropriately decorous tones, "Greetings, My Prince. It is an unexpected honor to find you here in Lendowyn."

Prince Dudley brought his hands up and

brushed them together as if he was trying to remove something distasteful. "I'm on an extended diplomatic mission for the queen. Grand plans of the crown and such." He leaned over and arched an eyebrow as he looked in my direction. "Still rescuing princesses, I see. Though isn't it a little out of character for you to truss them up and sling them on the back of your horse?"

"I am afraid that this girl is not what she seems, My Prince."

"Good," said the prince as he straightened up. His tone became darker. "Because what she *appears* to be is Princess Lucille of Lendowyn. And while I do not begrudge my servants the odd hobby, at this juncture the kidnapping of a member of the Lendowyn Royal Court by a servant of Grünwald would be . . . disruptive. The queen has plans." He took a step forward until he was barely a hand's breadth away from Sir Forsythe. His posture would have been intimidating if not for him being a head shorter than the knight. "You don't want to disrupt the queen's plans."

"No, My Prince."

"Then perhaps you could explain why you aren't taking this remarkable simulacrum of the Lendowyn princess back to the court of King Alfred the Oblivious?"

"That is a long story, My Prince." Sir Forsythe launched into a summary of the whole soul-transference business that, while largely accurate, made me out to be both more of a villain, and more of an idiot, than I remembered being. I tried voicing an objection once or twice, but Sir Forsythe's reach was long enough to introduce me to the back of his gauntlet without pausing in his storytelling.

I'd had enough.

"All lies!" I yelled. "I am the Princess Lucille of Lendowyn and I demand to be returned to my father."

Sir Forsythe raised his hand again but Prince Dudley shook his head. The knight froze, staring at me with a look of murder in his eyes.

"So," Prince Dudley said as he walked around the knight to face me directly. "You claim this is a fabrication, and you are actually the princess?"

"Of course I am. This man is a delusional lunatic." It seemed a plausible claim to me. "He saved me from a dragon, and then he clubbed me on the back of the head! Unless you want a diplomatic incident between our kingdoms, I suggest you release me now."

"Now isn't this an interesting development?" Prince Dudley smiled, giving his boyish face a disturbingly cherubic look. "The woman claims you are a liar?"

"Such audacity," muttered Sir Forsythe.

Prince Dudley bent so that our noses almost touched, and he brought a hand up to caress my cheek. I suddenly had a bad feeling about my improvisation.

"You said yourself how this would disrupt Queen Fiona's plans," I said, trying to inject as much royal steel into my voice as I could.

"Yes, Mother can be such a spoilsport at times." He shook his head. "But you really aren't the princess, are you?"

"Of course I am."

"No. I don't think so. Sir Forsythe doesn't have the wit to compose a credible falsehood. Also, I have wide-ranging experience in the world and its women. I have enjoyed princesses and prostitutes, and I would classify your attire as much more the latter than the former. Also, having met the princess on several occasions, I would have expected a few more tears." He let go of my face, and I felt my skin shudder in involuntary relief. He stepped back to address Sir Forsythe, "This explains the last one."

"What last one?" I asked, already getting uncomfortable pictures of the answer. My body was running around without me, and I couldn't come up with any scenario wherein it ran into Grünwald nobility and ended with a good result.

"I suppose you intended to sacrifice this soul cursed by the Great One all on your own?" Dudley continued, ignoring me. "You'd like to have the favor of his dark embrace all for yourself, you greedy bastard."

"Not at all," Sir Forsythe responded, "that honor should be granted to the third legitimate son of my liege, since he happens to be here."

Dudley waved over a couple of men from the circle of robed figures and gestured toward me. The pair untied me and roughly lifted me off the back end of the horse. They didn't do me the courtesy of flipping me over as they carried me, forcing me to stare at the cracked earth as I dangled between them.

Prince Dudley still talked to Sir Forsythe as his minions carried me up the hill. "The virginal flesh is a bonus. Though, the body *should* ripen a little for a feast day. I suppose we'll make do."

Suddenly I was being swung back and forth, and I barely had time to suck in a breath before I was arcing up through the air. My side slammed into something cold, hard, and unyielding. I groaned as someone pulled my shoulder, rolling me onto my back. I stared upward, the obelisk jutting up from somewhere past my head to loom over me, pointing up at a blank slate-gray sky.

Then a dozen robed figures surrounded me like wolves around a freshly slaughtered sheep carcass. Sir Forsythe's charm kept me from moving a muscle below the chain in the necklace, so all I could do was scream insults and obscenities as I felt their hands paw at the princess—at *me*— tearing off my leather. For some reason it pissed me off that they showed so little respect for it. The leatherworker in Doylen had been so proud of his workmanship.

Why was I thinking of that?

Even my own screams seemed far away from my thoughts, like I wasn't even here. Somehow, though, it made sense. It wasn't even my own body. Really, despite feeling the acolytes' hands yanking off my boots and leggings, in some sense I was just an observer watching the violence done to someone else. The paralysis only served to enhance the dreamlike dislocation. The part of my mind that continued to think along these terms wondered if this was really the case, why was I still screaming?

Apparently, one of the acolytes wondered the same thing, and, after cutting part of my undergarments off, shoved some of the shreds into my mouth. Unable to scream anymore, I could hear Prince Dudley idly talking to some of the other Nâtlac worshipers by my feet.

Someone was asking whether they should deflower the sacrifice before or after they cut out the heart. Prince Dudley responded that there was no reason why the deflowering couldn't happen before *and* after, something about the best of both worlds.

That was the point where the dislocated observer part of my mind decided to start screaming as well.

CHAPTER 11

I don't have a real clear memory of the next few moments. It seemed to last an eternity with me paralyzed, naked, and gagged on the altar, black-robed acolytes holding down my arms and legs as if I could move, Dudley at my feet undoing his breeches. At some point I remember hearing someone say, "At least it's not another wizard."

But, as Prince Dudley started climbing up to take the princess's virginity, a familiar shadow crossed above us. Dudley and the other acolytes looked up as a booming voice called down.

"I always thought you were overcompensating for something, Dudley."

Above us, dropping out of the clouds, was a black dragon gliding on fifty-foot wings, snaking its long neck down in our direction, opening a set of toothy jaws that could comfortably envelop half the altar.

One of the men holding my arms screamed like a little girl.

Prince Dudley's eyes went wide and the color drained from his face. He raised himself to his knees and slid backward off the altar, still staring at the sky. He reached down to the ground, where his breeches, belt, and scabbard had been left. He grabbed blindly for his sword, staring at the descending dragon.

It was a bad plan.

I didn't see exactly what happened, but his sword only came half out of its scabbard as something tangled up in his feet and he fell backward, naked sword between his naked legs. He cursed in pain as he dropped out of my line of sight and I winced inside.

Then my field of vision was filled by a wall of muscle and dragon scales. The dragon had landed with its feet straddling the altar. I saw a scaled forearm make a sweep and I heard an acolyte scream.

Its head—*her* head—bent down to look at me. **"Move! I'm trying to rescue you!"** Her breath blasted my naked skin with the scent of sulfur and brimstone.

I'd never been happier to have a dragon yell at me.

"I can't!" I called up at her. "Binding charm!"

The dragon uttered a word that I'm sure princesses weren't supposed to know. Then she knocked back a line of acolytes with another sweep of her forearm, raised her head, and belched three cannonball-size balls of fire after them. I heard more screams from beyond my line of sight.

"I don't believe this . . ."

She swung her tail and knocked aside another half-dozen black-robed figures as she reached down and grabbed me. She hugged me to her chest and flapped her wings, and suddenly we were airborne.

Below, I heard a familiar voice uttering an elaborate challenge up at her. We rôcketed up out of the gray mists of the cursed black forest, and the Dragon Lucille asked me, **"Did someone participating in a sacrifice to the Dark Lord Nâtlac just call *me* an unclean abomination?"**

I gulped air and yelled over wind whipping past us. "That's Sir Forsythe the Good. I think he's a bit confused."

She grunted and clutched me tighter to her chest, a gesture that probably would not have been nearly as uncomfortable with any other princess. As it was, I felt as if I was clamped between the thighs of an elephant wearing particularly baroque plate mail. It didn't help that I was naked and couldn't move.

At least she was warm, in stark contrast to the freezing wind tearing across my backside.

As she swooped up into the spinning blue cauldron of sky above us she said, **"I can't believe that heights used to make me sick to my stomach."**

I closed my eyes and said, "They still do."

The flight away from the black forest was all sickening lurches and bone-chilling cold. It was a miracle of self-control that I didn't empty my stomach during our escape—either that, or the ten-minute flight didn't give my body enough time to realize what was happening to it.

She landed on a plateau overlooking more mundane-looking woods and scattered farms and gently set me down on my feet in front of her. Of course, I promptly fell over. She grabbed me and held me up in front of a giant lizard face that may have been showing the first signs of panic.

"Are you all right?"

"Yes!" I gasped, struggling to breathe against her tight grip on me. I managed to croak out, "Binding. Charm."

She lifted me up and opened her hand so I was resting on her palm. It felt precarious because I was unable to move or shift my weight, but at least I could breathe again. I looked up at her face—her sharp, toothy, lizard face—and stared into eyes that should have been pitiless as any bird of prey's. It was the first time I'd gotten a chance to see the dragon's features in full daylight. It should have been horrifying.

It was, but not quite in the sense I expected.

Something of Lucille managed to leak out in the dragon's expression; concern, compassion, worry . . . whatever it was, it was just enough to shift the focus from the gigantic killing machine staring down at me to the young woman who was trapped inside it.

Trapped inside, and staring at her own body frozen in the palm of her hand.

And I'd thought *I* had it bad.

"The necklace," I told her. "Take it off of me."

The massive head nodded and came closer, squinting. Her other hand lifted above me, extending a finger tipped with a talon almost as long as my forearm. When it lowered in my direction, it didn't matter what I had seen in the dragon's eyes; if I hadn't been paralyzed I probably would have pissed myself.

The tip of her talon rested on my stomach and she slowly drew it up between my breasts until it hooked the charm and drew it back up over my head.

In response, my whole body shuddered and I clenched myself up in a ball on her palm.

"Oh, no! Is everything okay? Did I hurt you?"

"No. I'm just *freezing*."

"Oh."

She set me down again, and this time I was able to stand on my own, a little unsteadily. I rocked back and forth, hugging myself against the cold.

Lucille moved suddenly toward the edge of the plateau, and dropped out of sight.

"What? Princess?" I called out to her, the cold forgotten for the moment. I don't know what distressed me more, the idea of being stranded alone and naked in the princess's body, or the idea that the dragon might be suicidal.

I reached the edge of the plateau, and a steep drop by Lendowyn standards, just as Lucille flew back up the side. I stumbled back a few steps as she shot back over the edge, blasting me in a sudden downdraft. Clutched in her forearms was a large dead tree whose trunk had been weathered bone white.

"What're you doing?" I asked as she landed.

"I'm sorry. I don't seem to feel cold anymore." She dropped the tree down on a bare patch of ground, gulped, and exhaled a small holocaust onto the unsuspecting log. I didn't even need to move to feel the heat from the sudden conflagration.

"Thanks," I said, stepping forward and turning around to melt the frost off my chilled backside.

"I should have thought of that earlier," she said as quietly as a dragon could manage. After a pause, she added in a lighter tone, **"but I did think of something ahead of time."**

"What—" I began to ask, but she had slipped away again.

I guessed I'd find out soon enough. I paced alongside the fire, allowing each part of my body turns at being warm again. Naked, lost, and misplaced I might be, but I was incredibly grateful to be alive.

Lucille the Dragon had managed to truly outclass me in the princess-saving department, and she didn't even need a shady wizard to put her up to it. Even if it was her own skin she was saving, I still had to give her an order of magnitude more credit than I would've any other royal. "We'll get you your body back," I said to the fire. "At this point it's the least anyone can do."

I jumped as a massive bundle of something landed next to me, and the ground thudded as Lucille landed about ten yards away. I looked over at her and she had her head cocked inquisitively at me.

I turned to the bundle she'd dropped. It was a sheet of torn gray canvas showing signs of teeth and claw marks, tied into a rough sphere by a massive knot on top. "Okay," I said, and started struggling with the knot.

After a minute or so of struggling, she said, **"Here, let me."**

The ground shook at her approach, and then a large scaled forearm reached over me, and a pair of talons clamped onto a loose flap of canvas and tugged.

The bundle fell open, spilling its contents in front of me.

My eyes widened as a cascade of boots, underwear, cloaks, and all manner of clothing spilled out at my feet. The selection seemed random, and gathered in haste—I saw at least two boots that were obviously missing their mates—but it made me feel an uneasy mix of gratitude and inadequacy. Not only had she outclassed me today in the hero department, she was gaining ground in terms of thievery as well.

I turned to face her and asked, "How did you know they were going to strip me for a sacrifice?"

"I didn't. I just saw you were dressing me like a whore."

Oh, yeah, that. I resisted the urge to say that it hadn't been my fault. Instead, I rummaged in the dragon's haul to put together a practical traveling outfit. And, to my relief, the selection did not consist solely of long lacy dresses and shoes of doom.

As I got dressed I asked her what happened, and about the rumors I'd heard about the destruction of Ravensgate. She sighed, flopped on the ground with an earth-shaking thud, and rested her head on her folded forearms. The old me could have looked her in the eye, but in the new princess version I had to tilt my head up to see she wasn't meeting my gaze.

She'd turned her massive head away from me, to stare out over the rise. I'd never thought of a dragon as a terribly expressive creature. From what I had seen, their faces were largely capable of only three expressions: sleep, disinterest, and bowel-melting rage. But seeing the Princess Lucille staring out at the horizon, head tilted away from me, double-lidded reptilian eyes half-closed and unfocused, I couldn't help but see the giant lizard as horribly sad.

And guilty?

"You didn't really . . ."

"It wasn't my fault." If anything, that booming voice sounded close to tears. **"I was frightened. I**

didn't know what had happened to me. I woke up and the first thing I heard was so many people screaming. I opened my eyes and I was falling toward the ground, and everyone was running away from something terrible." Lucille shook her head slowly and closed her eyes. Next to me, her hand closed into a fist, causing her talons to dig into the earth, leaving a hole the size of a shallow grave. "I didn't realize they were running from *me*."

"I'm sorry." I looked up at her and both my pounding heart and churning stomach hadn't quite realized that I wasn't facing the monster they thought I was. I ignored my panicked body—it wasn't mine anyway—and stepped forward to place my hand on the back of her fist. I don't know if she could feel my touch through her armored skin, but it probably wasn't appropriate for me to hug royalty anyway, even if it had been physically possible.

She had crashed into the town center at Ravensgate, still terrified and disoriented. She destroyed a blacksmith and a bakery just by standing up, turning around, and trying to see what everyone was screaming at. When she saw what had frightened them, she had screamed herself—and accidentally discovered the ability to breathe fire. By then, yelling at the fleeing populace that she wasn't really the dragon didn't do much to assuage their fears.

Then, as she was desperately trying to stamp out the fires she had started, things got worse.

"Worse? How?"

She groaned and nodded as if her neck strained against the weight of the small mountain below us. **"Ravensgate is a border town, a crossroads for mercenaries, adventurers, militias, and privateers. Of course they would mass to 'defend' the town against an invading monster."**

Like the dragon's face, I'd never really thought of a dragon's voice conveying much beyond contempt or stentorian anger, but I could hear her words—booming as they were—dripping with sarcasm.

"They attacked you?"

She laughed. Even though I never heard a dragon laugh before—and that is an unnerving experience to begin with—I could tell there was little humor in it. **"They tried."**

"You didn't . . ." I had the brief mental image of the draconic princess finally snapping and slaughtering the town's defenders in a demonic fury.

She whipped her head in my direction, making me flinch. **"No! You don't think—I wouldn't . . ."**

I was suddenly more terrified of making her cry. "Of course you wouldn't. Tell me what happened."

From what Lucille could tell in the ensuing chaos, there had been three main groups of defenders—organized parties of more than ten people. The smallest of the three groups, in numbers and stature, were the mercenary fighting dwarves of the Graybeard Mountains. The next most populous group bearing arms against the reptilian invasion were the dozen or so members of the Greencoat Raiders, a ratty group of oceangoing privateers. Lastly, and most numerous, were over twenty members of the Lendowyn Militia.

"Lendowyn can afford a militia?"

"They're volunteers that fight for the king in exchange for whatever goods they can liberate from the battlefield."

"I see no way that could go badly."

Those were the three main forces. To that was added at least seven smaller groups of two to three armed adventurers. All converged to save Ravensgate from the invading dragon.

From the way she said "save," I began to understand exactly what must have happened. She confirmed my thoughts when she explained that, from all appearances, the dwarves had been drinking for most of the prior evening, and possibly the three nights prior to that.

"Their judgment was not in the best of shape. Not to mention their aim."

"Their *aim?* They missed . . ." I trailed off, because what I was about to say would have been terribly unflattering to a normal princess—even though, at the moment, Lucille was literally the size of several of the proverbial barn doors.

"First blood I saw was a small throwing axe embedding itself in the backside of the captain of the Greencoats."

"That . . . couldn't have been good."

It wasn't.

The Greencoat Raiders, being little more than officially sanctioned pirates, had pretty clear views on how to deal with that kind of insult, and engaged the dwarves in a counterattack that was not quite as badly impaired as the dwarves'. Lucille suspected they had only been drinking about half as long as the dwarves prior to battle.

Of course, once the dwarves and the Raiders engaged in open warfare in the streets of town, the Lendowyn Militia had to make all efforts to suppress the fighting, pushing the two forces into the merchant areas where the battle could be more profitable.

"They forgot me completely. By the time I flew away, half the town was on fire." She sniffed. **"I should have tried to stop them, but I was so scared . . ."** She buried her face in her arms and her whole body began shaking.

I walked around in front of her and strained to reach up and touch her on the side of her face I could reach over her scaled forearm. "It's not your fault."

"I should have tried to stop them." Even a sobbed whisper into her folded arms had a booming quality I felt in my chest.

"How, exactly? They wouldn't have responded to reason—and would it have been better to stick around to claw them or set them on fire?"

She paused, and after a few long moments said, **"No."**

I don't know how she managed to sound small and frightened, but she managed it.

"Leaving the situation was the best thing you could have done."

She lay there, still and silent, for a long time. Then, her eye opened and she blinked at me. I looked back at her dinner-plate–size reptilian eye, dwarfing the hand I'd placed on her cheek, and I realized that my heart wasn't racing anymore.

"Thank you, Francis."

"It's the truth. You did the best you could with a bad situation."

"It's awful."

"And call me Frank, please."

"Frank." She inhaled and raised her head from her arms, pulling away from my hand gently so I didn't have to scramble back. She moved with more grace than you'd expect of someone who'd just become a multiton lizard. **"I don't want to be a dragon."**

"I understand. I don't really want to be a princess either."

CHAPTER 12

Her head snaked around and faced me. **"Why not?"**

"I'm sure it's wonderful and all, but I'm a guy."

She sniffed and turned away, her nostrils loosing small curls of steam. **"I'm sorry, it's just . . . you're still human."**

"Uh—" I stopped short because she was right. Princess Lucille had really gotten the worst of this deal. By comparison, I was suffering a minor inconvenience. "I want to fix this too."

"I know."

I walked around in front of her until we were facing each other again. "So let's talk about how we do that."

She tilted her head in a nod, and lowered it until her chin touched the ground near my feet. White steam still curled from her nostrils, and I caught the slight scent of brimstone. I wasn't nearly as frightened as I should have been. **"How? The book wasn't there."**

"I know. But I was planning—before the court of Grünwald sidetracked me—to return to your father. Do you think he could help us?"

"Do you really think it's a good idea to travel to my father's castle together when every would-be prince in a hundred miles is looking to save you from me?"

I sighed myself. "It seemed more plausible when I assumed that you were running around in *my* body."

"You don't know the half of it."

"I don't like the way that sounds."

"Do you know anything about the Lendowyn legal system?"

"I've been in this kingdom for less than a week."

"Well, there was a royal proclamation offering my hand in marriage?"

"Yes, to whoever brought you back, along with the head of the dragon that took you."

"Of course."

"Well, if we get to your father and explain—"

"It's not that simple."

"Why not?"

"Because proclamations like that are enchanted and magically binding, to prevent the parties—my father, King Alfred in this case—from reneging. The only way it can be voided is by the hand of the wizard who drafted it for the court."

"Elhared?"

"Elhared."

"That does complicate things."

"There's more."

Of course there was.

It was bad enough that while Lucille was in the dragon's body, her own father had a price on her head, an offer that Elhared would have made difficult, if not impossible, for the king to rescind. The old coot seemed too smart to allow the king to muck up his plans that way.

No, the worst part was the structure of the Lendowyn legal system in regard to the nature of spells of the type Elhared had employed against us.

Some legal scholar in the mists of Lendowyn prehistory had made the observation that it opened too many cans of worms to provide a separate status to someone or something possessing the body of a Lendowyn citizen. Should someone be able to opt out of their taxes because they happened to suffer demonic possession? What would one do when the twelfth son shows up claiming all the inheritance because Dad decided to take up residence in his body? Then all manner of crimes could happen and the perpetrator could just claim that something or other was using his body when he set fire to his neighbor's sheep.

It was easier for everyone just to ignore the whole soul thing.

That meant, despite any evidence to the contrary, Princess Lucille had no real legal status at all except as an enemy of the state. For all intents and purposes, I was currently the princess and heir to the throne of Lendowyn.

She stared at me as she told me about that legal

wrinkle, and watched as the implications of it sank in.

I wasn't just wearing her body. I *was* her in every important respect. If I walked into the Lendowyn court and was entirely truthful with them about what happened and who I was—they would still have to treat me as Princess Lucille. Legally, even though I stood here in front of the *real* princess, *I* was the one who was a member of the Royal Court of Lendowyn.

I patted the tip of her nose. "I need a moment."

I took a few steps away, and half-sat and half-collapsed on the ground.

"Are you all right?"

I raised a hand. "A moment."

She had told me just how easy it could be for me to escape most of my problems. If I was willing to stick with the changes in my body—and Lucille was right in that it was nowhere near as bad as it could have been—all I needed to do was present myself to the Lendowyn court to get most of what Elhared had promised me. I would have just as much protection from the ritual angst of the Nâtlac cultists of Grünwald *as* the princess as I would have if I'd been married to her. Then there were all the perks of being royalty, even in a bankrupt kingdom.

All I had to do was abandon the princess to her fate.

A deep, shameful part of my brain whispered to me, *"She's a big girl. She can handle herself."*

"Frank?"

I couldn't look at her. I hugged myself and stared at the ground, my stomach churning with a toxic mix of self-loathing and self-pity.

"I don't blame you."

"What?" I turned my head to face her, suddenly terrified I had said something out loud.

"This isn't your fault. Don't blame yourself."

"What?"

"You didn't know what Elhared was planning."

"I should have."

"You risked your life to save me."

"Well, after pulling me off of that altar, I think we're even on that score."

"Frank, you faced a dragon for me. You're still my knight."

"Uh . . . There's one thing . . ."

I wanted to tell her the truth. I really did. But when I looked into her face, and saw the gratitude peeking from behind her reptilian features, the words disintegrated in my mouth. I couldn't tell her that her knight was just another fraud in this whole fraudulent mess.

"What one thing?"

I stood up and tried to compose myself. "I don't care what the law says. You're still the Princess Lucille." I bowed to hide how ashamed I felt.

"Thank you."

The way she said it made me feel worse.

*   *   *

Later on in the evening, the topic of conversation had thankfully traveled far away from myself and exactly how much of this debacle I had been responsible for. She had flown off to find us a meal, which gave me enough time to berate myself in private so I could devote my thoughts toward planning something potentially more productive than self-recrimination.

As we ate, I told her what I had come up with.

She lifted her nose from the roasted flank of her second wild boar and looked at me. **"So we don't go back to Father?"**

I shook my head. "No, not right now." I took what was left of the boar's leg she had given me and tossed it back to her. It must have been dragon reflex, but her head jerked and her jaws snapped shut on it way faster than something that size should have been able to move. I jerked back in shock.

She swallowed, bones and all, then turned her head to face me. **"I'm sorry, were you done with that?"**

"Y-yes."

"You were saying?"

I was still not quite sure about how to read her expression most of the time, otherwise I would swear she looked amused.

"To get this reversed we need the book, and we need to find my body."

"I suppose I can't have my body back until you have somewhere to go."

"Right, and it seems that if we find Elhared, we'll find both."

"Elhared? Didn't he blow up?"

"I thought so too. But someone came and took the book from the cave. Someone who wore the same size boots I used to. And hijacking my body was more or less what the old coot intended when he cast the spell of doom."

"You think it was him?"

"Yes, and I think he ran afoul of the same emissaries of the Grünwald court as I had." I explained the things I'd overheard when I was being taken for the sacrifice, especially the reaction of everyone when they heard that I was Frank Blackthorne.

"That explains the other one."

Of course, she asked the inevitable question.

"What does the Grünwald court have against you?"

"I—ah—disrupted one of their ceremonies."

"Disrupted?"

"I sort of . . . accidentally . . . stole the queen's virgin sacrifice."

"Accidentally?"

I swallowed and forced myself to bear the whole ugly truth. "Well the Ziggurat was supposed to be abandoned. But there they all were, chanting and waving sharp things around. I couldn't leave the poor woman there . . . Elhared used that whole mess to con me into—"

"I'm sorry."

"Trying and—What?"

"I misjudged you. I thought you were just try-ing to save me because of the so-called reward."

"That's what I was trying to say. I was in the Ziggurat because—"

"She wasn't a princess, was she?"

"No, but what I'm trying to tell you is that I'm—"

"You're a good man, Frank Blackthorne."

"Uh, thank you?" I wanted to finish, I really did. But my courage fled me. I couldn't bring my-self to contradict Princess Lucille's image of me. And it made me feel even worse for weighing the option of abandoning her.

"Anyway," I said, changing the subject, "if we find Elhared and drag him before your father, then I think we can fix this." I *wasn't* a good man, and the sooner we unraveled this mess, the better.

"That makes sense."

"Unlike us, he has no reason to return to Len-dowyn Castle—not without me—you—in tow to get his reward. He's probably laying low trying to figure out a way to make that happen."

"So how do we find him?"

I had an answer, but I didn't much like it. We had to talk to the last people who saw Elhared wandering around in my old body.

"Do you have any idea where the Grünwald diplomatic mission would be hanging out when they're not making sacrifices to their Dark Lord?"

*   *   *

The Grünwald mission made its home in the northern palace, which used to be the summer home of Lendowyn royalty until the costs of upkeep became more than the treasury could handle. For the last decade or so, the property had been rented to various other kingdoms—Grünwald being the latest and most lucrative tenant.

My response upon hearing this was to ask if the king had any idea how they spent their spare time. Lucille responded with a massive shrug. They paid well.

Of course they did.

Lucille flew us there just before daybreak the next day, to avoid the rather obvious sight of a dragon flying across half the kingdom in broad daylight. She landed us on a wooded hillside overlooking the palace. Our timing was fortuitous, as dawn had barely begun to break when a caravan of men and exhausted horses came down the main road toward the palace.

There was no mistaking the horseman in the lead. Sir Forsythe the Good was the only member of the company who didn't look dirty, exhausted, or wounded.

"That bastard's still alive?" came a terrifying whisper from behind me. Lucille's breath burned the back of my neck. I was about to say something about Sir Forsythe leading some sort of charmed existence, when I saw that the "good" knight was not who she referred to. In the midst of the party, Prince Dudley lay in a cart, bandaged from the waist down.

"I'll incinerate him."

I turned to her and said, "Not subtle, My Princess. Though I appreciate the thought."

"He was going to rape and kill me."

"I know, but he's the best lead I have on El-hared. We need to talk to him, not slaughter him."

"How do you intend to do that? Just sneak in there?"

"That's pretty much my plan."

"You're kidding."

I turned away from the palace to face Lucille. She had done her best to conceal herself behind the tree line, flattening her body against the ground so from a distance she'd just seem to be a small hillock nestled behind the trees. Her head lay on the ground next to me, tilted slightly in my direction, eyes staring right at me.

"I've broken into more secure places."

"Maybe, but you aren't built like a knight anymore, Frank."

Was I ever?

I had the urge to try and tell her again who I really was, but this wasn't the time for that. Instead I told her, "Sneaking, not fighting. And I think your body is better built for skulking around than my old one was."

She said **"Oh,"** as if she wasn't quite certain

how to take my comment about the usefulness of her body.

"Be ready to fly us out of here if we need a quick getaway." I didn't give her a chance to talk me out of it. I just started climbing down toward one of the rear walls of the palace.

She called out after me, **"You're very brave."**

I didn't know if that made me feel better or worse.

I wasn't kidding when I'd told Lucille that her body was better suited to thievery than my own. While I had built a typical skill-set for my profession, from lock picking to pickpocketry, being tall and lanky had always limited my ability to hide in the shadows. The princess's body, on the other hand, was petite, and not only made me much lighter on my feet, but also made it much easier for me to hide.

The princess's low profile was half the reason I was able to make it down to the walls on the shaded side of the palace unseen. The other reason was the fact the inhabitants weren't paying much attention. The palace appeared oversized for the Grünwald delegation, which meant they were understaffed for the size of the perimeter. Even with guards on the upper wall making rounds, there were four minutes out of twenty when my side of the wall was completely unobserved.

And again I found the princess's body adept at climbing, even a wall that didn't intend to have much purchase. I was able to inch up an inside corner where a tower met the outer wall, holding my weight up just with the pressure of hands and feet pressing against the angled walls. I just had to endure the sensation of the princess's boobs rubbing against the stone.

To quote Sir Forsythe, I had to take the bad with the good.

Scaling the wall took me the better part of half an hour, most of it spent halfway up, waiting for the guards on the wall to pass by my position. Near the top, I pulled myself up and through one of the tower windows. It was a maneuver I would have never attempted in my old body; the window was much too narrow. It was almost too narrow for the princess. While I could mash her breasts to fit through the opening, I discovered that her hips were not subject to that kind of deformation. I had to corkscrew myself to align her pelvis with the long axis of the window before I could slide myself through.

But I made it. I was in the palace.

Now I just needed to find Prince Dudley.

CHAPTER 13

It must say something about my state of mind, or my less-than-reputable history, but as I hunted through the half-used hallways of the Lendowyn Summer Palace, I felt more at ease then I had since I'd broken into Lord Nâtlac's Ziggurat. Despite being in an alien body, I finally felt as if I was in my element and I knew what I was doing.

It was just too bad that, given their financial situation, there'd be no priceless Lendowyn royal artifacts laying around for me to liberate—though, considering my legal status as described by Lucille, I wondered if I did take anything if it would count as theft anyway. I only appropriated a single dagger from a weapon display. I wouldn't have bothered, since I didn't even have a proper sheath for it, but the princess had omitted any arms from the wardrobe she had scavenged for me.

I slipped through the maze of hallways, operating counter to my own instincts, moving toward where I sensed people. After nearly fifteen minutes, I finally came to the portion of the palace that showed signs of habitation—furniture recently dusted, lamps and candles that had seen use in the last few hours.

My luck held, as I heard a whispered conversation before I came upon the speakers. The sounds came from around the corner of an intersecting hallway ahead of me and I edged up on the corner slowly as I tried to make out what was being said.

I heard an old woman's voice. "The soulless little twit has no respect for his elders."

"Agatha! Mind your words," someone else snapped in a loud whisper.

"She's right, Beatrice."

"I'm not saying she's wrong, Mabel. There are simply things that do not profit us to say."

I looked around the edge of the wall, ducking my head below eye level to avoid a casual glance. In the hallway beyond, I saw a trio of black-robed, white-haired old women. To my eye they looked exactly alike.

"Should I hold my tongue before my sisters? Will *you* tell the queen I think her son has less use than half a bag of fresh pig manure and is less pleasant company? Or that I've seen headless chickens with more aptitude? Or that the better part of him ran down his father's leg?"

"Agatha, *please*."

"Sister, I did not grow so old to be afraid that someone might take offense that I noticed that the prince has the intellect of a moldy turnip and the disposition of a leprous frog."

The third woman sighed and said, "Come, sisters, we have a poultice to brew."

As they walked on, away from me, I heard Agatha whisper, "If there is any justice in the world, it will *sting*."

I watched them walk away, and then looked up the hallway in the other direction. There was one ornate door that may have been where they'd just come from. Judging by Agatha's complaining, they most likely had just had to deal with Prince Dudley.

If my luck held, he was behind that door.

I edged up on the door, undoing the latch and allowing it to drift silently open. Beyond was a bedroom with a roaring fireplace, ornate tapestries, and a giant bed with a tasseled canopy. The bed's single occupant lay half-sitting on a mound of silk cushions. He didn't look in my direction. Instead, he stared into a teacup with obvious distaste.

"Crone! This tea is lukewarm!"

If I had any doubts of the bed's occupant, that put them to rest.

"Do you hear me?" Prince Dudley raised his voice as I slipped quietly into the room and edged to the side of the bed. "I need hot tea. *Hot!*" He fidgeted a bit, shifting his legs under the sheets. "And you bound my wounds too tightly. My leg itches."

He continued complaining, covering the sound

of my approach, until I was within arm's reach. He turned in my direction and yelled, "Crone!" at me.

"Nope," I responded. With a quick one-handed gesture, I lassoed Sir Forsythe's binding charm around his neck.

His eyes went wide and he opened his mouth to scream for help. With one hand I raised my stolen dagger as I covered his mouth with the other. That knocked the teacup from his now-paralyzed hand, spilling the contents over the sheets. His eyes went wider, began watering, and he started screaming against my palm.

"Oh, come on. You said it was lukewarm."

Muffled screams of agony kept coming from under my hand and I raised my dagger up to eye level. "What do I have to cut off to make you shut up?"

He shut up.

"Now, Prince Dudley, I'm going to lower my hand. As I do that, I want you to remember that you are more concerned with keeping all your pieces attached than I am. Understand?"

He nodded and I lowered my hand.

"W-what do you want?"

"Elhared."

"Elhared?"

"Are you hard of hearing as well as being a half-assed necromancer?"

"I don't know what you—"

I pressed the blade of the dagger against his throat and he sucked in a breath as he winced from the neck up. I noticed now that my weapon was more ornamental than anything else. I cursed under my breath as I realized that I'd be better off clubbing him with it than trying to use the sorry excuse for a blade.

Fortunately for me, the prince didn't know any better.

"Oh, yes. You mean the Lendowyn court wizard, don't you?"

"You know I do."

"Have you tried Lendowyn Castle? He has been known to frequent there."

"You're stalling."

"No, really. I'm trying to help. Why would I know anything about Lendowyn wizards?"

"'That explains the other one,'" I quoted back to him.

"Oh. Uh."

"What 'other one,' Dudley?" I pressed the dull dagger into his throat.

"Ack. Please, the whole ceremony—that wasn't personal. You just were in the wrong place at the wrong *oof*."

Cutting something off would have taken too long with the blade I had, so I'd just punched him in the groin with my off hand. Unfortunately, the princess's body couldn't put much force behind it. Fortunately, Prince Dudley could probably have been brought to tears by a five year old yanking his hair and kicking him in the shins.

"Elhared, Dudley. You know what happened to him, and to me. And you were the last to see him in his new body." I punched him again for emphasis. "You're going to tell me where the wizard went."

"Please, stop," he whispered, sounding as if he was on the verge of strangulation.

I held my position, my left fist raised. I glanced at the blade at his neck, and saw a deep dent where the dull blade pressed into his flesh. My knuckles were white, and I had forced it against him hard enough that the so-called point had actually drawn a bead of blood. If the dagger had any edge at all, Dudley would probably have been decapitated by now. I eased up a bit so I could understand what he was trying to say.

"Fell Green," he choked out.

"What?"

"Try searching. In Fell Green," he said between gasps.

"Never heard of it."

"Market town. Border. Sells things. You can't get. Elsewhere."

"Elhared went there?" I was wondering why I hadn't heard of this town "Fell Green," given the source of my livelihood. I made it my business to know every black market and smuggler's haven for two or three kingdoms in every direction. If some town specialized in marketing contraband anywhere in the area, I should have at least heard of it.

Then it struck me that the contraband I thought about, and the contraband Elhared and this little necromantic twerp would be in the market for, would be two *very* different things.

"You're talking about a wizard town?"

"What else?"

That did make sense. Though, despite Dudley having the backbone of a hardboiled egg, I couldn't help but think the information came a little too freely. Trusting anything this guy said seemed a fool's game.

I started to lean into the knife again, to press him for more details, when the door to the bedroom swung open letting in a stench reminiscent of what the gastric result of overindulgence of Mermaid's Milk must smell like.

I turned to see a familiar trio of old women, standing frozen in the doorway, staring at me with my knife at Prince Dudley's throat. The one in the lead, Mabel I think her name was, held a small cauldron the size of a human skull, from which drifted green-tinted steam.

"Ma'am," I said as calmly as I could manage. "As you can see, I have the prince hostage. If everyone stays calm and quiet, he won't get hurt. Do we understand each other?"

The three women looked at each other, then at me, and finally at Prince Dudley. I could swear I saw the ghost of a smile on Mabel's face before she dropped the steaming cauldron with a crash, spilling the foul brew everywhere. The women turned and ran down the corridor screaming, "Help! Murder!"

So much for stealth. I looked at Dudley, who was still gaping at where the women had been, and said, "I think you need to work a little harder on motivating your people." Then I clobbered him on the side of the head with the hilt of the dagger and retrieved the binding charm.

The princess may have had a shorter stride than I used to have, and probably wouldn't have been able to beat me at a flat run, but her body was nimble, and my escape through the suddenly populated halls of the Lendowyn Summer Palace was all dodging and quick shifts in direction. One corridor was blocked by rushing guards and I was able to quickly dive through a closing door, dodging servants as I ran across a banquet table to slip out the kitchens before the old me would have been able to turn around.

When I finally came to a door leading to the battlements outside, coming in was a giant bearded man holding a battle-axe. He wore the skin of a wolf tied around his neck as a cloak. The wolf looked as if it had been bigger than me in life and on this guy it looked small.

He grinned at me, taking a confrontational stance and readying his axe before the open doorway, the door swinging shut behind him.

I did something I never would have attempted

in my old body. I rushed him. The giant's eyes widened, as if this was the one thing I could have done that would have surprised him. He raised his axe, but he reacted too slowly to stop me.

I dove between his legs, rolled across the threshold onto the battlement, and leaped up to my feet before the guy knew what was happening.

My victory was short-lived. I was brought up short by a familiar voice coming from the other direction. *"Hold, intruder!"*

Of course Sir Forsythe was up here.

He ran toward me, across the battlements, shouting something about the fruits of deception. I looked behind me and, small consolation, the giant I had dodged had contented himself with blocking my retreat, leaning against the door to enjoy the show.

He had every reason to expect that show to be a short one. Sir Forsythe charged me, all blade and glinting armor, and I stood there in salvaged clothing holding a dagger that would do better service as a tent peg. I yelled at the charging knight. "You know, by Lendowyn law, I *am* the princess now. You don't want to cause an incident, do you?"

Sir Forsythe seemed unconvinced as he swung his sword at me. I dodged under his swing and jumped up on the outer wall, jumping from merlon to merlon around him, thanking whatever deity was listening that Lucille's body had good balance even when taking the top-heavy additions into account.

His sword chipped stone at my feet and I jumped again, yelling back. "Attacking me could be seen as an act of war, you know."

"Much as assaulting the prince of Grünwald?"

Damned if he didn't have a good point there.

I kept ahead of his swings, but I was running out of battlements. The wall swung out and came to a sharp point where I'd have to turn back and meet Sir Forsythe and his sword. "Come on," I said. "You can still rescue me. That was the original idea wasn't it?"

"Stand still, thieving harlot."

As I reached the corner, and the end of my straight-line escape from Sir Forsythe, I was gratified to see a shadow move quickly across the sky above me. I reached the corner and jumped out into the sky about fifty feet above the ground.

Just in time for Lucille to catch me in a bruising embrace.

As we flew away to the sound of Sir Forsythe's curses, Lucille said, **"That blond ass *did* call me an unclean abomination."**

CHAPTER 14

"I don't understand why you're so calm."

I paced around Princess Lucille, shaking my head. "We have other things to worry about." We had come to ground deep in the forest, in a clearing caused by a long-ago fire. It was isolated from any roads, far from any observation by brigands, cultists, or would-be knights.

"What if I hadn't been in time to catch you?"

"If you hadn't been there, I wouldn't have jumped."

A draconian fist slammed into the forest floor in front of me, the force of the impact almost knocking me over. **"Frank,"** she snapped at me. **"It isn't just your own skin you're risking."**

"I—uh—"

"You could have killed yourself, and lost me any chance—" She sucked in a breath and I saw her lower jaw trembling.

Damn. If there was anything more disconcerting than having a dragon angry at you, it was watching one about to cry.

"I'm sorry, Princess."

"You can't die. You're all I have."

"I'll be more careful."

The fist in front of me unclenched, and she raised the tip of a talon so that the side of it brushed gently against my cheek. **"Please."**

I placed a hand on her talon to steady myself as I stepped back, mostly so I didn't stumble and make it look like a panicked retreat from her. Not that I didn't trust her. I trusted her enough to jump off a castle wall into her embrace—I'd had no choice, but even so. It wasn't trust so much as a healthy respect for a natural weapon the size of a short sword touching me so close to my neck.

After all, I'd just promised her I'd be more careful.

"Fell Green," I said, changing the subject.

"Yes?"

"You know the town?"

"In a way."

Lucille only knew the town because her presence in the royal court made her aware of it as a point of friction between Lendowyn and the Duchy of Dermonica, regarding which one had jurisdiction over the town.

"Both rulers trying to claim it?"

"No, as I understand it a war nearly broke out because Dermonica continually tried to insist it was on our side of the border."

"Of course . . ."

"The legends that have it moving around by itself don't help matters."

Because it would be too easy if our destination had a set geographic location. I could picture Prince Dudley laughing at us, and I found myself wishing all manner of unfortunate infections on the man.

To make it worse, I didn't know if the status of the wizard town of Fell Green made his assertion about Elhared's location more or less likely. It certainly sounded like the type of place a dark mage might run to ground.

"Do you know where it's *supposed* to be?"

"On the border."

"So how long is the border with Dermonica?"

"Less than a hundred miles along the Fell River."

"Well, I guess that narrows it down, doesn't it?"

In the late morning it seemed straightforward enough. Fly out to the river and follow it until we saw the town. She had even gotten the hang of gliding along with the wind so that we felt almost still—so it was only the terrifying height that made me sick to my stomach.

Nausea aside, it was the swiftest form of travel I had ever experienced. We covered the length of the Dermonica border in less than four hours.

The problem was a distinct lack of any population center larger than an isolated inn or cattle farm.

"Are you sure this is the Fell River?"

"I know the geography of my kingdom."

"Then the town. Are you sure it's on the river."

"I told you! It moves!"

"Please, don't get upset, I wasn't trying to—"

"It's hiding from us."

"I just want to make—" I stopped.

"What?"

"A wizard town. Of course it's hiding from us."

"Pardon? I was speaking metaphorically. We could have missed it."

"No, maybe it doesn't actually move. Maybe the wizards just have it well hidden from the casual traveler, some massive enchantment to conceal its real location."

"Well that's just great. How do we find it then?"

"We look for the things they can't hide."

However well camouflaged Fell Green might have been—even if it was completely invisible—the fact remained that there was no mundane town of any substantial size along this stretch of the Fell River. Apparently, the only real commerce between Lendowyn and Dermonica was in invective.

That meant it was likely that any well-traveled roads in the area would be leading to Fell Green, since it seemed that the unseen town was the only destination of note. As the sun began setting, we found what seemed to be a likely prospect, a crossroads where three marginally maintained paths led to a wide dirt avenue cutting through the Dermonica forest in the middle of nowhere.

"Why don't you land there?" I pointed out a clearing close to the crossroads.

"Shouldn't we follow the road?"

"Aren't you tired?"

"Honestly? It—" She paused so the only noise was the rustle of wind by us. **"I enjoy it. Flying."**

"Honestly? I don't." I glanced toward the sunset and squinted my eyes against the wind. "I'm freezing, dizzy, and this town doesn't sound like the kind of place best approached at night."

She sighed and descended.

Unlike other lizards, dragons apparently had substantial reserves of body heat. It probably had to do with breathing fire. So, as the sky faded to purple, I was lying against her for warmth. She curled around, chin resting on her tail so I was surrounded by a wall of muscle and dragon scale. It was actually sort of cozy in an objectively terrifying sort of way. I asked her for any more information she had on Fell Green.

Her sigh resonated along her neck beneath me.

"I told you all I know. I was the princess, at best I was a prop when it came to diplomacy. At worst I was a bargaining chip."

"Was it really that bad?"

"Frank, what was the price for my own rescue?"

"I see what you mean."

"It never was all sunshine and rainbows being my father's daughter. Gods. You have no idea how

suffocating it was, how stubborn he is about forms and appearances no matter how bankrupt we were. The volume of rules of etiquette is so large and heavy, I still believe that they built the royal library around it when the castle was constructed."

"No wonder you enjoy flying."

I felt her chuckle rather than heard it.

"And you wondered why I wouldn't want to be a princess."

"I did, didn't I?"

She was silent a long time as I watched the stars coming out above us. There was a rustle and a large leathery wing eclipsed the sky, coming to rest against the curve of her tail and plunging me into darkness. I felt a surge of terror as my heart pounded in the sudden darkness, broken by her words, **"Good night, Frank."**

"G-good night," I responded, as I realized she was providing me with a makeshift shelter. If I turned my head, I could see the sky past the top of her wing. This was probably the safest, and warmest, place I could spend the night in this forest.

Rather thoughtful of her, actually. Even if my racing heart would have appreciated some warning beforehand.

As I closed my eyes and tried to relax enough to sleep, I heard a rumble deep in her throat, a sub-vocalization that she probably didn't even intend me to hear.

"I still don't want to be a dragon."

*   *   *

In the morning, we took up a watch for any travelers along the highway who seemed to be going away from anything important. Or, more accurately, Lucille engaged in her newfound love of flying while I waited by the crossroads with my feet firmly planted on the ground.

Personally, I didn't think it was necessary for her to fly over the incoming roadways to alert me of approaching traffic; that was the point of me stationing myself at the crossroads—to meet and question them, not hide. However, since she suggested the idea, and the other option would have her staying put in the clearing so as not to scare away any merchants or travelers, I decided to indulge her.

She'd been through enough. Why not let her enjoy what little freedom this debacle had granted her? Even if it was unnecessary.

I watched from my position, and saw her as a small mote drifting in the sapphire-blue sky. She was so high that only a keen observer could tell her from a bird. I smiled as I watched her do loops and turns and stomach-churning dives.

I smiled because I wasn't with her.

It might be her idea of fun, but envisioning myself riding her as she executed those maneuvers was close to my definition of the exact opposite of fun.

Then I saw a small burst of light near her, and she changed direction back toward the clearing behind me. Someone was approaching, and they had come earlier than I expected.

"I suppose I should have some sort of plan," I whispered to myself. So far, the plan had been, "think of something when the time comes." Now that that time had come, I realized that seemed tactically a bit weak.

The caravan rolled into sight before I could come up with anything more substantial. The first wagon came to a stop upon seeing me standing next to the crossroads. A large bald lump of a man looked down and said, "Ho, what misfortune has waylaid such a maiden so far from civilization?"

Unlike Sir Forsythe, this man did not radiate sincerity.

Having no plan except the blatantly obvious, I stepped out into the road and addressed him. "No misfortune, I merely lost my way to Fell Green." I usually had no problem faking sincerity myself, but hearing myself talk was enough to tell me that I was seriously off my game. Maybe it was because I was telling the truth.

"That is no place you wish to go, young lady." He delivered the admonition with a predatory grin that rivaled Lucille's current incarnation for show of teeth. Though the dragon would win on points for having teeth in substantially better condition.

Again I tried to find the reserve of royal command that should be hidden in this body somewhere. "Perhaps you can tell me the way and I'll judge for myself."

I sounded as commanding as a four year old with a wooden sword.

"Oh, we can do better than that." The bald slug of a man raised his hand and, behind the lead cart, several men jumped off, weapons drawn. "If such a place is your desire, I suppose we can accommodate you. There's always room for more merchandise."

As more men dismounted, the canvas covering the wagons fluttered aside, briefly revealing ranks of chained female prisoners huddled inside.

I finally settled on a workable plan. What it lacked in originality, it made up for in simplicity.

I ran for it.

The plan had one fatal flaw; these guys were expecting such an eventuality. I felt a weighted rope swinging to wrap my lower legs from behind. I tumbled face-forward into the road, one of the men jumping on my back before I could roll over to face him.

By my count, this was the third time some overly aggressive males had taken me captive since I'd taken residence in the princess's body. I was getting tired of it.

So was Lucille.

The forest to our immediate right exploded into flame, sending smoldering branches and leaves blowing across the road. I heard horses scream and panic behind me as something massive thudded onto the ground ahead of us, and I craned my neck to look up. Princess Lucille faced my attackers, wings spread, talons gouging massive ruts into the roadway, mouth showing teeth backlit by a maw glowing with brimstone and anger.

"Let him go!"

I have no doubt that they would have done so immediately in the face of such demonic fury, if it wasn't for the pronoun confusion. The guy on top of me just didn't understand what the screaming dragon wanted. Unfortunately for him, no one provided him with an explanation before a scaly forelimb batted him away to tumble into the burning forest.

Once he was off my back, I was able to turn and sit up. "I wouldn't move," I yelled out at the men, who hadn't had the time to gather the wit to run. The horses drawing the wagons were barely in control, rearing and dancing and showing the whites of their eyes.

"Do what Frank says," ordered the dragon from behind me. The horses *loved* that, but it only engendered confused looks from the men.

I pulled the rope off my legs and stood. "She means *me*, people. And if you all drop those weapons, no one will have to get crispy."

From the back, one man threw a sword at the ground with enough force that it stuck upright in the road in front of him. "That's it. I quit."

The bald man looked down from his effort to keep the horses in check and said, "But, Stavros—"

"'But' nothing!" He pointed at the dragon. "What idiot has us try and snag an enticingly nubile young thing left so conveniently alone on the road to a nefarious den of black magic and necromancy? One who couldn't see a trap if he was hanging by his ankle over a pit full of stakes and shadow vipers, that's who."

The other men in the entourage dropped their weapons and slowly backed away from me and the dragon. I cleared my throat as loudly as I could manage, and they all stopped moving. Then I turned to whisper to Lucille, "Can you back off a bit now? You're spooking the horses."

"But—" she tried to whisper, and her objection was cut short by an equine scream of pure terror. Instead she nodded, beat her wings, and launched up into the sky to circle above us.

One of the men stooped to start to retrieve something, and I said, "You don't look so stupid that I have to *tell* you that's a bad idea."

The ringleader finally got his team of horses under control. He chuckled nervously. "I suppose an apology is in order?"

CHAPTER 15

The only moral I can draw from this part of the story is that, if you are to engage in a career of highway robbery, it is extremely advantageous to partner with a dragon. That, and Stavros had a good point about being wary of unaccompanied nubile young women found at forest paths leading toward infamous cities of dark magics.

I freed the "cargo" from both wagons while Lucille watched from the sky with a literally smoldering gaze. The two dozen half-naked women I unchained were very appreciative, and I received a number of hugs and kisses. I don't think anyone has invented a language to describe exactly how confusing the sensations from *that* were to me at the moment.

The men replaced the women, chained in the first cart, and the ex-prisoners got the trailing wagon to take themselves toward some outpost of civilization. I also bequeathed them most of their former captors' weapons, boots, and clothing. I was in a generous mood.

They also wanted to take some of their former

hosts with them, including Baldy. I drew the line at that. "We'd both hate ourselves in the morning," I said. I told them they'd have to content themselves with the clothes, weapons, and the chest of gold on the second wagon.

They weren't hard to convince.

Once they were safely on their way back in the direction the small convoy had come, I climbed up on top of the remaining cart and took a seat next to Baldy. He kept staring up at the sky, where Lucille was doing slow circles above us. When I took my seat and looked up, she tilted her wings, almost like she was waving at me.

I shook my head and turned my attention to Baldy.

"So," I said, "You were going to take me to Fell Green, now, weren't you?"

"You know, they don't appreciate random strangers—"

He stopped because I placed the point of a dagger just above his kidney. It had come from one of Baldy's subordinates, and unlike the one I had liberated from the palace weapons display, this one actually had an edge. "Funny," I said, "I don't think Lendowyn *or* Dermonica appreciates slave trafficking." A small red dot stained the linen shirt where I had poked him.

"They were indentured servants, perfectly legal."

"Like I was going to be?"

"Well . . . uh . . ."

"Please don't make me get my one outfit all bloody."

He didn't put up much of an argument.

Baldy drove the wagon down the road for several miles. We traveled mostly in silence, because whenever the man opened his mouth he filled me with a desire to get stabby. When I thought about our destination, Baldy's profession, and how folks like Dudley usually got their sacrifices. . . . It just reflected well on my self-control that I hadn't disemboweled the guy already.

After about an hour of travel, we emerged from the trees onto a meadow bordered by what looked to be one of the wider spots of the Fell River. The road headed right toward the shoreline, to a wide bridge of black stone that crossed the river. The bridge was an impressive piece of work, and out of place so far from any sign of civilization.

I stared at the arches over the river, and the opposite shore that was barely in sight. Baldy pulled the wagon to a stop just short of the bridge. "Must be on the Lendowyn side," I muttered to myself.

"You don't know?" Baldy asked.

I prodded him with the dagger again, just because it made me feel better. He sucked in a breath and shut up.

"Why are we stopped?"

"We have to pay the toll."

I was about to ask "to whom?" because the entire area seemed empty of anyone. But, in the space of my short exchange with Baldy, a figure had appeared on the bridge out of nowhere; an emaciated man, wrapped in black rags, leaning on a staff. His eyes were the same shade of gray as his stringy hair, and clutched in one clawlike hand he held a wooden bowl.

The man hobbled up to Baldy's side of the wagon and shook his empty bowl in our direction. "Alms?"

That answered that question.

Baldy glanced at the dagger sticking him, then at a chest by his feet. I reached down and opened the chest and pulled out a leather coin purse. "How much?"

Baldy sighed. "A crown a head."

I held the purse up in front of Baldy with my free hand and said, "Pay the man, then."

"Are you sure you want to—" a poke ended Baldy's train of thought and he started rummaging in the purse.

If the beggar noticed Baldy was a hostage, he gave no sign of caring. His expression didn't change at all from the blind stare he'd greeted us with.

Not until Baldy filled his bowl with coins.

The old beggar looked at his take, then back at us. Gone was the staring senile visage, replaced by irritation. The old man's grip visibly tightened on the staff, and he stood straighter. "You ain't trying to smuggle someone in without payin', are you?" He gazed at Baldy with an eyebrow cocked in a way to suggest that his gray-clouded eyes weren't blind at all.

I got a feeling I didn't want to annoy the man.

I put some pressure on the hilt of the dagger and said, "You forgot someone."

"What? I counted everyone."

"Nope." I said, nodding upward.

Baldy followed my gaze, looking up to see Lucille doing lazy circles and loops in the sky above us.

"Oh, yeah. Dragon. Right."

The beggar stared upward as well, jaw falling open as the last coin clattered into his bowl.

In response to that last coin, the air over the bridge shimmered, darkened, and turned opaque. It was like watching a mirage disappear as you approached it; the view of a bridge arching over the river vanishing as if it had never been there.

Fell Green was not on the Lendowyn side *or* the Dermonica side. It was actually on a long dagger-shaped island in the middle of the river, an island that had been invisible until now. The bridge, now much shorter, met a road that crossed the body of the island, and Fell Green squatted behind massive stone walls that dominated the entirety of the island to the west of that road.

Baldy shook the reins and started the team of

horses across the bridge, leaving the beggar/gate-keeper staring up, slack-jawed, at Lucille.

Once across the bridge it now seemed that the island was much wider than the river that flowed around it. I tried not to think about that too much. Baldy's wagon followed the road between a high stone wall covered with black-leaved ivy, and a dense forest that competed for ominousness with the woods where Dudley performed his devotions to the Dark Lord Nâtlac.

Between the two, I gave the woods here the edge for subtlety, inducing dread without any obvious theatrics. No burnt tree trunks clawing at an ash-gray sky from a field of crushed bone. These woods were lush, leafy, and a little *too* healthy. Something about the shades of green just seemed a bit off.

Once we came in sight of the gate to the town, I relieved Baldy of the last of his gold and ordered him to stop the wagon.

"Now," I told him. "This is where we part ways." I pointed the tip of my dagger down the road ahead of us. "Keep going, unless you like the idea of being set on fire by an angry lizard."

As I climbed down from the wagon, Baldy said, "I need the keys to unchain my men."

I shook my head. "You need incentive to go to the next town and find a blacksmith." I waved my arm and Lucille began descending. "I suggest you get going."

He looked up at the descending dragon and snapped the reins. The horses didn't need to be told twice, and the wagon vanished down the road at a furious gallop as Lucille set herself down in a clearing next to the road.

"I think we make a good team," I told her, hefting the bag with the remnants of Baldy's finances.

"This island came out of nowhere."

"Yeah, I can see why there's some argument over jurisdiction."

She turned her massive head toward the wall. Her eyes narrowed and thin trails of steam curled from her nostrils. I saw commotion along the top of the wall as multiple guards seemed to be rushing to cover the section across from us.

"He's in there?"

"That's what Prince Dudley said—"

"Let's get him." Her voice was a near-growl, and her talons sank into the earth. Her muscles were so tense that I could almost hear them vibrate.

"Calm down."

Her head whipped in my direction and she yelled at me, **"Calm down!"** Her breath was so heated that I thought I could smell my eyebrows burning. Her jaws snapped shut on the words like a trap designed to catch the deity of all bears and bearlike creatures.

There was less than an arm's length between us, and I felt the vibration from her jaw slamming shut in the back of my own skull. I must have completely internalized the fact that she was the princess, because I didn't immediately flee in terror.

"Yes. Calm down."

The fact that I stood my ground must have made an impression, because she froze, staring at me. Her mouth opened to say something, but nothing came out but a few wisps of brimstone-flavored steam.

"First, we're here on the word of Prince Dudley. While he was under threat of some serious pain when he said we could find Elhared here, do you actually trust him?"

"Uh . . ."

"Second, this is a wizard town. If you noticed, they've been massing on the wall since you landed, and I suspect they have a slightly better equipped and organized defense than Ravensgate."

"But . . ."

"Lastly, if a dragon storms the gate of this town, and somehow makes it past the town defenses to the point of doing a house to house search—we'll ignore the logistics of how *that* would actually work for the moment—do you think Elhared will conveniently stay put for you to find him?"

The rage had sapped from her. As immobile as much of the dragon's face might be, it was becoming surprisingly easy for me to read her expressions now. If I had to describe how she looked at me after my tirade, I'd probably call it "pouty."

"But I want to help."

I shook my head and patted her nose. "You've been helping. There's no way we could have gotten here without you. It's just that quietly hunting down one guy in the middle of a town does not play to your strengths at the moment."

She settled down on the ground, resting her head on her folded forearms with an intimidatingly resonant sigh. **"You have no idea how much it annoys me that you're right."**

"Cheer up. I'm sure we'll get a chance for you to lay waste to a small army before we change you back."

"Now you're mocking me."

"I wouldn't do that to someone who could bite me in half."

She turned her head and snorted what might have been a draconic chuckle.

"Really, you've handled more than your share. You saved me—us—from being a sacrifice. You saved a bunch of women from those slavers. That's not even mentioning traveling here in the first place. There's a time for subtlety and diplomacy, and there's a time for intimidation and cracking skulls. Right now, your job's the latter."

"I never really was ever that assertive."

"I think you're doing well."

"Really?"

"You make an excellent dragon."

"Thank you, I think."

"And you're still helping. After your unsubtle arrival, you think the town guard's going to give me any grief?" I gestured up toward the wall, where a few bucket-helmeted guards peered down across the road at us. "Who's going to mess with a girl with a pet dragon?"

She lifted her head and cocked it. **"Pet?"**

"Uh—figure of speech."

Lucille launched herself again, to orbit the town at what we hoped the guards would perceive as a safe distance. And, as I predicted, the guards at the main gate were very polite and helpful with directions—though some of that might have been habit given the kind of powerful masters of dark sorcery who must regularly pass through here. It's never a good idea to roust someone who could turn you into a toad. Lucille's presence probably just suggested I was part of the small club that belonged here.

So, without incident, I entered the black heart of the necromancers' haven of Fell Green.

It wasn't that bad.

I got a lot of stares, since I was a young woman traveling alone. But apparently, *because* I was a young woman traveling alone, most of the potential troublemakers seemed to follow the theory of Baldy's ex-minion Stavros: *it's a trap.*

The marketplace tended toward the obscure and obscene in terms of spell components—I could have easily replaced the flattened pixie that Elhared had used as a bookmark. However, there were also more than enough merchants selling mundane gear appropriate to my chosen profession. I took the opportunity to lighten Baldy's purse a bit, at least for the sake of more easily pumping a few merchants for info on the possible location of the unfortunately not-so-late Elhared the Unwise.

I was in luck. Elhared was a known and not particularly loved fixture of this town. I listened to several anecdotes of his activities prior to my meeting him. His status as a skinflint was something of a local legend. I suspected that meant Lendowyn's financial difficulties predated him skimming the treasury. I even heard from someone who had spent several weeks on a custom replica sword for the wizard, only to be stiffed on the last payment.

I didn't bother relating the fate of that sword.

I followed the endless marketplace, and the Elhared stories, to the less nice quarter of Fell Green. As things got scruffier, I was glad for the practical attire Lucille had salvaged for me. I was receiving many fewer lewd propositions than I had with the leather I'd originally purchased. I was also glad that Lucille was orbiting the town, keeping an eye on me. Periodically, I glanced up at the sky to check her position. Despite what I had told her about subtlety, given the population I mingled with at the moment, it was comforting to have that sort of backup.

Finally, as I talked to a merchant selling virility potions so noxious that they made impotence seem attractive by comparison, I had success. The old crone set down a steaming vial of lumpy brown liquid and pointed a crooked finger across the street at a tavern named The Harpy's Teat.

"The old bastard just went in there an hour ago."

CHAPTER 16

Up to now, I had been relying on an aura of confidence that was one part con game, one part knowing how to walk around this type of neighborhood, and one part the knowledge that Lucille was above me, watching. It had worked so far, no one questioning the presence of my doubly misplaced self.

I walked across the threshold of The Harpy's Teat, and most of that seemed to evaporate. Half the eyes in the place glanced in my direction when I entered.

This establishment gave me a healthy appreciation for the charms of the dockside tavern where I had first met Elhared. I'm certain that I would have some difficulty finding worse smells along the wharf, and by comparison with the clientele here, the patrons of The Headless Earl were guests at a princess's tea party. Some of the beverages being served made Mermaid's Milk look positively appetizing, and the vile concoctions the old crone was selling across the street didn't seem that bad in retrospect.

And, unlike The Headless Earl or that dockside tavern, most of the patrons here weren't human. Walking into those other dens of comparatively bland iniquity as an attractive young woman would raise all sorts of worries. Walking in here, under the dirty gazes of ogres, goblins, imps, and the more feral types of fairies, I not only had to worry about potential rapists, but about someone desiring to gnaw on my bones after the fact.

My hand slipped down to my belt to rest on the hilt of the dagger I had liberated from one of Baldy's minions. I wished for the fake *Dracheslayer*. Useless it might have been, but at least it had *looked* intimidating. For a few moments, I suspected that the crone across the street had sent me in here as some sick form of entertainment.

One of the nearest goblins—hairless, green-skinned, wiry, and with hands and feet a size and a half too large for his body—wiped the drool from his lips, got unsteadily to his feet, and weaved toward me.

"You losht, darlin'?"

It was hard to tell if the stench was from the goblin's breath, or from the flagon he held a little too loosely in his hand as he gestured at me.

"No." I answered quietly as I pondered ways to quietly extricate myself without escalating things. I figured, right now, most of the eyes on me weren't yet focusing with predatory intent. At this point it was probably mostly curiosity over what in the Seven Hells someone who looked like me was doing in a place like this.

"Well, I'sh got a seat for you right here."

"No, thank you."

As my eyes adjusted and I saw deeper into the establishment, it became clear that, while the nominal business here was providing alcohol, the real business was the operation of various games of chance. Several ogres had already lost interest in me, and were turning back to their card games, and while I had the undivided attention of one goblin, a dozen others were ignoring me in favor of a large game of dice. In the rear, a slick-looking elf took wagers in front of a giant wheel of fortune illustrated with pictures painted by a Tarot aficionado with some very peculiar fetishes.

And, in front of that wheel, chanting for it to land on the three of tentacles, was the old fart Elhared.

The crone *wasn't* setting me up.

I took a step forward, and a large, sticky green hand landed on my shoulder. "You not goina turn down my hoshpitality."

I've said before, all things being equal, I prefer subtlety. If I hadn't just seen my quarry, I might have engaged the inebriated goblin in another round of witty repartee as I quietly excused myself from the situation. Instead, I drew my dagger and spun around, bringing the hilt up between the goblin's legs. His yellow eyes widened in surprise as he froze and exhaled.

Goblins are reportedly more tolerant of pain than humans, so I pulled my fist back and slammed the pommel of my dagger back into the goblin family jewels again.

He dropped the tankard. It clattered to the sawdust-covered floor, spilling its foul contents.

The goblin hunched over and started emitting a low groan. I took his hand off my shoulder and turned him around. "You're drunk," I told him. I took two steps to get him started back toward the table he came from. "If you're going to puke, puke on your friends."

Safely freed from my admirer, I turned back toward the tavern. Judging from the reaction of the clientele, my dealing with the goblin *had* been subtle by local standards. I noticed a few places where money changed hands, and most of the eyes that had been watching my little domestic drama returned to more interesting subjects.

Most, but not all.

Elhared was looking right at me. His eyes were wide with recognition, and he mouthed something that was more obscenity than incantation.

We stared at each other for what seemed like a short eternity. It was less than a second, but it was long enough for me to realize what was wrong with this picture.

That was *Elhared's* body, not mine.

Oh, crap.

Ersatz Elhared bolted over the gaming table,

away from me, scattering chips and causing curses all around. I ran after him.

It wasn't the crone who set me up. It was *Dudley*. Dudley was the one who knew about all the displaced souls running around, and it probably amused him no end to send me after the wrong Elhared. Unless it really was the original Elhared I was chasing, and not a dragon with a gambling addiction.

Given where I'd found him, and the old man's state of flight, that seemed unlikely.

I vaulted over my own set of gaming tables and followed him through the kitchens—and the less said about them, the better. We emerged into an alley behind The Harpy's Teat, and I caught up. It wasn't a particularly impressive feat. Despite her short stride, in reasonable footwear, for a short distance, Princess Lucille could probably outrun Frank Blackthorne. Catching up to an old man in heavy robes, aged somewhere between seventy and dead, wasn't that difficult.

The fact I tackled him to the ground may have been more impressive, if you didn't take into account that not only was my quarry ancient, but was inhabited by someone whose only previous experience in physical conflict was predicated on having large talons, jaws that could bite a warhorse in half, and outweighing any potential opponent twenty-to-one. So it wasn't really a fair fight.

I straddled his chest, and after a brief slap-fight, I had him pinned to the ground. After trying to lift me off of him and failing, my imitation Elhared's literal last gasp was to suck in a breath, open his mouth, and exhale long and hard in my face. While the eye-watering stench of old fish and bad teeth was unpleasant, it was nowhere near as disabling as intended.

I stared at the dragon-in-Elhared's-clothing incredulously.

With a sheepish look and a barely audible voice he said, "Yeah. Right. That wouldn't work, would it?"

"Enough playing around. Where's the *real* wizard?"

"What real wizard?"

I slapped him so hard that my own hand went numb.

"Ow! That really hurt."

"Where's Elhared? *And* the book?"

"I don't know!"

I raised my hand to slap him. From behind me came a sickeningly smooth voice. "Isn't this a sight?"

The speaker could have been referring to himself. When I turned my head, I saw an elf with slicked-back hair and a garish outfit that was all pastels, ruffles, and lace. His makeup was designed to enhance the androgyny of his already indeterminate features. Flanking him were two more elves in similarly outlandish garb, all swirls and points and engraved floral motifs, though since their outfits were constructed of leather, studs, and chain mail, they were much more practically dressed. Those two also got points for crossbows of ivory-inlaid ebony and engraved brass. The weapons may have looked over the top, but they appeared functional—especially since they were pointed in my direction.

Elhared the Fake redoubled his efforts to throw me off of him, muttering inarticulate grunts that may have been an attempt at producing native draconic obscenities with a human larynx. Both efforts were about as successful as his attempt to breathe fire.

"Please," said the lead flouncy elf. "I would appreciate calm. I do not like to inconvenience my customers. It is bad for business. However, your abrupt departure from my establishment in the midst of an ongoing game resulted in a balance due to the house. We cannot allow even the appearance of someone avoiding a debt to us." The elf's smile was bloodless and much too wide for his face.

"Look," my phony wizard pleaded, "You know I'm good for it."

"Yes," the elf hissed. "That is the other thing. I've heard a bit of your dialogue with the young miss here, and it seems to raise questions about the stake the house has provided to the presumptive court wizard of Lendowyn."

Discretion is the better part of keeping one's skin in one piece. I raised my hands off of faux-Elhared and slowly got to my feet. "I'm sure we can discuss things in a civilized manner and get this all sorted out. Why don't we just lower the crossbows before something happens that everyone here will regret."

My glance upward was involuntary, but the elf noticed it.

"I presume you are looking for your traveling companion?" I didn't think it was physically possible, but the damn elf's smile got wider. "A separate issue, but the dragon is currently indisposed."

Pretend-Elhared was in the midst of getting to his feet himself, and he froze. "Dragon?"

"Damn it all," I whispered. Dudley must be really pissing his pants in amusement now.

"We take our debts very seriously," the elf told him.

I looked at our imitation wizard and said, "How idiotic can you be, coming back to the same guys you already owe money to?"

"I was on a streak, damn it."

The elf clapped his hands and the back alley vanished around us.

CHAPTER 17

Fell Green might have been a wizard town, but there was more than sorcery keeping it from prying eyes. It wasn't completely in the world of men. Just as its visible manifestation straddled the river between Lendowyn and Dermonica, its essence straddled the mists that separate our world from the fae realms.

At least that was our elven host's explanation why they really didn't give a crap who was royalty and who wasn't.

Human authorities didn't have any jurisdiction with the world of elves; no diplomatic relations, no extradition treaties, no cultural exchanges. Changelings were the primary trade goods, and any tourism was generally one-way. Fell Green was about as close as anyone wanted to get, and as our recent experience showed, even at that remove, dealing with the fae rarely had a positive outcome.

The elf and his guards pulled us through the mists, to a place as far from Lendowyn court intrigue as was the moon. In fact, we could have stood on the moon for all I knew. The ground was made of silver sand that glowed a milky white. Above, a different sky simultaneously held its own sun and moon that stared down on us like a pair of accusing eyes. We followed a road made of gold that led toward a vast city that could have been made of spun sugar and spiderwebs, towers reaching as tall as the city was wide.

"Look, don't you see," Elhared the Lesser groveled. "I'm the court wizard. I have money. The entire Lendowyn treasury—"

That should have confirmed any suspicions about this Elhared's true identity. The real wizard would have had more sense than to brag about access to an empty vault.

Our hosts remained unmoved by his pleas as they marched us off the main road and up over a hill on the outskirts of the great city. When we crested the hill we came into view of a massive arena buried in a bowl scooped into the ground below us. We descended a broad staircase to the circular floor, and faced a series of golden cages that ranged from the tiny to the humungous.

One of the latter held Lucille.

As the elven escort shoved me into a human-size cage, Lucille said, **"Oh, Frank, they got you too!"**

"Looks that way," I muttered more to myself than to her. The door locked itself behind me with a sound more like a crystal chime than the shutting of a prison cell.

"And Elhared . . . Oh. That isn't, is he?"

The counterfeit wizard fought his elvish captors as they tossed him in another cage. He yelled, "I *am* Elhared! Court wizard of Lendowyn! That is the Princess Lucille! The king shall hear of—"

The chief elf made a lazy gesture and suddenly the ranting went silent. I saw the wizard's face contorting, and his lips moving, but no sound came from the cage.

The elf sighed. "My, that person is tiring."

"What's going on?" I asked him. "What are you doing with us?"

He strode up to my cage, drawing a lace handkerchief from his sleeve. The primary purpose for it seemed to be to provide him with something to gesture with. "See?" He addressed the silently screaming ex-dragon Elhared, "It *is* possible to ask impertinent questions in a civil tone."

"Impertinent?"

He turned to face me. "Questioning your betters. Speaking out of turn. Working among mortals has made me more than typically munificent in the face of such crass behavior." He whispered to me in a conspiratorial tone. "Be grateful that I'm not the judge."

"Judge? What's going on here?"

"You are on trial, of course."

"Trial—" I paced around the inside of the cage. "Look, there's been a misunderstanding."

"There is *always* a misunderstanding. No one

ever *intends* to steal the food from our table. Somehow it just happens." The elf unfolded his palms and blew across them, making his handkerchief flutter. "It has been my experience that mortals properly understand very little—"

"No. I mean we aren't who you think we are."

"Is anyone? If you have a defense, I would reserve it for the judge." The elf leaned over to whisper again, as if sharing some great secrets of the universe. "And a word of advice, do not interrupt him. I find you amusing, but that capricious old fart would just as soon slit you open to water his garden." He straightened up and smiled. "Not that it wouldn't be amusing in its own right."

The elf turned and waved his armsmen to follow as he left the arena, leaving us caged and alone. Whatever the elf had done to silence Elhared the False, he hadn't bothered to dispel. The dragon in the old wizard's body was shouting after the elf, gripping the bars and trying to shake them.

I wondered if he knew no one could hear him.

"What's happening?"

I turned away from the furious silence of the fake wizard and toward Lucille. She was in the largest cage available, and still she was hunched over and curled up, barely fitting in the space. The bars looked wire-thin and inadequate for containing her, but gouges in the ground and scorch marks told me that she hadn't left her cage untested.

"Some sort of elvish court."

"Why? What did we do?"

I hooked a thumb back at the pretender Elhared. "Not us, *him*."

"Elhared?"

"No, the dragon. Did you know about the dragon's gambling problem?"

"Tell me you're kidding."

"Before the spell went haywire, the dragon said that Elhared had bought his service with a promise to cover his gambling debts."

"And?"

"These are the folks he owed money to."

She shook her head, as much as she could in the too-small cage. **"Then they should have me, or him, right? Why are you here?"**

"Our draconic genius here was trying to use Elhared's line of credit as a court wizard to win back his prior losses. I'm here because when he saw me, he ran out on one of their games—"

"He was gambling with them *again*?"

"Like I said. He has a problem."

"Wonderful."

"*Silence!*" The word was punctuated by a loud crack that resonated through the ground and the bars of my cage. Shouting at us was a huge elf. He stood at the top of the entry stairs clad in a garish uniform dominated by an embroidered midnight-blue cape held on by brooches the size of dinner plates. In his right hand he held an intricately carved, silver-tipped ebony staff nearly twice his own height and the diameter of a small tree. He shouted, "*Silence!*" again, and slammed the tip of his staff against the stone stairs, generating a flower of sparks and another resonant crack that echoed through the arena.

I realized now that the arena wasn't empty. The seating for spectators was in shadow, so I had to squint to see the audience from our brightly lit spot on the arena floor. Still, I wondered how I could have missed the crowd on my way in.

"The court of the most high Timoras, lord of all realms under the hill, is in session. The Grand Inquisitor of the Winter Court shall preside and pass judgment."

Much as I tried, there was no way I could interpret that statement as something positive.

"All rise for the Grand Inquisitor."

I almost expected a trumpet fanfare. What we got was five more cracks of the bailiff's staff on the steps, slamming like cannon fire.

After the bailiff's showmanship, the Grand Inquisitor himself was a bit of a letdown. He was the least flashy dresser so far, clad in black robes, the only color in his ensemble a tricornered cap in deep crimson. Short and wide for an elf, he was also the first elf I had ever seen who showed any signs of age, to the point where he wore a pair of spectacles that drew attention to the slight creases that framed his stormy gray eyes. He strode in without much ceremony and stood in front of pseudo-Elhared's cage.

"Speak to the court—" he started to tell the fake

wizard. I saw a lot of mouth movement, but I couldn't hear a thing.

The Grand Inquisitor sighed and made a gesture with his left hand.

"—so it's all a big misunderstanding."

"It is always a misunderstanding," the Inquisitor said quietly to himself. In a louder voice he said, "Speak to the court. Identify yourself and justify your actions. Bind yourself to the truth or face censure."

"Yes. Yes. Of course," Imitation Elhared said to the Grand Inquisitor. I could see perspiration beading on his brow, and he cast several furtive and not well-hidden sidelong glances in my direction. "You see, I am the Wizard Elhared of the Royal Court of Lendowyn, of course. I have a generous stipend from the crown, so there should be no issue in paying the small debts I've incurred." He stroked his beard with such nervous enthusiasm that at any moment I expected him to start wringing the flop-sweat from it. "Now you're wondering why I ran from the Princess Lucille here." He gestured in my direction. "There's a simple explanation for that, really . . ."

Yeah, the explanation is you're stalling.

"You see . . . uh . . . the princess had been kidnapped by an evil dragon. I was as surprised as anyone to see her walk into your establishment. Shocked really. And the first thing I thought of was, I had to rush to notify the king."

The Grand Inquisitor nodded. "I see."

"She wasn't chasing me, you see. She recognized me, of course, and knew I would be able to lead her back to Lendowyn Castle and her rightful place in the royal court."

As he said that, he looked right at me in a way that made me feel dirty. I knew instantly what he was getting at. If I backed him up with his asinine excuse for a story, he'd back up my own claim for the Lendowyn throne. All I had to do was stand by while Lucille the Dragon took the fall for the old dragon's debts. I don't know what pissed me off more, the thought that Elhared the Make-Believe thought I would be the kind of ass that would cut a helpless woman loose just to save my own skin, or the fact that I spent several seconds weighing the costs and benefits of the idea before rejecting it out of hand.

He kept spinning his ever more elaborate fabrications to the point Lucille couldn't take anymore.

"Lies!" she screamed with a rage that turned my spine to butter. I could smell the brimstone from my cage. I was suddenly concerned for the safety of everyone present. **"Nothing but lies! He's—"**

Her shouts were cut short by the thunderclap of the bailiff's staff. The Inquisitor made a slight gesture and quietly said, "Contempt."

Lucille froze in mid-rage. Even the smoke curling from her nostrils had ceased movement and hung stationary in midair. I glanced from her frozen effigy, back to our pretend Elhared, and I caught the barest hint of a smile.

Oh, you bastard.

While it had appeared that he'd been spinning a gratuitously implausible tale, I suddenly realized the old dragon had dealt with elves before. Probably had dealt with the elvish judicial system before. He might have been spinning a web of lies that could challenge the work of the demon-spiders of Hsilb, but he was also trying to bait a reaction from Lucille—pushing her to react, just so the Inquisitor would shut her down.

The ugly suspicion was confirmed when the Inquisitor concluded his interview with him, and announced that the dragon had forfeited the right to testify. It was my turn.

The Grand Inquisitor walked before my cage and stared at me over his spectacles. "Do you corroborate the wizard's testimony? Shall we release you both back to Lendowyn?" While the Inquisitor's back was turned, the ex-dragon wizard looked at me and made a "get-on-with-it" gesture.

I silently asked the universe to stop handing me prime opportunities to betray the princess. "Yes, about that testimony . . . The 'wizard' is absolutely right in that there exists a kingdom called Lendowyn, whose royal court does include a wizard by the name of Elhared, and a princess by the name of Lucille. I'm afraid everything else he said is a very intricately imagined pile of crap."

The counterfeit wizard winced as if I'd struck him. He grabbed the bars and pleaded with me. "*Princess*, these elves do not recognize Lendowyn law. Do not say something that threatens your royal immunity."

Another thunderclap from the bailiff and another contempt gesture from the Inquisitor, and he was frozen just like Lucille.

"Go on," the Inquisitor told me.

I hesitated a moment. The message had been as clear as it was brief. If I revealed the truth, I'd abandon any favor my princessness might give me. The elves would treat me just like they would the thief Frank Blackthorne.

Of course, I could spin another lie to compete with the ex-dragon's. But, even though that was my forte, I couldn't really class that one in the category of good ideas.

So I did the opposite. I told the whole, naked, unvarnished truth. I'm not sure exactly why I needed to, but it came pouring out of me, from the moment Elhared conned me in a dockside bar, to the point where I tackled his body outside an even less reputable establishment.

I might have just been really sick of the ex-dragon. It also might have been that I didn't want to see Lucille condemned because of a lie. It might also be because this was an elven elder on his home turf, someone with enough power to freeze a dragon in mid-rampage, and it seemed to be the epitome of poor judgment to lie to the guy.

It may just have been that I had never stopped to explain myself or who I really was to Lucille, and at the very least she deserved to know the truth. When I was finished, I was looking into her frozen eyes, not the Inquisitor's.

"I'm sorry," I whispered to her.

A thunderclap echoed though the arena as the bailiff continued in his effort to beat the ground into submission. My two fellow defendants unfroze. The current Elhared shook his bars and spat at me. "You stupid bastard. We could have walked out of here. You'll pay for this. I'll find you—"

I was more concerned with Lucille, who had obviously heard and understood everything as well. She stared at me, and I realized that she had begun sobbing. **"You lied to me."**

Damn it. I didn't lie, I just hadn't gotten to the part where I wasn't really a knight in shining armor. And really, to be fair, given that Sir Forsythe was the best example of the genre locally, she should have been grateful.

The Grand Inquisitor spun around and addressed the spectators. "Testimony has concluded. Judgment will now be rendered."

CHAPTER 18

I had expected elven justice to be inscrutable. I didn't realize how inscrutable.

The Grand Inquisitor pointed a finger at the ex-dragon who was still shouting invective at me. "You have lied to the court and have defrauded the blood of the fae. Your debts shall be paid in the service of your person to the Winter Court for a term of one year for each golden sovereign so owed; should you expire this sentence will pass to your descendants by blood."

The newly sentenced Elhared the Fake did not take the news well. He howled at the Inquisitor, "You can't do this. Let me go. I'm in a position where I can pay you back. I just need to get back to the castle. You understand, while I'm in this body I *am* Elhared, as far as the law's concerned. Just let me go . . ."

The Inquisitor wasn't listening to him. Instead, he pointed a finger at Lucille, who at the moment made the most dejected picture of a dragon possible. "You have been determined to possess property that belongs to the fae by right. You shall suffer no additional punishment, and may leave as you will at the termination of the original terms of service."

Her head rose and she shook it in confusion. **"What? What property? What service?"**

"The prior owner of that body wagered its service to the fae. We are owed a dragon."

"What? He wagered with you, I didn't."

The Grand Inquisitor turned toward me, ignoring the cries of protest from the dragon.

"It wasn't me!"

He pointed a finger at me and I could feel my heart stop beating for a moment. I had no idea what punishment I was in for, or what crime I may have committed; all I knew was that I wasn't going to like what the Inquisitor had to say.

I was right, but not in the way I thought.

"You," said the Grand Inquisitor, "are free to go."

I opened my mouth, but no words came out. The bars slid into the ground around me until I stood, unrestrained, on the arena floor.

Needless to say, this didn't go over that well with my former fellow prisoners.

"You're just letting him go? He admitted to you that he was a thief, an outlaw—"

"He has stolen nothing from us," said the Inquisitor. "Unlike some—"

He had to sidestep a jet of flame. **"He was supposed to be a knight. And now you're just letting him go?"**

"Lucille, I didn't mean to—"

I had to dodge some fire myself.

"You're letting him go? In my body? He lied to me!"

The Inquisitor was unmoved. He brushed off his robes and said, "Frank Blackthorne has not lied to us."

Another thunderclap from the bailiff's staff ended the court, and the Grand Inquisitor walked back toward the exit, leaving me standing there dumbfounded.

"Wait a minute!" I ran after him. Behind me I heard dragons former and current cursing after me.

"Just wait!" I interposed myself between the Grand Inquisitor and the exit.

The bailiff raised his staff and looked about to give me a taste of what the floor was getting, but the Grand Inquisitor raised his hand, stopping him. "What is it, Frank Blackthorne?"

"Why release me and not her? Lucille's done nothing to you."

"She is in the possession of our property."

"She hasn't wagered anything with you."

"That has little to do with it. She is in receipt of property that was forfeited to us. It is our right to recover that property. Beyond that, actions on her part are irrelevant."

"It isn't property. It's her! You're imprisoning an innocent woman."

"True," the Inquisitor admitted. "But when the

dragon wagered the last of his gold, he wagered his service in thrall to the fae crown. The elf king is owed the service of a dragon for the next thousand years."

"A thousand—" I took a step forward and felt the bailiff's staff smack painfully across my boobs. I stumbled back and the Grand Inquisitor strode past me. As he walked by he said, "You should take your leave while you are still free to do so."

I called after him. "This isn't Lendowyn, you can't hold her accountable for something the prior occupant of that body did."

I think I heard the Inquisitor sigh. He turned around. "We do not hold her responsible." He took a step forward, and his voice rose slightly and his eyes hardened. "But understand this, Frank Blackthorne, and if you are wise you will take this truth to your grave. The fae do not absolve debts." He reached out and touched a finger to my chest just above my collar. His finger on my skin felt icy and remorseless. "We will *always* be paid. This does not change based on any hardship on your part. It does not change should you decide to die in our debt. And it certainly does not change should some random mortal choose to inhabit what is owed us. To this point I have shown considerable lenience because you have done the fae no ill. But my tolerance for your insufferable questioning has worn thin." When he withdrew his finger I realized with a gasping wheeze that

I'd been holding my breath. "The princess's unfortunate luck is not our problem. Nor is it yours, Frank Blackthorne."

"Really?" I muttered. "Have you taken a good look at me?"

He started to turn away, and against my better judgment I asked, "Can't you do something for her?"

His voice rose in volume and lowered in tone. "You question the judgment of this court?"

I raised my hands. "No. No. Never. It's done. Verdict and all. I understand. You get a dragon for a thousand years. It's yours. But, can I talk to you outside your capacity as Inquisitor?"

"Grand Inquisitor!" the bailiff intoned.

The *Grand* Inquisitor looked at me and sighed. He looked over at the bailiff and said, "You're dismissed."

The bailiff saluted with his staff and took a step back into the shadows. Before I saw where he disappeared to, the Grand Inquisitor waved me along to follow him.

We walked past the entrance to the arena, across the broad golden road to a hillside overlooking the spun-sugar city. Other elves were about, but unlike any other city I'd been in, no one could be considered to be in a hurry, and no one seemed to show any curiosity at my presence. The looks I received were cursory at best.

I guess I should have been grateful. Most of my

life, any undue attention I received in a strange place was always a bad thing.

Above us, the strange sun and moon had drifted together to the point where they nearly touched. The Grand Inquisitor stopped at a line of smooth, polished stones at the crown of the hillside. The stones were about thigh high, perfectly cubical, and displayed various colors; from a stormy blue-black granite to something with the color and markings of a star sapphire. He sat on the sapphire cube, and gestured to me to take another seat on a cube of speckled ruby.

"You can't challenge the court's ruling," he told me as I sat. "There is no appeal."

I nodded. I knew the fights I could pick, and directly challenging the elvish legal system was not one of them. "I know. But aren't there other options?"

"Like what?"

"Aren't you guys renowned for your skills in magic? Isn't there someone here who could take her and put her in the right body?" I looked down at myself and smoothed the drape of my dress where it fell over the princess's thighs. "I mean, since we have it right here."

I think the Inquisitor's eyes widened slightly. "Are you seriously suggesting that?"

I shrugged. "She doesn't deserve being trapped in some stupid wager the dragon made."

"Even if you could pay the fees of such a service, what would you have done with yourself?"

"Well if you put the dragon back where he belongs, you can stick me in Elhared . . . You'd have no reason to hold either of us then."

He stroked his chin as if considering it, but he finally shook his head. "No, Frank Blackthorne. Even if you found a willing mage under the hill . . . The dragon is too valuable a commodity to risk just to salve your mortal conscience."

"What? *Why?*" I stared at my knees and tried to ignore the quaver in my voice and the way my vision blurred.

He explained that it would be very dangerous for even the most skilled practitioner to do such a spell to unenchanted individuals, more so now that everyone involved suffered from a prior spell. Without an exact duplication of the prior rite—in other words, without Elhared's evil spell book of evilness—it was possible that an attempt would just completely sever a soul's connection to the material realm.

"Dead dragons aren't particularly useful," he said.

Not unless you want to marry Lendowyn princesses.

"It is over. Even if I were moved to release the dragon, that decision was never in my hands."

I raised my head and looked at him.

"Whose hands is it in, then?"

The palace of the Elf-King Timoras, lord of all realms under the hill, sovereign of the Winter

Court, was not that difficult to find. All one had to do was stand somewhere in the fae realms and walk in the direction that got colder. Wherever in the realms you were, a thousand paces in that direction brought you to the aptly named Winter Palace.

In my opinion, they went a little overboard on the theme. You entered the frost-covered palace and found yourself attempting not to slide and fall on a floor made of ice, walking between icicle columns that supported a roof that appeared to be the better part of a blizzard frozen in place—so to speak.

As easy as it was to find the place, getting an audience with the elf-king himself was somewhat more difficult, even when I name-dropped the Grand Inquisitor and said he'd sent me. With all the functionaries, viceroys, and guardsmen who shunted me from one to the other, I began to expect that Lucille's terms of service might actually conclude before I got anywhere.

But, as long as it may have seemed to me, it ended up being less than a day. I think. It was hard to tell since the elves never seemed to sleep, and what glimpses I got of the sky never did give me any hint how to tell night from day.

All I knew was that, when I finally got an audience with the elf-king, I was exhausted and ravenous. Unfortunately, what little I knew about the fae realms told me that eating or sleeping during a visit would not be the wisest thing to do.

Then again, no one had accused me of having an overabundance of wisdom.

They escorted me into a mostly empty room dominated by a dais and a massive icy throne. The long-limbed monarch sprawled on the throne, leaning against one arm while his legs draped over the other. An elaborate fur-trimmed brocade cape cascaded from his shoulders, over the arm of the throne, to pile on the floor. A crown graced his brow, cocked at a slight angle as he stared up into the unmoving blizzard of a ceiling. His hand cradled a silver chalice and raised it toward me in a somewhat mocking gesture. "A toast to what isles of distraction we can find in the great ocean of tedium."

"Your Highness," I said in a way that I hoped was properly deferential.

He cocked an eyebrow in my direction and said, "Your Lowness." He tossed the chalice behind the throne where it landed with a clatter. "One of my endless retinue must suspect you have something of interest to say. Unfortunately, they are rarely correct." He swung his legs around so he was in a normal sitting position, showing suddenly how tall he actually was, a head taller than any average elf, who were abnormally tall and lanky to begin with. It made it easier for me to keep the appropriately submissive gaze, since I'd have to strain the princess's neck to look him in the eye. "Are you afraid, young lady?"

I bristled at the address, even though my reaction made no objective sense. "Young lady" wasn't nearly the least appropriate thing he could have called me at the moment—it was technically correct after all. I shook my head and told the truth. "I've been too preoccupied to think of it, Your Highness."

"Oh, please dispense with the formality. It is so predictably boring. Did anyone tell you what the price is to petition me?"

"No, Your—no."

He chuckled.

Now I was afraid. I looked up and found his eyes. "What is the price?"

He clapped his hands. "There we go."

I was tired, and hungry, and my nerves were frayed. I couldn't keep up the façade anymore. I snapped at the elf-king, "What game are we playing now?"

He stood up so quickly I felt a chill breeze as displaced air blew past my face. He bent and grabbed my chin, tilting my face up as he bent down. His lips brushed my cheek, the skin so cold it burned. Then, his face next to mine, he whispered into my ear. "Entertain me."

I stumbled a few steps back. "What?"

"Entertain me. That is the price. Tell me anything. Request anything, but . . ." He straightened up and pointed a finger at me. "Do. Not. Be. Boring."

CHAPTER 19

The elf-king looked me over, his face grave as a marble cenotaph, finger pointing at me as if he was some apparition manifesting to single me out for some special damnation.

I couldn't help it. I started giggling.

In my normal body I'd like to think I might have controlled the impulse. Giggle fits were not the most manly of afflictions. However, I suspect even if I had had my full measure of masculinity at hand, I still would have been unable to withstand the inherent ridiculousness of the situation.

The elf-king lowered his finger and arched an eyebrow.

"T-that—" I raised my hand to hold off any questions as I gasped for breath. "T-that . . . shouldn't be a p-problem."

"I'll be the judge of that, young lady."

The "young lady," made me start giggling again.

He looked down at me as I tried to gain control, "Was I unclear? *I* am the one who desires amusement." His grave expression made me start again.

Damn it, I'm going to get myself killed doing this.

For some reason, that thought was even funnier.

He looked down at me as if I had gone completely mad, which was evidently the case. Then he strode back to his throne and plopped himself down. "Young lady, this is becoming tiresome—"

"P-please—" I held up my hands in a pleading gesture. "D-don't call me 'young lady.'" I took a couple of deep breaths. "My name's Frank Blackthorne."

"Frank? That is an unusual name for a mortal woman."

I held my breath to kill the giggles and spoke through clenched teeth. "That's because it isn't."

"Explain."

I closed my eyes and took a deep breath and asked, "Your people told you nothing about me or why I'm here?"

He made a dismissive gesture. "Some random mortal who passed through the Grand Inquisitor's court. Acquitted for some inexplicable reason. You aren't unique."

"Really?"

"Every one of them will end up here with the same tired pleas." He raised his voice in a mocking tone, "'Please, please, Your Highness. I'm innocent, give me passage back home.'" He leaned forward, folding his arms across his knees. "All I ask is an entertaining story. Is that so much? Yet they all end up so bland I end up with a firstborn or something equally ridiculous just to provide a guide out from under the hill."

I'd been too preoccupied to have thought that far ahead.

"That isn't me," I told the elf-king.

"Is that true? Frank? There is more to you than an unusual name?"

"You have no idea."

"And you aren't here to plead for a way home."

I shook my head. "No."

"Why are you before me then?"

"I want your dragon."

The throne room was silent for a few long moments. My words hung in the air, wrapped in my clouded breath that was almost motionless. The elf-king stared at me, eyebrow arching.

"You have captured my interest, Frank Blackthorne."

If nothing else, the elf-king seemed to find my travails amusing. This was the second time I'd related my story in a short period of time, but I found it cathartic to complain about the farce my life had become. I didn't begrudge the elf-king his laughter. I was laughing just as hard at times, though in my case it was nerves and exhaustion. In the elf-king's case, he seemed to find anything involving Sir Forsythe and the Royal Court of Grünwald absolutely hilarious.

In retrospect, that really should have been a clue.

I concluded my story with a bow, feeling like the cliché bard in the ballad who, after regaling the crown with an incredible tale, is granted his heart's desire. I certainly seemed to have achieved the goal of entertaining the elf-king.

"So," I asked him. "Now you know everything, will you please release Lucille to return with me?"

He laughed and applauded my performance.

"Of course not," he said.

My smile froze on my face. "Why not?"

"You earned yourself a guide back to the world of men, but the dragon? *Seriously?* I have a millennia of service due from that creature regardless of who inhabits its skull, and all you've done is assure me that I now have a most unique and interesting dragon."

I shook my head, all the effort and fatigue crashing into me at once.

"Oh, come on," the elf-king said, "Why do you care? You *do* realize that your role as the hero was all a sham. You were never intended to save the princess, really. Your straining against that destiny is probably the most amusing thing about your fate."

"What do you want?"

"What do *I* want?"

"For the dragon. What do you want from me to release her?"

He'd been leaning forward during my story, and now he slowly sat up straight and cocked his head. "I thought I made it clear. I *want* the dragon."

"A wager? Aren't you elves into that? Some sort of diabolical bet? Is that what you want?"

He laughed, but I heard more pity in it than amusement. "Frank Blackthorne, you have nothing with which to stake such a wager. Besides, the house always wins."

"But—"

He held up his hand in the first regal gesture I had seen from him. "Desperation is not becoming. Accept your own good fortune and depart in peace, before this becomes a tiring exercise."

I swallowed and clenched my fists. "So there's no argument that would convince you to release her?"

"No."

"In my current body I have all the legal rights and possessions of the princess of Lendowyn—nothing she has?"

"Mortal kingdoms do not interest me."

"Nothing I could give? Nothing I could do?"

"No."

"There's nothing—anywhere—that you desire more than the service of that dragon?"

The elf-king sighed. "There's nothing that *you* have or could give me."

"Ah. Nothing I personally have at the moment. But, perhaps you should reconsider what I might *give* you, given my talents and some time."

Silence fell across the throne room again, and the elf-king looked past me at something only he could see. Slowly he smiled.

"Perhaps." I had the bad sense to count the elf-king's smile as a sign of victory. "So, Frank Blackthorne, what would you be willing to steal?"

"What do you have in mind?"

"There is a ring of great importance—"

Of course there is.

He rubbed his finger absently as he continued. "It once belonged to me. However, I cannot recover the ring myself given the conditions under which it was lost. It is however one thing worth more to me than a pet dragon."

"You want me to steal it for you?"

"No. I would not ask that of you. It would violate the terms of my agreement to directly pay any agent to act on my behalf to retrieve it for me. I only relate this to you to answer your question of what I desire more than the service of that dragon."

"I see."

"Once you return to your own world and resume your life of thievery, should you come across this object and decide on your own initiative to liberate it from its current owner, I would remain blameless."

I watched him effortlessly bend the terms of that past agreement beyond recognition and I realized that this was the same guy with whom I was trying to strike my own deal. If I'd felt I had any choice in the matter, I would have been slowly edging away at this point.

The elf-king kept explaining. "Should you also return with this object and offer it to me, I would be obliged to reward you in an appropriate manner."

I nodded. "So, perhaps you could provide some more detail on this ring, just in case I come across it when I get home."

"Nothing remarkable to it. A simple gold band. The importance lies in the terms of the wager in which it was lost."

"Wager? I thought the house always wins?"

"*Eventually* it does."

Inevitably there was a catch.

There always was.

The ring in question, whose value the elf-king could only quantify in terms of the symbolic and the sentimental, happened to reside on the left hand of Queen Fiona the Unyielding, Monarch of the Kingdom of Grünwald, High Priestess of the Cult of the Dark Lord Nâtlac . . .

. . . former fiancée of the Elf-King Timoras.

The betrothal, I inferred, had gone less than well. So no wonder he found the incident with the entrails so amusing. I shouldn't have been too surprised. The world of royalty was a tiny little cesspool where everyone was either trying to sleep with each other or trying to kill each other or trying to do both simultaneously. Still, I couldn't help but be slightly in awe of a universe that somehow managed to keep making things even *more* complicated.

The only bright spot was that, because of the vague circumstances under which the elf-king lost the ring in question, I wasn't subject to any official agreement with the fae. So there was no wager, no terms, no contract that could be reinterpreted in creative fashion. Everything I had seen about the way the elves conducted business was telling me that this was a *good* thing.

The elf-king summoned me a guide who could have been the first one who had brought me here from Fell Green, all pastels, lace, makeup, and aggressive androgyny. My guide led me from the steps of the frigid Winter Palace and toward the smell of fresh-turned earth.

"So did the young lady enjoy her stay under the hill?" he asked with a too-wide smile. If he wasn't the first elf, he must have been a sibling.

"I've had more relaxing trips."

He chuckled. "Are you tired? Perhaps you should lie down and take a short nap."

"I think not."

"Oh, a shame. Mortals are never really here until they take their meal and rest upon our shores." He turned and gave me that unnerving smile again, "I guess you know that."

My feet began crunching on the golden path,

and I looked down and saw dead leaves drifting across. I looked up and somehow a forest had sneaked up around us without me noticing. It was the most natural thing I had seen in this place, the autumn canopy hiding the too-close sun and moon from view.

We walked a little farther, to a clearing in the wood. In the middle of the clearing a low ring of white stones sat waiting for us.

"Go to the circle, close your eyes, and turn widdershins within it three times and then walk straight for twenty paces before opening them. Then you will stand upon your own ground."

I took a step toward it and felt the elf's hand on my shoulder.

"*Exactly* three times, and *exactly* twenty paces."

"Or?"

"Or you end up somewhere else." The elf extended his other hand palm up, offering me a small elaborately carved wooden whistle on a loop of leather cord.

"What's that?" I asked.

"The king has granted you free passage back under the hill. This is the key for your return."

I picked up the whistle. "I just blow into it?"

"And the path back here will appear to you." He took his hand off of my shoulder and I hung the whistle around my neck.

I walked toward the circle and glanced back at

the elf. "Close eyes, turn around to the left three times, then walk forward twenty paces?"

"Yes."

I nodded, took a deep breath, and walked into the circle.

CHAPTER 20

I followed the elf's instructions, and when I opened my eyes, the sky was back to normal. I stared up at a sky the purple-blue of twilight with just a dusting of stars above. I didn't know if it was sunset or sunrise, but either way, I felt a great relief no longer being in an alien land worried about any misstep trapping me . . .

. . . which meant I immediately started wondering what the catch was. The past few days had been enough to make me suspicious of anything that seemed to go well.

I stood in a forest that could have been in Lendowyn, or anywhere else with a similar climate. I found my way to what appeared to be a major road. I kept to the side, using the woods for cover, partly because I was still a young woman traveling alone, mostly because I was tensed for the possibility of Sir Forsythe or someone like him attempting to save me.

The road was well-traveled. As I followed it, several mounted travelers and a half-dozen wagons rode past me, all in the same direction I was going. None noticed me, or if they did, they didn't bother to stop. The wagons themselves gave me the first clue that not everything was going as well for me as it appeared. All of them were loaded down with harvest vegetables, melons, squash, pumpkins . . .

Problem was we had walked into Fell Green in midsummer. I'm no farmer, but I know better than to expect to find a twenty-pound pumpkin anywhere before midautumn. And as the sky lightened above me, I could see the forest canopy had turned brilliant shades of scarlet.

Unless the place where I stood kept a different calendar of seasons than Lendowyn, my two-day ordeal under the hill had cost me at least as many months. Possibly more.

Possibly much more. How did I know that the autumn around me belonged to the same year I left? I tried to tell myself that it made no sense to assume anything was worse than it appeared, but recent experience had been nothing but an extended lesson in the prudence of pessimism. However bad things appeared, they were more than likely worse.

But the universe, cold bastard that it was, always made certain that it was worse in a way I didn't expect.

I had become so preoccupied with the possibility that anything between a year to a century had passed me by, that I didn't spare any thought to *where* exactly I might be. Not until I emerged from the woods and faced the city I had been heading toward.

The place was vaster than anything in Lendowyn. A crooked crag of rock supported an angular black keep that loomed over a crowded walled city. Outside the massive blocky walls, a second city sprawled outward over a flat plain, surrounded by farms and meadows. Closest to me, a large portion of the meadows/pastures between the extended city and my rise by the woods had been given over to a tent city. Colorful banners and streamers hung everywhere, marking this as a festival day.

The devices and coats of arms I saw on many of the banners told me clearly whose harvest festival this was, even if I hadn't recognized the black keep lording over everything.

"Welcome to Grünwald," I muttered to myself.

Of course, if I was serious about recovering the elf-king's ring and saving Lucille from a millennium of servitude, I would have had to come here sooner or later. It's just that I would have preferred the latter. I was hungry, exhausted, and I wanted to have at least some time to plan exactly how I was going to accomplish retrieving something off the finger of the ruler of a kingdom where everyone wanted me dead.

Actually, that was an exaggeration. The *whole*

kingdom didn't want to kill me, just the armed portions with the legal right to do so.

At least, with the festival below, there was already a crowd to lose myself in even at this time of the morning. It was large enough that a strange face in its midst wouldn't arouse any suspicion. I sighed and walked down to join the party.

I had to work my way too close to the city wall, and the city guard, to find an inn with a spare room. But whatever insanity I was about to attempt, I was going to attempt it after some rest and regrouping. According to the innkeep, I was lucky, it was only the second day of the harvest festival. By midweek people would be sleeping in the streets.

Yep, that's me, lucky.

But, in a sense, the innkeep might have been right. The harvest festival was some warped providence, and I could make use of it to cover my theft. And the fact that it still had six full days to go meant that I had some time to plan things out.

I paid the innkeep out of the measure of slaver gold I still had, thanks to the elves' disinterest in confiscating my possessions. Then I retreated to the tiny little room that he had left for me. It was windowless, and the bed was no more than a mat on the floor, but it was thankfully free of secret passages for any would-be assassins, kidnappers, or thieves.

Even so, I took the one chair and used it to bar-

ricade the single door. I seemed to have success-
fully avoided recognition, but a little paranoia at
this point couldn't hurt.

I stepped away from the door and stood still for
several moments.

Then I started shaking.

"Damn it all," I whispered and hugged myself.
"Damn Elhared. Damn the dragon. Damn the
elves." I closed my eyes because my vision was
blurring again. "Damn me."

I was going to make this right, and beat the hell
out of Elhared in the process.

I was overwhelmed with the same sense of loss
that had plagued me off and on since I'd woken in
this body, but, strangely the image that the emo-
tion brought to mind wasn't from the memories of
the old Frank Blackthorne. It was the recent memory of me attempting to comfort the Dragon Lucille
after she had saved me from the altar of Nâtlac.

The dampness on my cheeks burned, and I
blamed the princess's body. I couldn't help but
think she had handled the transition better than I
had. She certainly seemed to make a better dragon
than I did a princess.

I shed my boots and stretched out on the poor
excuse for a bed.

In order to free her, I needed a ring off Queen
Fiona's hand. Nothing to it, thievery is what I did.
And given the festival, the queen would almost
certainly be making an appearance.

Simple.

I closed my eyes telling myself I was going to brainstorm some sort of plan, but exhaustion claimed me and I fell into a deep dreamless sleep.

I woke twelve hours later, feeling a now-familiar disorientation. I took care of the normal necessities upon waking, dispensing with the modesty I'd been clinging to. I was stuck in Lucille's body, and I decided that going through the normal process of hygiene wasn't an abuse of the privilege.

I took my waking meal in the inn's common room as the rest of the guests were having their dinner. The house was roasting something vaguely pig-shaped on a spit, and the smell reminded me exactly how ravenous I was. I barely noticed a couple of lewd propositions in my preoccupation to get a meal.

I retreated to the end of one long table with a bowl of root-vegetable stew with a chunk of roast something floating on top, a hunk of black bread, and a tankard of ale the size of my head. I would have preferred to be alone, but I satisfied myself with the end seat on the far side of the table, putting an empty spot between me and my neighbor, a bald pile of fat molded in the vague shape of a man.

Fortunately, that gentleman was more interested in the large leg of animal he was consuming than he was in me, and his bulk blocked me from the view of everyone else on our side of the table.

I emulated him and bent over my meal in rapt concentration. I needed to formulate a plan. I needed to get close to the queen. Close enough to lift the rings on her fingers. I needed to get close, unobserved by her guards and retainers.

I was a skilled pickpocket, and given Lucille's smaller delicate hands, I suspected my skills hadn't diminished. So if I got close enough I was sure I could pull it off. But it should happen in the open to give me a chance to escape. I had a whistle back to elf-land, but I didn't know what form the path would take, or how long it would take to appear. The ability to get a running start would be a plus.

Best would be pulling it off without anyone noticing, but I doubted that would be possible outside the keep, and I didn't think attempting to slip in would be worth the risk. This wasn't like finding Prince Dudley in a half-empty palace in the middle of nowhere, this was the seat of power in—

"Hey!"

I looked up from my meal, which was already half gone. I glanced at my oversize neighbor, who was still focused on his own meal.

"Yes, you!"

I turned my attention across the table. Facing me was a leathery old man with a gap-toothed grin and thick gray hair pulled back into an extremely long braid. He pointed at me with a hunk of black bread and narrowed his eyes at me. "Just arrived, eh?"

I nodded, uncomfortable at the attention. The last thing I needed was another proposition. The events from The Harpy's Teat were still fresh in my mind.

"For the festival, I take it?" he asked.

I pondered graceful ways to slip away. I was constrained by the fact that I did not want to abandon the remnants of my meal, since it was my first in what seemed like days. So I nodded again, and quietly continued eating.

"Traveling alone?"

This time I didn't nod. Instead I shifted the grip on the knife I'd been using to serve myself in case I needed to use it in a hurry. The man-mountain to my left proved not completely oblivious, as out of the corner of my eye I saw him set down his animal leg and turn his attention, ever so slightly in our direction.

"A young lady should be careful. The land is full of brigands, murderers, rapists . . . *thieves.*" He hissed the emphasis on the last word like it was an accusation.

Oh, crap.

I've done enough acting in my life to keep the shock from leaking into my expression and body language, but it didn't keep gap-tooth guy from being inordinately pleased with himself for his subtlety. He leaned back in his chair and chuckled.

The large man was glancing from me to him then back to me again. I think I saw his eyes widen a bit, but he wasn't my concern at the moment.

"Careful, yes," said the gap-tooth-guy. "There's a particular fugitive you should be concerned with. Someone named Francis Blackthorne. The Grünwald throne has offered a hundred gold crowns and a title to the person who captures him."

I swallowed very slowly.

Gap-tooth-guy continued. "He must be a very bad person to be worth so much."

I straightened up and said, "Well the man would be a fool to come into the capital city, wouldn't he?"

"Oh, yes he would be. But take care, as I believe he's shown an interest in young ladies like you. Steals them away in more than one sense."

I bet you're proud of yourself for that one.

He stood up and clicked his heels and presented me with a short bow. "If you wish, I can provide you protection from the dread Francis Blackthorne. The third room to the left upstairs. I work for considerably less than a hundred crowns."

The gap-tooth-guy sauntered away from the table with a bounce in his step and, undoubtedly, a song in his heart.

The large wall of man next to me had turned to focus his attention wholly on me. The attention was unnerving, and the last thing I wanted was another proposition.

He opened his mouth to say something and I cut him off. "I have no idea what that was about."

I got up and retreated from the common room before this guy tried striking up his own uncomfortable conversation.

Gap-tooth-guy was a problem. He obviously knew my backstory, and it had propagated far enough that I had more to worry about than just the Grünwald guardsmen. In a sense I was lucky that my gap-tooth-guy was too clever by half. He had recognized me—recognized Princess Lucille—and instead of waiting to take me by surprise, he had come up with this blackmail scheme.

I still held my knife and the hunk of bread, and I realized I had abandoned the rest of my supper.

"Damn," I said as I walked outside.

I wiped my knife clean on my hunk of bread and finished eating it as I sheathed the knife. Outside the inn the light had faded toward evening.

I had two options. I could disappear back into the city and find other lodgings. Or I could confront the guy. If it wasn't for the fact that I needed to get close to Queen Fiona, I would have chosen the former, hands down. However, I had no doubt that if I vanished, my gap-toothed adversary would notify the Grünwald court of my presence. That would make an already difficult situation worse.

I was left with confronting the guy.

However, I wasn't about to walk through the front door into an obvious trap. Not when the guy was lucky enough to have rented a room with windows that opened onto a narrow, secluded alley. At least, that's where I estimated his room to be given his instructions and what I knew of the layout of the inn.

I scaled the wall to the second story, under what I thought was his room. I peeked through the window—

Damn.

Wrong room. I peeked in the window and looked straight into the eyes of a well-endowed prostitute who apparently was just starting her workday straddling some guy who, judging by bits of armor strewn about, was a functionary of the city guard. She locked eyes with me in mid-grunt.

I let go with one hand so I could put a finger to my lips before ducking back under the window. I paused, tensed, under the window, waiting for a reaction. I was relieved to hear the sexy-time sounds continue unabated.

I guess that's the measure of a professional, how you deal with the unexpected while you're working.

I held my position while I remapped the interior of the inn in my head. I knew I wasn't on the wrong side of the building, which meant that I had miscounted windows. Either a room or two had more than the one window, or—more likely given the brief glimpse I'd had of the room beyond the assignation-in-progress—I had missed

that one of these windows opened onto the hallway at the head of the stairs.

I moved laterally to the window to my immediate right, and slowly peeked inside. I was re-
warded with a view of gap-tooth-guy. He sat in a
chair, facing away from the window, toward the
door. His braid hung over the back of the chair,
almost to the ground, and a crossbow rested
across his knees.

A crossbow? Really?

I decided that he was not the smartest guy to
have tried to blackmail me.

I climbed up to crouch on the sill outside the
window. Lucille's body had an advantage in light-
ness, balance, and dexterity that allowed me to
stand on a thin ledge that never would have supported the original Frank Blackthorne. I stood
there perched on the tips of my toes, maintaining
balance with the fingertips of my left hand while
I slid the dagger slowly between the window and
the jamb.

I used the dagger to slowly, quietly lift the latch.

The window hinged outward, so I had to sidestep all the way to the edge as it swung out. I had
a stupid grin on my face. It felt good to be indulg-
ing my skills as the old Frank Blackthorne would,
without worrying about dragons, or elves, or
princesses—

Or boobs.

I'd slid fluidly aside to let the window silently

open past me. I'd even sucked in the princess's nonexistent gut to give the window enough clearance.

And I mashed it into my right tit. I didn't do it hard, but the unexpected resistance threw my whole body off-kilter, like miscounting a set of stairs in the dark and finding the floor too early.

I managed to keep from yelling, but I dropped my dagger so I could grab the window frame and keep from tumbling into the alley. The clatter was enough to alert gap-tooth-guy. He spun around, knocking the chair over as he stood to point the crossbow in my direction.

He fired.

CHAPTER 21

If the man had had any sense, he would have taken a moment to aim, possibly declare some sort of ultimatum. But, luckily for me, my gap-toothed adversary was something of a moron. I don't even think a skilled bowman could spin around from a seated position into a firing stance and bring a twenty-pound crossbow to bear on a target and fire with any accuracy, even if the target was less than three paces away.

He did come close, if only by accident. The bolt smashed through the window inches from me, throwing glass across the princess's inconvenient bosom.

Now that he was armed with an unloaded crossbow, he was considerably less of a threat. As that realization dawned on him, he tossed the crossbow aside and dove for the dagger I had dropped inside the room.

That gave me the perfect opportunity to jump down and land on his back. I felt some satisfaction as he squealed like a girl. But the squeals continued as he threw me off him. As I slammed into the wall I realized I was hearing the prostitute next door.

He came at me with the dagger, and I rolled away and sprang to my feet.

We circled, facing each other. "Aren't you full of surprises," he said, gesturing with my dagger.

Great, he likes to talk. "What are you trying to accomplish?"

"Oh, come on, Francis, there's a price on your head."

"Why the stupid charade downstairs?"

He laughed. "Please, I know better than to think I could collect that reward. Too much history between me and Grünwald. First official I came to would vanish me and claim the prize."

He probably had a point there. The guard enjoying himself next door would probably be first in line to cosh this guy in the head and take me to Queen Fiona himself.

We kept warily circling each other. I tensed myself, waiting for him to make a move. "Then what's the point of this? I don't have any money, so blackmail is pointless." That was a lie. I still had a good portion of slaver gold left, but I wasn't about to tell this guy that.

"No it isn't. You have something I'd very much like to have." He licked his lips.

We had now completely reversed positions, my back to the door, his back to the window, the upended chair between us.

"You must be kidding me," I said.

"Oh, please. After what happened to you, the experience must be . . . *unique*. With the body of a *princess*, no less. Let me experience that and no one will be any the wiser."

Oh, hell no.

"It's a mutually beneficial situation, ain't it? Tell me what it's like, Francis."

I ran forward, grabbing the chair.

"Don't call me Francis!" I yelled at him as I slammed the chair into his knife hand. I tried to knee the gap-toothed pervert in the groin, but he swung his leg to deflect my blow and tip me over. I lost my grip on the chair and it fell back into the room, dagger embedded in the seat.

That was the least of my problems. This guy was twice my size, and was strong enough to throw me across the room.

As his hands grabbed my throat, I realized rushing him had been a bad idea.

"Got you," he said, and I couldn't catch the breath to raise an objection. He pinned me to the ground, grinning and washing me with breath that matched his rotten teeth. "I think I get to call you anything I want now." He leaned forward and whispered into my ear, "And I like 'Francis.'"

The bastard licked my cheek, and it was enough to make my whole body shudder. I felt something long and thin brush my hip. *What? That can't be what I think it is.*

Thank the gods, it wasn't.

I reached a hand down and it was the end of the guy's long braid.

You work with what you got.

I grabbed it, twisted it around my wrist, and yanked.

"Ack!" he said as his head pulled back from my face. The shock made his hands loosen to the point I could breathe. I balled my other hand into a fist and started slamming it into the side of his head. There wasn't much force behind it, but by yanking his hair with the other hand, his face gradually turned to meet my blows.

He caught my fist in one hand and started squeezing. "You're going to regret that."

I responded by pulling harder on his hair. He cursed and reached around for my other hand. That freed my neck, and my head.

So I slammed my forehead into the bridge of his nose.

I think it is good advice not to head-butt someone if you don't know what you're doing. The impact blurred my vision and sent a painful shock all the way down my spine. Warm blood gushed across my face and I had no idea whose it was.

As my own brain rattled dizzily in the princess's skull, I heard that my talkative captor had been reduced to monosyllables, every other one sounding like the word, "Kill." I might have been dizzy and half-blind but, as he released my fist to grab his face, I could feel that my attack had backed him off me enough so I could move. I bent my legs and pushed myself out from under him to scramble unsteadily to my feet.

He grabbed for me with the hand that wasn't clutching his face and I dodged backward. My backside pressed against the windowsill. The breeze from outside brushed the hair against the nape of my neck.

He took another swing at me, and I leaned backward, half-flipping and half-falling out the open window.

Dizzy as I was, I would have plunged to my death if I hadn't still held the guy's braid wrapped around my wrist. I fell down about four feet before we both jerked to a stop.

I hung there for close to a minute, as my head cleared, waiting for some sign of movement or commotion above me. All I heard was heavy breathing and grunting from the pair in the neighboring room above me.

Once my head was clear, I found purchase on the wall and let go of the guy's hair. When I let it go, it slid slowly upward until I heard a soft thud above me.

I climbed up, peeked into the window, and grimaced.

One problem solved, I guessed.

I climbed back into the room, stepping over my gap-toothed assailant. He wasn't going to get back up. My abrupt exit at the end of his braid, combined with his abrupt stop at the base of the window, had done fatally unpleasant things to his neck.

"Damn it," I whispered. I hadn't wanted to kill the guy. Not to *start* with, anyway. All I wanted was to discourage him a little. Tie him up so he was out of the way until I accomplished what I needed to do, something like that.

Maybe I should have given the guy what he wanted, distasteful as it was. Given his inclinations, I might have tied up a willing victim.

I righted the chair and pulled the dagger out of it. I sat down and faced the guy. His eyes stared blankly off to my right, above the hand that was still clamped over his broken nose. I kicked the crossbow that still rested between us. "You weren't very bright."

He didn't move.

"Seems like I'm not very bright either."

He didn't have a response to that.

"What am I going to do with you?"

My one-sided conversation was interrupted when the door to the room burst in. A man the size of a small mountain stormed in, stumbling, swinging a mace almost as big as I was. I scrambled back from the onslaught, brandishing my dagger as the man swung, spun, took a misstep, and fell on his back in the middle of the room, his bald head landing in the gap-toothed corpse's lap.

"I don't believe this." I stared down at the huge man on the floor. I recognized him from the dinner table downstairs. He was out of breath, panting. He wore leather armor that appeared hastily pulled on, several sizes too small for him. "Who are you and what are you doing here?"

"I am Brock," he said between breaths. "My Princess. Brock here. To save you."

"Of course you are." When no threat appeared forthcoming from the pile of would-be hero on the floor, I sheathed my dagger. I walked to the door and looked out into the hallway to see if anyone was responding to the brief commotion. No sign of anyone, and the only sounds came from next door.

I envied that pair for their blissful ignorance, if not for their inevitable chafing.

I closed the door and latched it.

"Brock thought the door would be locked."

"Uh-huh."

"Brock heard a scream."

I rubbed my temples and sighed. "You probably heard the lovebirds next door. I don't remember any screaming in here."

"Brock is confused."

I righted the chair and sat down again, looking down at Brock the Hero. "You aren't the only one," I said.

He slowly sat up, shaking his head. "This is not what Brock expected." With me in the chair and him seated on the ground, our eyes were about on the same level.

"What exactly did Bro—did you expect?"

"The shaman told Brock his destiny. A princess in a far off land would be in danger. He showed Brock visions of a dragon, and a kingdom, and a princess more lovely than anyone Brock has ever seen."

I whispered to myself, "Brock needs to get out of the village more often."

"Brock saw you, Your Highness."

"Why doesn't this surprise me?"

"Brock is here to save the princess."

"You aren't the only one," I repeated.

Brock had come from a barbarian village far to the east, past two mountain ranges and one rather large desert. He wasn't the best regarded member of the village; being large and slow, he wasn't much use for the hunt. He'd been subject to taunts and pranks by his peers all his life. He couldn't count the number of times he'd been abandoned in the forest, his so-called brothers laughing as they outran him.

So when the village shaman shared a vague vision with Brock about saving a princess, Brock took it as a sign to leave—even though Brock knew quite well that it was probably the tribe's way of getting rid of an embarrassment.

I might have come to terms with the universe

having a practical joke at my expense; I wasn't ready to have the joke involve other people so literally.

"You came all this way by yourself?"

"Brock has learned how to be alone."

"Well I have some good news and some bad news. The bad news is that I'm not the princess."

Brock shook his head. "No, Brock saw you in a vision."

"I'm sure you did. But for the moment I'm a thief named Frank Blackthorne and the both of us are a little out of our depth."

He gave me the "Brock is confused" look. I empathized with the guy.

"The good news is I *am* trying to save a princess."

Brock was a bit smarter than he seemed. I only had to go over the backstory twice before he got it—and I got the feeling that the second go-round was an attempt to catch me in any inconsistencies. It was clear, however, that I had gained an ally whether I wanted one or not.

He did make it easier to dispose of an unwanted body.

Also, I had to admit that it was helpful to have an errand boy. The presence of both Brock and the late gap-toothed-guy here showed that I was nowhere near as anonymous as I needed to be. I needed some protective coloring, and I didn't want to risk going out and getting it myself. So, when dawn came, and Brock the Barbarian returned without the inconvenient body, I had another mission for him. I gave him a bag of coins and a list of things to get from the marketplace for both of us. Then I hunted down the innkeep without venturing into the common room where someone else might recognize me. I paid for another two days in advance out of the funds I'd liberated from the gap-toothed guy, plus a little extra for discretion's sake.

Then, I discreetly asked for a favor.

He took the extra coins and nodded, smiling.

I retreated to my room and, about an hour later, I heard a knock that was way too subtle to be Brock. I opened the door and caught my visitor in the midst of a yawn.

She froze, mouth open, and stared down at me.

"You?" she finally whispered.

I waved her inside. "I figured you worked here. This kind of place tends to frown on outside contractors."

She shook her head, rippling a mane of curly black hair. "Honey, it's nice to have an admirer. But you're a girl."

"What," I said, "my money's no good?"

"It's not my area of expertise."

Even though she was still rubbing sleep from her eyes, I found her very attractive. Too attractive. I hadn't been able to have an intimate moment with anyone since the virgin, now "ex-," that I had rescued from the Nâtlac cultists of Grünwald. Expertise or not, I was sorely tempted to help her with some on-the-job training.

My cheeks started burning, and my guest's expression went from befuddlement to an amused smirk.

"That's not why I wanted to see you," I said quickly. "I just want to buy your time, and your silence." I tossed her the rest of the gap-toothed-guy's gold.

She grabbed it out of the air. "Why me?"

"From what I've seen, you're observant, discreet, and have some contact with the city guards in this town."

The coin purse disappeared somewhere into her bodice. "Correct on all three. You've bought my time. What else is it you want?"

CHAPTER 22

I had a plan.

I wouldn't go as far as saying that it was a particularly good plan, but I had managed to cobble together something plausible in twenty-four hours. And I didn't have any more time to come up with anything more airtight since, according to my informant, the queen was only going to make an appearance for the jousting tournament. That would be the only time I would be able to use the festival as cover to get close to her.

Not that it would be easy in any event. That area of the tent city wasn't open to commoners, and everyone entering the festival town itself fell under the scrutiny of the city guard making sure all the proper taxes were paid. Then, of course, there was the problem of the wrong people recognizing me, either as a thief or a princess.

However, thanks to Brock's shopping trip, I had the means to deal with that last concern.

The morning of the queen's appearance, I transformed myself. I wrapped my boobs—more uncomfortable than it looks—and donned a motley outfit of garish yellow and green checks. I braided the princess's hair—again, not as easy as it looks—and tucked the unfortunate result under a big floppy hat. My face I disguised under a thick coating of white greasepaint. I drew new lips on top of that in black, as well as shadowing my eyes until they looked like holes into my skull. That I covered with a black domino mask.

The result was a vaguely androgynous jester character who shared only height and weight with the princess.

I left the inn with Brock, who wasn't only a new ally for me at this point, but another element of my disguise. Those on the lookout for Frank Blackthorne or the Princess Lucille were looking for a woman traveling alone. Not for a huge bear of a man, masked and cloaked, holding up a chair with a juggler clad in garish motley and white makeup.

When I had mentioned disguising ourselves as street performers, he had been somewhat skeptical.

"Are you sure people would believe that?"

"I'm a fair acrobat and juggler. The right costume and no one would question it."

"What would Brock do? Brock is not a performer."

I had looked him up and down and said, "You're an attraction all by yourself."

"Brock cannot *do* anything."

"No? How much can you lift?" I had asked him.

Turns out, despite being slow and clumsy, he was just as strong as he looked, and could hold a chair steady while I sat, juggled, did handstands, and otherwise made a literal fool of myself. Our act was good enough that people threw money at us. We may have made a profit by the time we were halfway to the tent city.

I felt pretty proud of myself. I had a talent for disguise, but that was as the old Frank Blackthorne. I didn't know if those skills would translate as well as the physical ones. The closest I'd come to disguising as woman before now was the one time I had to dress in drag to escape the harem of a southern sultan who was rather upset at the loss of a jewel-encrusted ceremonial dagger.

Turns out that just like the acrobatics and climbing, the only major difference was having a set of boobs.

But our disguise was a little *too* good.

We were only one of dozens of acts making our way down the main road. And, like every other performer, we were obliged to stop whenever a crowd of enough interested people congregated. So I noticed when a trio of other performers would stop at the same time we did.

It also attracted my notice because the trio was rather mismatched; a fellow juggler on a pair of stilts, a fire-eater in a leather vest and baggy pants, and an actor in a tragedy mask who appeared to be dramatizing the death of the last Grünwald king.

"I think we're being followed," I whispered to my supporting act as I bounded off the chair to collect the latest round of public donations.

"Brock doesn't see who?"

"Stilts, Flame-boy, and Tragedy."

I couldn't see his expression behind his mask, but I could hear the confusion in his voice. "Brock only started learning the language. Can you explain?"

I retrieved the last coin from the dirt and gave a bow. "Head toward that alley," I said as I scrambled up to return to my perch on the suspended chair. It gave me a better bearing on our shadows. I cursed because Tragedy had already lost himself in the crowd.

Brock headed toward the alley I had indicated, and I saw Stilts and Flame-boy abruptly end their performances to follow us.

"Okay, maybe the actor was just some random hanger-on." I said, keeping watch behind us as we slipped between a stable and a blacksmith's. "Two on two's better odds anyway."

We were deep between the buildings, out of sight of the street, when Brock came to an abrupt halt. "What is—"

I was interrupted by someone saying, "Bravo!"

I turned around so I was facing forward, and

looked down on the gentleman with the Tragedy mask. His arms were flung wide, and in one he held a wicked-looking short sword.

Not some random hanger-on, I thought.

"Magnificent act," Tragedy said, bowing in our direction. "Quite the eye-catching pair you make."

What gave us away? I couldn't figure it out. Was the princess just that recognizable?

Flame-boy and Stilts caught up with us, blocking our retreat.

"What should Brock do?"

"Wait a moment," I whispered. "What do you want?" I called down to Tragedy.

"To honor you, of course."

Brock started to lower my chair and Tragedy whipped the short sword around to point at my face.

"Please remain seated for the duration of the program. I am loathe to provide a swordsmanship demonstration to a nonpaying audience." Brock slowly raised the chair back into place.

Tragedy made a show of stroking the chin of his mask. "Where was I? Oh, yes, you're being honored."

I heard chuckles of amusement from behind us and I looked as Stilts idly tossed one of the clubs he'd been juggling from one hand to the other and Flame-boy brandished a pair of burning batons.

"You have been chosen, by vote of the membership, for induction into the Brightwood Performers' Guild."

My first feeling was relief. This was just straight extortion; none of these characters actually knew who I was. There was some slight chance of extricating ourselves without attracting any more attention. I sighed and picked up my purse. "I assume there are some dues involved?"

The point of the sword lowered. "You are wise as well as an excellent performer."

Stilts piped up, "Heh. He knows it's hard to juggle with busted fingers."

I could tell why Tragedy was the spokesman for the group.

"How much?" I said with my most reasonable voice. "Half?"

"Sorry," Stilts said. He reached over Brock's shoulder and snatched the coin purse from my hands. "We's got to take it in advance. Fines for registering late."

I was perfectly willing to let bygones be bygones and let them take what they wanted, but when I wrapped up my boobs, I had stashed the elven whistle in the purse. That wasn't something I could give up, since I didn't have a Plan B for my exit after thieving from the queen.

I stood up on the chair. "I'll pay you, but I need that pouch."

"You should have considered that before you attempted to shortchange the Performers' Guild." Tragedy was brandishing the sword again. "Please seat yourself."

"Brock," I said, "Chair him."

I sprang off onto Brock's shoulder as Brock swung the chair at Tragedy. Stilts backpedaled with his massive stride, to give Flame-boy space to demonstrate his skills in my direction. I leapt as Flame-boy puffed out his cheeks. The distance of my leap managed to surprise all three of us. Advantage to the princess for having a higher leg-strength-to-weight ratio than I expected.

I arced across the alley, followed closely by a spray of fire from Flame-boy. Stilts dodged quite ably to the side to avoid a collision with me, a maneuver that would have been more impressive if he had kept my purse out of my reach, and if he hadn't dodged into the Flame-boy's dragon impression.

I hit the ground in an ungraceful tumble, but I landed with my purse in hand.

Behind me I heard Stilts calling out, "Idiot."

I spun around and dodged just in time to avoid another spray of fire. Stilts no longer paid me any attention; he was attempting to reach down and beat out flames that were spreading up his long pants. Flame-boy stood between me and Brock now, flame-tipped baton in one hand, ceramic flask in the other. He was in the midst of taking a swig, fueling his next attack.

I reached into a sack on my belt and pulled out one of my wooden juggling balls and pitched it at his face. It struck him in the hand, shattering the flask and splashing his face and chest with the fluid inside. Whatever was in the flask must not have been pleasant to get in the eyes, because Flame-boy screamed and covered his face . . .

Dropping the baton . . .

Flame first . . .

Into the puddled remains of the flask at his feet.

His scream raised several octaves as his boots were engulfed in fire, and he ran blindly in my direction. I dodged to the side, and he slammed into a wall. "Brock!" I yelled.

He turned away from the crumpled form of Tragedy.

"We need to go!"

He tossed aside the splintered remains of the chair and ran toward me.

"No, you's not getting away like that!" Stilts yelled down at me. He had beat out about half the open flames, and had decided that was enough. He took a couple of impressive strides in my direction, easily outpacing Brock, who resembled a mountain in terms of speed as well as size. Stilts bent and swung a club in my direction—

Just as the blinded and stunned fire-eater stumbled face first into Stilts' still-smoldering knees. The remnants of the stilt fire was enough to ignite the fluid that doused Flame-boy's upper body, and he screamed, burying his burning face into Stilts' trousers trying to smother the flames.

Stilts might have been skilled, but he wasn't

able to keep his balance like that. He toppled over just as Brock scooped me up and ran back toward the street.

By saying "ran," I am being generous. The only reason we lost our pursuit was because they were all either unconscious or on fire.

We managed our way to the tent city with a few minor alterations in our act, accommodating the loss of our chair and one of my juggling balls. And we managed to avoid any more recruiters from the Brightwood Performers' Guild. We stationed our last performance in front of one of the auxiliary entrances to the tent city at the fringes of town. There was much less of a crowd to lose ourselves in, but there was only one guard manning the entrance.

One *particular* guard.

I had some worries as we extended our performance twice. But my friend from the inn finally showed like I'd paid her to. She had not only been useful in determining the best way to sneak into the upper-crusts' side of the festival, it turned out that her inside knowledge of the city guard was particularly thorough when it came to *this* city guard. She managed to monopolize his attention so thoroughly that even Brock had time to slip in past him.

We were now inside the perimeter of the tent city around the tourney field, but not quite where

I needed to be. We had slipped into the service half of the temporary city, where all the supplies and servants were housed for the festival. A strongman and a juggling harlequin might have fit in on the streets within the city proper, but here our dress was out of place—unless there was an unannounced clown joust scheduled that I wasn't expecting.

As soon as we were past the guard, I led Brock between a pair of supply tents, ducking between a web of interwoven anchor ropes to find a safe place to slip in and plot out my next move.

I found a good hiding spot, a quiet tent that, when I pulled the canvas up to peek inside, was filled with stacks of oak barrels. I held the canvas up and waited for Brock to maneuver his way past all the ropes between the tents. Where I had ducked and weaved through most of them, he had to lift his legs up and step over them. In some cases he had to swing his leg over ropes that were nearly eye level on me.

Slow as he was, I would never want to be chased by the guy. He gave the impression of a deliberate avalanche.

After a nerve-racking wait, Brock caught up with me. It was too much to pull the canvas up to let him in, so we had to sneak around to the proper entrance and slip inside when no one else was looking. Fortunately, there were not many people back here, and at the moment they were concentrating on unloading a wagon into one of the other storage tents. They shouted at each other in a language I couldn't decipher.

While those people were occupied, I ushered Brock inside and closed the tent flap behind us. Large barrels flanked us, stacked along each wall of the large tent. I could guess their contents pretty easily. The whole tent had a yeast-mildew smell like the basement of an old alehouse.

I whispered to myself, "So far so good."

Brock reached up and removed his mask and smiled. "What do we do now?"

"Give me a few moments."

The smile faltered. "What is your plan now for Brock to save the princess?"

I held up my hand and shook my head. "Hold on. I need to think."

"Brock thinks you have no plan."

"No, I do have a plan." Unfortunately we had reached the part of my plan that simply went, "Step 4: Think of something."

I know, it's a bad habit of mine, but things never follow the a script anyway.

"Then what is it?"

"I'm improvising," I snapped in frustration.

Brock shook his head, sighed, and sat down on one of the oak barrels. The aged wood creaked in protest. "Brock should not be surprised."

"Could Brock stop talking about himself in the third person? It's annoying and I'm trying to think."

"What do you mean?"

"Do you hear me referring to myself by name all the time? *I* do this, *I* do that—not *Frank* does this, *Frank* does that."

"Brock—*I* apologize. This is not how Brock's people talk. B—I just learned this language."

"I thought your accent was a little strange." I took off my floppy hat and freed my hair. The oak casks had given me the germ of an idea of how I could mingle with the high and mighty. I would just need to get from where the ale was stored to where it was served. "Sorry I snapped at you. How long did it take you to learn?"

"Brock has only been here two weeks."

"Two—you learned this language in two weeks?"

"It took Brock longer than usual."

"Longer—usual—how many languages does Brock speak?"

"Brock hasn't counted." He closed his eyes and, after mumbling for a moment, said, "Twenty-seven."

"You know twenty-seven languages?"

"No. Brock *knows* thirty-three. Brock can only *speak* twenty-seven of them. Six of them Brock can only read, since the languages are dead and no one speaks them anymore."

I stared at him a moment and then I shook my head. "You're a surprising man." I reached into my pouch and pulled out a cloth and began removing the makeup from my face.

"You are improvising now?"

"Yes."

"And you know what Brock can do?"

I looked him up and down and said, "Ditch the cape and the mask—you know the language those guys by the wagon were speaking?"

"It is spoken in small land to the north of—"

"I know exactly what you can do."

CHAPTER 23

As a mode of travel, I do not recommend riding within a hastily emptied oak barrel carried by a gigantic multilingual barbarian. It is even more unpleasant than it sounds. You can barely breathe, and every breath you do manage is saturated to the point it's like trying to suck air through a barkeep's cleaning rag. Then there's the fact that the inside is too slick to hold yourself up against all the bouncing and shifting.

Brock did good. Once the accessories we'd added for the sake of the performing arts were removed, his normal attire fit seamlessly into the population of servants and laborers who worked on the backside of the royal games. He was intimidating enough that no one bothered to challenge him, especially since he seemed to be carrying a barrel of ale toward thirsty noblemen. His language talents were helpful, in that he could get directions from his imported peers without having any extended interaction with a Grünwald foreman, or anyone else who might combine the realization that something was amiss with the inclination or authority to care. I heard someone challenge him twice; each time Brock responded in that strange northern tongue I couldn't understand. The people challenging him apparently didn't understand either, and were too busy to bother dealing with him.

It felt as if I rode in that barrel for half the day, but it probably only amounted to a quarter hour at most. Eventually, the world tilted around me, spilling the remaining dregs along with myself, toward one end of the barrel as it hit the ground.

The impact set the end above me askew. We'd had to pry one end of the barrel free to get me inside, and doing so had ruined the barrel, leaving that end only loosely attached. We'd wedged some rags around it to hold it in place, but apparently there were limits to how long that could last. I drew my dagger and crouched in an inch of dirty ale, hoping that there wasn't anyone other than Brock about to see the lid go cockeyed.

A large hand reached in and lifted the broken end of the barrel off of me. Brock looked down and quietly said, "You can come out."

I sprang out of the barrel and assessed my surroundings.

We were obviously in the working part of the tent city now. This tent was packed with barrels, but unlike the storeroom we'd come from, half these barrels were empty. I was gratified that Brock had the presence of mind to stack our barrel with the empties.

Also in this tent were racks of large mugs and trays, and a space with rags and a large washbasin. That was good, since I now smelled more like a brewery than was appropriate. I headed toward the basin and told Brock, "Keep an eye out for anyone coming."

"If they come?"

"Warn me, look busy, and don't speak the language."

He nodded and took a station by the entrance.

By the basin I stripped off the saturated jester costume and started washing the excess ale off of me. Brock looked in my direction, turned several shades of red, and went back to looking out the tent flap.

What else could I do? I needed to change outfits again if I needed to get anywhere. And if nothing else, it is hard to express the relief I felt after unwrapping my chest. Twice, Brock warned me of people coming. Both times I crouched, clad only in my dagger and wet undergarments, behind a stack of barrels while Brock anonymously moved barrels from one side of the tent to the other. Each time, the servers ignored Brock and went about their business, retrieving and filling tankards of ale, depositing trays of empties by the washbasin.

The third time, the server came to wash the empties and refill the rack of tankards. I watched her until I had a good estimate of her size and shape. Slightly taller than the princess, and a bit more endowed, but generally workable.

"You'll do," I said as I leapt from my hiding spot to point the dagger at her. "Don't scream," I said as Brock set down a barrel and grabbed the woman by the shoulders.

"What is this?" she cried, eyes widening at me.

"It's one of two things," I said. "It's where my large companion knocks an innocent woman unconscious and shoves her in a barrel. Or it is where a not-so-innocent woman avoids a blow to the head and makes some extra money for very little effort."

She looked at me, then turned to look up a Brock, then back at me again. "How much are we talking about?"

We were talking all that was left of the slaver gold, plus about half the take from our street performance. It pained me, but I wanted this woman's discretion as much as I wanted her clothes, and I was paying her to allow us to tie her up and sit in a barrel for what might be a few hours at least. That should be worth something.

Once we settled on an amount, she was quite helpful. She fixed my hair, which was apparently a hideous mess. And she helped properly fitting the bodice—during which time I discovered that this woman wasn't nearly as well-endowed as I had thought. Her bodice and low-cut chemise combined to do absolutely miraculous things to the princess's cleavage.

I had been worried that someone might recognize me once I slipped into the crowd with my face uncovered. Looking down as she tightened the laces binding me, I realized that my worries might not be such an issue, at least for half the population. It also gave me a convenient place to stash the elf whistle.

"There," she said after adjusting everything. "Now you don't look too frightening." She reached down and smoothed my apron. We had traded undergarments, and my old chemise, despite being cut more modestly, was still wet and clung to her in some rather distracting ways. Again I was reminded how long it had been since I'd shared intimate company with a woman, and that feeling—more than the bodice thrusting my cleavage toward my chin—reminded me of exactly what I lacked at the moment.

As much as I told myself that what I was doing was for Lucille's benefit, I was really motivated by selfishness. Of course I would do just about anything to return her to her body; it was the only way I could return to my own.

The woman gave me an inscrutable expression and touched my cheek. "You're really too pretty to be waylaying serving wenches."

"I'm not waylaying you," I said, clearing my throat. "I'm bribing you, remember?"

She laughed. "Are you saying you wouldn't have followed through on your threat if I'd started screaming?"

"It would have been the huge barbarian who waylaid you. That's what I brought him for."

"I see."

I hunted for a good place to conceal my dagger, and settled for my upper thigh. I fumbled with it a moment, before my most recent contract employee reached down and said, "Let me."

She slid my hand away and started working with the buckle to fit the sheath snug against the skin. She quickly managed it, but left her hand against my inner thigh. "You haven't even asked my name."

"I'm sorry," I told her, "I've had other things on my mind."

"Evelyn," she said.

"Uh huh." I reached down and removed her hand. She squeezed it for a moment. "I'm afraid we're going to have to tie you up now."

"I know." She looked into my eyes, and what I saw there . . .

Let's just say, I didn't know if it was a good thing or a bad thing. Whatever it was, I didn't have the time to deal with it right now. Instead, Brock and I tore apart enough dishrags to tie together to make credible restraints, bound Evelyn hand and foot, and Brock gently set her down into the barrel I'd arrived in. Last I put the remains of the harlequin outfit in with her. She looked up at me with a half-smile and said, "I normally work in Brightwood, at The Three-Legged Boar. If you ever want to return my clothes."

I nodded and Brock put a clean dishrag into her mouth as a gag. I lifted up the barrel lid. I hesitated a moment, then I told her, "My name's Frank." I put the lid in place over a very puzzled expression.

I did not want to ponder any of the implications of what Evelyn had said—mostly because entertaining certain ideas would be admitting to myself that my current princessly state was something more than a temporary affliction, and that wasn't anything I was ready to deal with on any level.

Instead I filled a tray with a full supply of ale tankards and walked with Brock out of the tent.

"What does Brock do now?"

Good question.

"Keep posing as a servant. Carry things around and work your way toward the tourney field. At some point I'm going to get close to the queen. It'd be nice if I can do this without being noticed, but there's more than likely going to be some sort of commotion. I'll probably be yelling. A lot. If that happens, I want you to ready some sort of distraction. A big one."

He smiled. "Brock can do this."

"Wench!" Someone shouted in our direction.

I turned and saw an old man hooking a finger in my direction. "No fraternizing on the job. Get those drinks out here."

"Got to go," I smiled at Brock and moved in the direction the crotchety old guy indicated.

As I passed the old man, he slapped my butt. "Speed it up, missy," he said with a cackle. From that point on I knew that serving girl wasn't going to go on my list of favorite disguises—though my earlier speculations were borne out by the fact that the old man was so fixated on my bodice that he was oblivious to the change in its occupant.

Welcome to the world of the highborn and noble, I thought as I stepped over some scion of some great house or other who had passed out in a pool of mud, piss, and vomit. I weaved through a population of titled nobles, courtiers, and diplomats, all personal guests of the Grünwald crown, and I think I could have exchanged most for any random denizen of The Headless Earl. The only differences seemed to be clothes, diction, and the cost of their indulgences. That, and I suspected the thugs at The Headless Earl were more polite to the servants.

Then again, what would you expect of a crowd gathered to watch men of knightly virtue beat the crap out of each other?

Between me and the field of honor was a good two to three acres of drunken lords, princes, barons, and whatnot from a dozen different places. Even though the arms of Lendowyn were notably absent from the serving tables, there were probably more than a few people present who may have actually met the Princess Lucille at one point or another. Unfortunately, I saw no way to get close to the royal pavilion, and Queen Fiona, other than through this mass of inebriated nobility.

Thin as it was, my disguise held up. There was the noble disinclination to notice the existence of common people, especially servants. And there was the general intoxication of the populace. Then there was the last line of defense, my cleavage-emphasizing bodice.

I drew a lot of unwanted attention, but none of it because anyone recognized me.

Still, as I dispensed tankards and dodged lewd dukes and groping earls, I began to recognize that my serving-wench persona was unlikely to get me too close to the queen. Close to the royal pavilion, the long open-air serving tables gave way to benches of seats for spectators. That area seemed much less rowdy, and my protective coloration would stand out. I didn't see any of my fellow wenches carrying tankards into the stands. Then there was the pavilion itself, which was its own building in the midst of the stands, separated by brightly painted canvas walls from the less-royal spectators.

I worked the tables close to the tourney field,

occasionally using my skills at clandestine acquisition to keep my tray populated with full tankards. I didn't want to run out and have to return for more. In many cases all I needed to do was lean over slowly as I collected empties, and no one would notice the empties weren't.

As I played my role, I kept one eye toward the royal pavilion, looking for means of surreptitious entry. I saw half a dozen ways to enter unobserved, and all had the same problem. The queen faced the field, on a dais, in front of everyone. Behind her was a tightly packed group of advisors, nobles, and guardsmen. Even if I made it into the pavilion, there was no route from inside to the queen—over, under, around, or through—that would escape notice from her entourage. Even then, there was another serious problem. To the right of Queen Fiona, standing at attention, was her champion.

Sir Forsythe the Good.

Of course he'd be here.

I turned away, afraid that even at this distance, Sir Forsythe might recognize me. That complicated things even more as I tried to think of any possible way to get to the queen without him seeing me. Cleavage alone wasn't going to be enough camouflage to get close enough to snatch the ring. Nâtlac aside, Sir Forsythe probably thought himself too pure of heart to be distracted that way.

I could hide within and wait for the queen to

leave the festivities, but that would give me a very small window of opportunity, in a tight space that was probably even more tightly packed with guardsmen. And, more likely than not, Sir Forsythe would be there as well.

This was looking less and less possible. Worse, I could see the rings glittering on her hand. So close . . .

I watched as the next pair of knights took the field. They strode in front of the pavilion. They were dressed in full plate armor that shone in the sun, the type of overly engraved nonsense that only got worn when nobles dressed up to play at war. Good at looking pretty, not so good on the battlefield.

Behind them, their squires led their warhorses. All of them came to a stop before the queen. The knights removed their helmets and handed them to their squires, both young men, boys really, wearing broad hats and tabards embroidered with their knights' colors. The knights turned from their squires to kneel and pay their obeisance. The queen stepped down from the dais to stand before the kneeling knights and provide royal sanction to the contest.

Then she held out her hand so the knights could show her proper respect, and they both placed a chaste kiss upon her jeweled hand.

I now had an absolutely insane idea.

CHAPTER 24

It was impossible to get close enough to the queen unseen. My next best option was to do so unnoticed.

Even in a skirt and bodice, I was gratified to find my ability to sneak around the clusters of tents was unimpeded. Unlike princesses, working women tended toward sane footwear.

I worked my way around the back of the stands, and into the service area of the tent city around the tourney field—toward the smell of horses. The staging area for the main event wasn't hard to find, with ranks of tents flying the colors of noble houses and stinking of manure.

I think there's some sort of metaphor there.

I didn't know the schedule of events, but it was also easy enough to find a knight who was going to the field soon. I just had to find a team of men gathering to strap a beefy gentleman into a tin can.

Seeing that, and the knight's colors, meant it was likewise easy to identify the matching squire, alone and waiting by the knight's horse. Again, the squire was little more than a boy with a dusting of adolescent hair on his lip and several youthful blemishes across his face.

That made attracting his attention into a nearby supply tent *extremely* easy. A few years older, and he might have been slightly suspicious of the flash of leg and bosom that attracted him inside. But, the young male brain being what it was, he wandered into my clutches almost as if he'd been ensorcelled by some evil mage.

It almost made me feel guilty.

The most difficult part of the whole enterprise was stripping the clothes quickly off his unconscious body and getting dressed before his knight was completely poured into his armor. I didn't have time to get fancy by strapping down my breasts again—probably a good thing, between the harlequin outfit and the bodice, they were on the verge of open rebellion anyway. And I didn't braid my hair, instead I just shoved it under the squire's cap, which was a size or two too large anyway. Between the baggy shirt and the tabard, my shape was more or less hidden. The boots were loose, but I only had to walk a short distance.

The elf whistle I hung round my neck under the tabard to keep it handy.

I was just about to tie up the naked squire when I heard a clanking approach. I had to run clumsily to go untie the bored warhorse from the tent stake the squire had used, and station myself in the squire's place.

I'll be the first to admit that this was nowhere near my most effective disguise. I wasn't as tall as the lanky teenager I replaced, I had a better complexion, I was lumpy in all the wrong places, and a thick lock of my hair had come free from under my cap to dangle in front of my face. Standing there, in retrospect, I realized there was no way my impersonation should work.

I stood frozen, refusing to breathe as the knight walked into view with a retinue of servants.

And for once, the universe was on my side. His servants were too preoccupied manhandling the knight up on the horse to pay me any attention. My nominal task was to keep the horse steady during the operation, but the warhorse in question was so well trained that he might as well have been a rock. The knight himself was too handicapped by his own obnoxiously plumed helmet to notice I existed.

Once their man was in place, everyone retreated to several paces behind the horse and the knight, leaving me my place in the lead. This was good, in that I probably looked a little less out of place from the back than the front.

We all stood still, waiting for the call for our guy to get jousted all to hell.

Even though I had no idea who this knight belonged to, I was again aided by the well-trained mount. When a herald somewhere shouted about the champion of house such-and-so, the until-then immobile horse pawed the ground and I knew to start leading it toward the field of so-called honor.

Throughout my career of going places I should not be, to retrieve things I should not have, it has been a useful tool to use the human tendency to see exactly what one expects to see. Many times if someone is presented, without fanfare, a scene that is almost what should be there—but not quite—they will be disinclined to observe closely the actual discrepancies.

My march across the tilting field, toward the royal pavilion, had to be the ultimate test of the premise. Here I was, a barely disguised out-of-place young woman, leading a warhorse toward the queen herself, under the watchful eyes of thousands of spectators, scores of whom should recognize me for one reason or another if they had cause to look closely enough.

Each step I silently prayed to whatever forces were in charge of my fate to just get me a little closer. Each step, just a little closer. And, to my amazement, my brazen effort worked. The inevitable recognition never came, no noble stood from the stands to point an accusing finger and shout, *"It's her!"*

Or, for that matter, *"It's him!"*

As we came to a stop in front of the pavilion,

and my knight dismounted, even Sir Forsythe seemed oblivious to my presence. My knight did me the favor of removing his helmet and handing it to me without even looking in my direction. I held it, the plumes making my nose itch, but further obscuring my face from the pavilion and the stands. He walked in sync with his opposite number, to kneel before the queen as the prior combatants had. It was hard to believe that I had gotten this far, and as Queen Fiona strode from the dais to give the royal imprimatur to the current round of ass-kicking, I readied myself to dash in front of the queen.

And, as she lowered her jeweled hand to receive her knightly devotion, a naked young man with a bleeding scalp ran onto the tourney field screaming, *"Treachery!"*

I took that as my cue. I tossed the helmet I held to the side, ran up in front of the startled queen, and echoed the knight's gesture, taking her hand, and giving it a chaste kiss as I palmed the three rings she wore. The oversize cap tumbled off as I raised my head. Our eyes met, and as the queen stared at me in shock, I said the first thing that came to mind. "I'm sorry about the entrails, Your Highness."

From behind her, Sir Forsythe drew his sword and scowled at me, *"You!"* he cried out as eloquently as could be expected. Other members of the queen's retainers scrambled out of the pavilion, and the knight kneeling next to us grabbed for me. He was surprisingly quick for someone wrapped in a fancy tin can, but he ended up with a gauntlet full of my tabard.

I ducked out of the tabard and ran for the horse, which seemed the quickest mode of escape available. I vaulted onto the saddle, swinging my leg with enough force to send one of my ill-fitting boots flying off into the face of one of the knight's servants. I sat on the horse, snapping the reins with the hand that didn't hold the rings, trying to kick it into motion.

The horse only moved to turn one eye to me and give a dirty look.

Damn horse was *too* well trained.

I was now trapped on top of the animal, surrounded by the knights' retainers on one side, the queen's on the other. Someone grabbed my leg and I pulled free, losing the other boot as I stood up on the saddle. Sir Forsythe waded toward me through the crowd.

At the top of my lungs I screamed, "*Brock!* If you're going to do something, do it *now!*"

He already had.

From my vantage, I saw the horses before I heard the hoofbeats. Four chestnut mares were loose, and, galloping from the confines of the tents by the knights' staging area, one headed for the tourney field, three others toward the crowd.

Then came the warhorses.

"Oh, crap."

I don't know where Brock found four mares in season, but he had found an efficient way to make the knights' mounts break training. Only six had broken free of their grooms to give chase to the mares, but ten hoses galloping through a crowd of drunken nobles was pretty significant as far as distractions go. The sudden stampede was enough to give pause to the people surrounding me and the horse I was on.

One of the mares galloped wildly down the jousting field toward us. The beast under me snorted, and I barely had time to drop back down and grab the saddle beneath me before my mount decided that the game had begun, knight be damned. He reared, throwing the knight's men to the four points of the compass, and started galloping toward his prize.

For a few strides it was as if I was part of a joust, an invisible opponent on top of the much smaller mare, our paths separated by a yard-tall hedge. Ahead, on our side of the hedge, the naked teenage squire stood, eyes wide in shock, unmoving.

I screamed "Move!" at him. A pointless gesture since, by the time the word was out of my mouth, the horse was upon him. The only thing that saved the squire was the fact that my mount, intent on a mounting of his own, decided just before reaching him to vault the hedge.

I took that moment to jump off, seeing no way

my ride could end well. I rolled along the field and up against the hedge. I did a quick inventory, making sure I still clutched Queen Fiona's three rings in my fist. I had a panicked moment when I couldn't find the elf whistle's strap around my neck, but then I felt that it had fallen into my shirt.

As I dug around in between my boobs for my escape, naked squire-boy decided to come to his senses and jump me. "It's all your fault!" He pinned my shoulders to the ground and landed a knee to my stomach, knocking the breath out of me.

Out of the corner of my eye, I saw the crowd by the pavilion regrouping and heading in our direction, Sir Forsythe in the lead.

My hand found the elf whistle under my right boob.

"Why?" cried the boy on top of me. "Why did you do that to me?"

Somewhere on the other side of the hedge I heard equine squeals and farting noises.

At least the day's going well for someone.

"Nothing personal, kid," I said, slamming my ring-filled fist into his overexposed nether regions. He gasped and fell off of me.

Sir Forsythe and crew were nearly on top of me as I put the elf whistle to my lips and blew so hard I thought my lungs would burst.

I fell backward as part of the hedge vanished behind me. I found myself looking down a tunnel through the hedge, burrowing much deeper than the hedge was wide. I didn't need any prompting. I was pulling myself into hedge before I rolled off of my back. Something shook the hedge above me, and I saw the tip of a long blade descend from above to stab between my knees.

Then I pulled myself a foot or two deeper, and the branches grew and closed up the opening between me and the tourney field.

CHAPTER 25

On the other side was a rather bored-looking elf. I looked around and saw the circle of white stones. I looked back at the elf and it was almost as if he hadn't moved since I'd left. "Well, that took longer than I expected."

I got off of the ground, pulling up the squire's ill-fitting breeches. "Well, I'm gratified in your confidence in me."

The elf provided his too-wide smile. "Oh, nothing like that. I just expected that you'd require escape from some foul end long before now." He held out his hand. "If you would."

I stared at his hand blankly.

"The whistle," he said. "That was a loan."

"Oh, yes. Sure." I gave him the whistle. He curled his hand around it and turned to leave.

"Shouldn't you take me back to the elf-king?"

He turned around and arched an eyebrow. "Whatever for?"

I opened my other hand and showed three rings. "I thought one of these was the point of this."

His eyes widened and he looked down. "You actually—"

He paused, composed himself, and said, "Of course. Follow me."

I don't know why I should have been surprised that they hadn't expected me to accomplish anything. That kind of game was something the elves were known for. It was one reason why it was a bad idea to wager with them. But, for some reason, I *was* surprised.

I had tumbled back into the world flush with victory and a sense of accomplishment, and I found out that my elf guide had expected me to give up and retreat the moment I struck some difficulty.

In the Winter Palace I again found that I had exceeded expectations. The elf-king greeted me in his throne room, dismissing some other, less interesting, visitors with a wave of his hand. The trio of goblins did not want to leave, and elven guards appeared out of nowhere to remove them by force.

"You have to listen to us—" the goblins shouted at the elf-king. "It's all a misunderstanding—"

It's always a misunderstanding, I thought.

"You arrogant fae prick!" one of them shouted before they were dragged out of the throne room, leaving me alone with the elf-king. He sighed and swung his legs down from the arm of his throne. "That was boring and predictable. Especially after your testimony this morning. No one seems to measure up."

"This morning?"

He shook his head and muttered, "Mortals." He stood and said, "Time is a bit more leisurely under the hill. There is a reason your kind always seems in such a hurry."

I already had that impression, but it was nice to have it confirmed. For each hour I stood here, something like a whole day must pass in the real world . . . it might have even been worse. Time here might be as flexible as the geography.

"I find it surprising that you gave up on your quest so early. I expected some magnificent stories when you came back. Horrifying, demoralizing stories." His grin was somewhat disturbing.

"They didn't tell you—"

"Oh, please. Surprise me, Frank Blackthorne."

I held out my hand and opened it. The trio of rings glittered in the cold blue light of the Winter Palace. The heavy signet ring clouded slightly in the cold air as my breath touched it. Next to it was a ring made of tangled gold and silver filigree, dotted with diamonds. Opposite that was a plain gold band.

He looked at my hand and said, "Indeed."

The elf-king reached over and I closed my hand, shaking my head. "Remember? This was done on my own initiative."

He looked up and his voice hardened. "Give me that ring."

"Not before agreeing on its price."

"I underestimated you, Frank Blackthorne."

"I gathered that. In retrospect if you thought there was a reasonable chance of me getting this ring, you wouldn't have let me out of here without some compensatory debt that only handing this over would resolve."

"You want the dragon, I know."

"At this point, it's not just the dragon."

"You pressure me in my own palace?"

I shrugged. "I swiped the rings off of Queen Fiona's hand in front of all the nobility of Grünwald and half the surrounding lands. After that, haggling with you is not particularly intimidating."

The elf-king glared at me for a moment with a stare that should have melted the icy structure around me. But the ends of his mouth twitched. Once. Twice.

Then he burst out laughing.

He spun around, whirling his furred cape. "You!" he shouted at the frozen blizzard in the ceiling. "Are! Not! Boring!" He whipped the cape aside with a flourish and plopped himself down on the throne. "Oh, I wish I had seen that old bat's face when you relieved her of her baubles." He clapped his hands. "Now, Frank Blackthorne, haggle. What is it you demand of the Lord Under the Hill to grant him his heart's desire?"

"First off, I want to know what you *can* give me."

He arched an eyebrow. "And I should help you in your attempts at extortion?"

"Negotiation."

"Let us not quibble over semantics."

"Can you undo the wizard's spell?"

"Frank Blackthorne, I would gladly do so to earn that bauble you hold. I would end with both dragon and the ring. But alas, I cannot do this without your wayward wizard, and where he might be, I cannot say."

"The Grand Inquisitor said as much."

"Such things are more dangerous than they seem. The mortal soul is not designed to traipse between bodies. That is the province of gods, demons, and undead spirits."

I sighed. "And if something goes wrong—"

"I can assure you, you would not be joining the ranks of gods or demons."

"Why, damn it? Elhared couldn't be that great a wizard, he worked for Lendowyn! How did he pull this off in the first place?"

The elf-king shrugged. "I'm sure he's mediocre at best. But you said he read from a book—so I doubt it was his power or skill. He was probably invoking the skills of some demonic entity or other. Souls are their specialty after all."

When he said "demonic entity" all I could think of was the Nâtlac-worshiping court of Grünwald, which makes it all that much more embarrassing that I did not immediately piece together the whole comedy of errors right there.

I do have an excuse. I was tired, frustrated, standing in ill-fitting squire's garb, and all I could think of was Lucille still locked into a cage in the wrong body . . .

I was not fit to negotiate with someone who was supernaturally adept at deal-making. In retrospect, that was obvious because I didn't suddenly become suspicious when the elf-king smiled, stroked his chin, and said, "But . . ."

"But what?" At that point, I didn't know it, but I was doomed. There was part of me that knew I should push my leverage for all that it was worth. I might have listened to that voice if I had been there only on my own behalf. But I wasn't going through all this for my own sake. It wasn't only Lucille anymore either. I was worried about Brock. I hoped he had managed the equine distraction without being caught, but I didn't know. Worse, given the time difference, several hours had already passed back by the tourney field. All these worries boiled within me, freezing the part of my mind that should have been devising a foolproof set of demands.

"I can offer you a promise that, should you return to me with the other principals, preferably with the book in question, I can set things back to your liking."

"You can?"

"With the book, and the collection of correct bodies and souls, it would be trivial. Without the book, it would only be a matter of strongly querying the wizard as to its content. Casting such things does leave an impression."

"So if you have Elhared, you can do this?"

"Of course, is that enough for the return of my property?"

"Wait a moment," I said, realizing I was on the verge of being conned. "That doesn't sound like much of a deal. You get the ring in return for a *promise* to do something, *if* I bring the misplaced old coot back here. If I get my hands on Elhared, and especially his book, it sounds as if any competent wizard could do the same thing."

The elf-king spread his hands. "I never claimed otherwise."

"And you're omitting a guide out of this place, or a way back."

"Can you blame me for attempting to negotiate things in my favor?"

"No, this is what you're going to do. You're giving me that promise. You're also releasing the dragon. The dragon and the princess who currently inhabits it are both completely free, all liens upon either body or soul are permanently and irrevocably released, and she is free to go as she will."

The elf-king nodded, the smile barely shifting. "Obviously."

"You'll give us both free passage and a guide to return us to the mortal world without delay or interference."

He sighed. "This is why people are more fun on the first visit. They come back and know too many of our little games. Not an issue, even though I will miss bargaining with you again."

"You'll give us a means to return with Elhared once we retrieve him—"

The elf-king held up his hand, "Simply so I can fulfill that first promise?"

"What else?"

"Why not this instead?" He pulled out a small silver mirror from his pocket and held it up.

"And that is?"

"A means to contact me directly. No travel involved. You find your wizard and speak my name to the reflection, and I can take the wizard's body and appear to you. Avoids all the bureaucracy, not to mention hiring a guide back."

I just knew that the elf-king had an ulterior motive, but when it came down to it, avoiding a return under the hill was a good thing. "Fine, the mirror will do for that. Any way you can get us close to Elhared, even if you don't know where he is."

"As close as possible."

"Also, I had a companion who assisted me in recovering these rings—"

"This begins to border on tedium."

"His name is Brock, and I need to know he's safe—"

The elf-king's smile was gone. "This I will tell you free, Frank Blackthorne. The man you know as Brock is safe as can be for a man whose destiny has yet to be fulfilled. He shall remain unharmed until he saves his princess."

He leaned forward, coming close to scowling at me over his steepled fingers. "Are there any more demands?"

I was at a loss. I had already gotten what I thought I wanted from the elf-king, but it seemed wrong to end it at that. With this much leverage, I should get something for my own efforts.

I looked down at myself. My feet were bare and streaked with mud, I wore the squire's long shirt that had pulled out of my breeches, and it sported streaks of mud and leaves. The squire's breeches hung down on me, bagging around my ankles now there were no boots to fit them into. "I want a chance to clean myself up, and some new practical traveling clothes that actually fit me."

The elf-king couldn't stop himself from laughing again, despite still glaring at me. "Yes, yes, of course. You'll have the finest clothes of elven manufacture if only for the amusement you've given me."

"We have an agreement?"

"Yes!" He clapped. "More than that. You have my pledge, my vow, and my solemn oath. Your every request will be met." He stood and extended his hand. "The ring?"

I opened my fist and looked at the three rings I'd liberated. "Which one?"

"The one on the right."

I picked up the plain band and the elf-king's face went paler than usual. "No! *Not* that one. My right, your left."

I dropped the plain band and picked up the filigree ring to the elf-king's obvious relief. When we were talking earlier, I'd suspected that the elves' definition of "plain ring" was somewhat different than mine.

I handed it to him and he shook his head. "I thought I'd outsmarted myself there for a moment."

He probably had.

I knew that I had been conned, but only because I had allowed myself to be. I knew there were a lot of other uncomfortable demands I could have made upon him. Judging by the relief he showed upon receiving his ring, I probably could have gotten most of them. I made the mistake of believing that I had used that threat to negotiate just what I wanted, without any strings.

Looking back, my naïveté is somewhat embarrassing.

"Frank Blackthorne, you will always be welcome here." He held up the ring so it glittered in front of him. "You, and the complications you create, are fascinating."

He called for some guards to escort me, and as they led me away, he called after me, "Remember, Frank Blackthorne, I always keep my promises."

They took me to a room in the palace that, while frigid, was warm enough for me to clean myself off. Once I got the last of the mud and ale off of me, and felt human again, it sunk in that I was thinking of this as cleaning *myself* off—not the princess. I didn't know what was more uncomfortable, the realization that I was now thinking of this body as my own, or the impulse I had, upon that realization, to force myself into thinking that body was alien territory and I needed to be embarrassed or ashamed of treating it so casually.

I was very happy that they had clothes waiting for me.

As I got dressed, and fumbled with some of the more feminine undergarments, I kept muttering, "We need to find my body. We really need to find my body."

Once I was dressed, I left the palace chamber and my elvish escort led me back to the arena where Lucille and Elhared the Fake were still caged. Lucille took one look at me descending the wide steps back down to the arena floor and turned her massive lizard skull away from me. At least as far away from me as she could manage in the tight confines of the golden cage.

"I'm not talking to some lowly thief."

I took it as a good sign that she wasn't crying or breathing fire in my direction. "I came back to free you."

She grunted. **"I've heard that before."**

"Hey!" yelled Elhared the ex-dragon from his own cell, "what about me?"

"Really, I am." I told her.

"And it worked so well the first time."

The bailiff met us at the foot of the stairs and bellowed at the now-empty arena, *"By proclamation of King Timoras, most high lord of all realms under the hill—"*

"I went through a lot to get the elf-king to do this."

"So now you're making deals with the elves?"

"—release all claims, debts, and liens upon the prisoner—"

"I think some gratitude is in order."

"—irrevocably and in perpetuity, under the hill and in mortal lands—"

"I'm sure you think following the last dragon's example is a great idea."

"I wasn't gambling for you. I got the king something he wanted—"

"Stolen, no doubt."

"—immediately without let or hindrance. So says the king!"

The bailiff brought his staff down with a thunderous impact that shook the arena floor and vibrated Lucille's cage into nonexistence.

"Come with us."

"I'm not going with you."

"Don't be ridiculous. I'm taking you back home."

"Home? I'm a dragon! What home do I have?"

"We're going to get our bodies back."

"What if I want to stay a dragon?"

I walked around so I stood in front of her face. I resisted the urge to slap her nose in frustration. Instead, I sucked in a breath and said, "I'm sorry."

"Sorry?"

"I'm sorry I lied to you, even if it was a lie of omission. I didn't mean to. Yes, I'm a thief, a somewhat accomplished one in fact. But, once I got to know you, I just couldn't bring myself to say so . . . I cared for you and I didn't want you to think less of me."

"Hiding who you are wasn't the way to do that."

I shrugged. "I don't know what to tell you. It was kind of nice for someone to think of me as heroic, even if it wasn't really true. I can understand if you want to part ways. But you probably should come back with me so you aren't stuck in elf land."

She lifted her head on her serpentine neck. She looked down at me, then turned to look around at the bailiff and the elf guards. **"What did you give the elf-king?"**

"A ring. Something he lost in a wager with Queen Fiona."

She whipped her head around to stare at me with shocked reptilian eyes. **"You stole from the Queen of Grünwald?"**

"Right off her hand. I don't think she was happy about it."

"They want to *kill* you."

"They can only kill you so much. I just gave them another reason."

She sighed with a belch of brimstone. I didn't think it was possible for a dragon, but she muttered something inaudible.

"What?"

"I'm sorry," she said.

"You're sorry?"

"I shouldn't be mad at you. I am, but I shouldn't be."

"Don't worry about it," I said. "Let's just get out of here."

"Yes." She stood up and stretched, almost like a cat. Her joints popped like a spastic ogre cracking a bullwhip.

"Look," came a pathetic plea from the remaining cell. "I'm sorry too. We're all sorry. Can you please get me out of here now?"

We ignored him as the elves led us up the arena steps.

"I'm sorry I vowed revenge—" I heard the crack of the bailiff's staff and didn't hear any more from Imitation Elhared.

"Thank you," Lucille said as we left the arena.

"You're very welcome."

"And you *are* heroic."

"No, I'm a huge bundle of questionable motivations. But thank you anyway."

Our elven escort led us to a completely different enchanted glade for our exit. We didn't even have to close our eyes. Instead, as we walked down a wide path, a silvery mist came to envelop us, obscuring everything but the shadows of the elves accompanying us.

"I still think dealing with elves is a bad idea. It never ends well." She tried to whisper, but there's no question our escort could hear every word.

"Princess, could you be just a little less bigoted?"

Our guides brought us to a stop within the mist, and the lead elf said, "We have arrived."

The mists had begun clearing and I saw a normal full moon above us, in a normal sky. "See," I told Lucille. "Back safe and sound."

The elves retreated, and the lead one touched my arm. "The king offers his apologies."

"For what?"

"Keeping his promises."

The mist withdrew, revealing ranks of armed soldiers surrounding us. The mist kept retreating, exposing a whole army underneath the moon's glare.

In front of us, flanked by two figures in plate armor, was Queen Fiona herself.

"See," Lucille said. "Back safe and sound. Still think dealing with elves is a good idea?"

CHAPTER 26

The queen took a step toward us. "I did not expect that prancing clown of a king to abide by his agreements. Not after that unfortunate display on the tournament field. I must say I am pleasantly surprised."

I looked from Queen Fiona, and to the retreating elves. I asked through clenched teeth, "What agreements?"

The queen laughed. "That trifle you stole for him, it was a token of fealty. To me. I had a pledge from him to deliver you to me, should it ever be within his power to do so."

"Wait a minute. I took that ring, and broke whatever bond you had over him. You could still coerce him to do this? What was the point?"

"Mistress," said the last elf, "you are correct, but the agreement Queen Fiona speaks of predates your meeting with our king."

"Wait. Crap. He was in league with you before I—Then he convinced me to—That bastard set me up!"

The queen folded her arms. "I'm sure he found

it amusing to 'return' you to me just to steal his token."

"Again, the king gives his apologies, but he does fulfill his oaths. You are back in the mortal realm, free to go as you see fit. Any further hindrance is not the responsibility of the fae." With that, the elf guides disappeared as one, leaving us "free to go" surrounded by the Grünwald army.

"Lucille," I said, "fly, get out of here!"

"Not without you!" She scooped me up with a forelimb and spread her massive wings.

Queen Fiona was unimpressed. "There are three hundred archers trained on you. Put the princess down if you care for her to continue living." She walked up to us, flanked by her metal-plated knights. While their faces were hidden under full helms I recognized the device on the right-hand knight as belonging to Sir Forsythe.

Unfortunately, I also recognized the sword carried by the left-hand knight.

Lucille froze in place, wings still spread. **"I can roast them."** She almost managed a whisper.

"Archers," I whispered back. "And you see that sword?" The left-hand knight carried a twin of the ill-fated *Dracheslayer*.

She snorted, **"That worked so well last time."**

"I think Grünwald might be able to buy a better sword than a freelancing wizard financed by a skim of an already bankrupt treasury."

She slowly placed me back on the ground. I stumbled slightly, kicking up some dust and what looked like a fragment of bone. *No, someone has to be kidding.*

I looked around, and saw the carved standing stones, and the altar, and how most of the queen's army seemed to be standing outside the lines of a rather distinct circle marked on the black, blasted ground. I looked up again, and the moon was nearly overhead.

Let me guess, a midnight sacrifice? And I wonder who it's supposed to be?

"Now, Francis Blackthorne, you have something I want back." The queen stopped in front of us. "Return it and the dragon might live."

"Don't give that bitch anything."

The queen looked up at Lucille and said, "And I might just leave something standing when we march on Lendowyn."

I could feel Lucille tense, and I was about to warn her not to do something stupid, but she looked back and forth and stayed put. Next to me, her claws dug deep into the ground.

I fell back on a long history of being backed into corners.

When in doubt, stall.

I stepped between the Lucille and the queen and held up my hands. "Sorry, you'll have to take this up with the elf-king, I've already given it—"

"Not some stupid engagement ring! At this point the fae bastard can choke on it for all I care! You know the ring I'm talking about."

As it was, I knew exactly the ring she was talking about. I reached into the pouch matching my fresh elven ensemble and felt the two rings I had left. One was a heavy signet ring with the royal seal on it, the other a plain gold band. The gold band felt warmer than it should have, and the elf-king had pointedly wanted nothing to do with it.

I squinted at the queen as I pulled a ring out of the pouch. *Ring of power maybe?*

Next to me, Lucille tried to whisper, **"We can't let them invade. The militia can't take on an army."**

The queen had no problem hearing her. "Especially since Prince Dudley has already hired them away," she responded.

Well, that explains why the twit had been in Lendowyn.

"The ring, Francis. It will be so much less messy than searching your corpse."

No, something else is holding you back, because that would have been your Plan A.

Was it the site? Some ritual requirement that they hold off on cutting out my heart until the appointed hour?

"You need it," I whispered, hefting the ring in my hand.

"Give it to me!" she shrieked.

"Do you need it to kill us, or do you need it to kill us *right*?"

"I'll slaughter both of you and raze Lendowyn to the ground. Every man, woman, child. Burn every building, salt every field, erase it completely from existence. If. You. Don't. Return. It. *Now!*"

Next to her, the knight with *Dracheslayer* spoke in a disturbingly familiar voice, "Your Majesty, that was not the agreement."

"Archers!" she screamed. *"Ready!"*

So much for stalling.

I hefted the ring in my hand and tossed it. "You win. Catch!"

"Frank, no!"

There was something deeply satisfying watching Queen Fiona abandon all pretense at dignity and dive after the glittering ring. She sprawled on the ground with an outstretched hand to catch the tumbling bauble. It landed on her palm, and she started cackling.

"What did you do?"

The queen got to her knees and stared down into her palm, and the laughter ceased.

"I improvised."

She turned toward me, holding the signet ring, face contorted with fury. *"This is the wrong ring!"*

"I know," I whispered as I reached into the pouch and slipped the too-warm gold band onto my own finger.

*   *   *

You might wonder exactly what your humble narrator must have been thinking at that point. After all, I had an obvious magical artifact, one that gave the *elf-king* pause, one that had belonged to the Queen of Grünwald and High Priestess of the Cult of the Dark Lord Nâtlac. A ring she was, to understate things a bit, rather anxious to retrieve.

Dark magical rings that inspire that kind of avarice do not have a great reputation for making things go well for their wearers.

To top it off, I stood upon a site that was most probably consecrated to Lord Nâtlac, and I probably still counted as a virgin sacrifice, if only on a technicality.

So, admittedly, putting that ring on, *there*, counts as the least intelligent thing I have done in this narrative. And that's after setting a rather high mark for self-destructive idiocy.

So, what was I thinking?

I wasn't.

I was running on pure instinct. We were in a corner, evil had triumphed and was about to grind us into the ground. What *else* was I going to do?

Everything changed when I put that ring on.

I don't just mean the fact that the entire Grünwald army disappeared, along with Lucille, the stone circle, the moon and the sky. I meant that when I blinked I was on my hands and knees on a cobblestone floor staring at a pair of large but sensitive hands that did not belong on a princess.

For one ecstatic moment I realized that I was me again. I wore my own body, and I had on the same clothes I wore when I had first wandered into that nameless dockside tavern. Between the buzzing and disorientation I managed to convince myself for nearly half a minute that everything was back to normal, and everything I remembered happening was just some adverse hallucination caused by the Mermaid's Milk.

Then I realized the buzzing wasn't in my head. Something like a mass of insects was making the sound from just beyond my peripheral vision. It started making the skin itch along my spine. I was suddenly very reluctant to lift my head to see beyond the patch of cobblestones below me.

Then one of the cobblestones blinked.

My vision had been a bit blurred because something in the air was making my eyes water. I pulled my hands off the stones and wiped them off on my shirt.

"Oh, crap."

The cobblestones weren't stones. The texture was hard and uneven, but every stone had some feature of a face or body, as if some humanoid creature had been compressed to this shape and had been set in place. The stones still lived. I could see limited movement, blinking eyes, lips baring teeth, a wriggling finger . . .

I pushed myself stumbling to my feet so I wasn't touching those things anymore. I couldn't tell exactly where I was. The rusty light was enough to see by, but everything beyond my immediate surroundings disappeared into impenetrable darkness. All I saw was the living floor, and a pair of pillars—or trees, or stalagmites, irregular and ropy with veins—disappearing into the darkness above. As I stepped back, a long tongue emerged from a mouth in the floor and began to lick my boot.

"Crap. Crap. Crap."

My eyes didn't just water anymore, they burned. The air was heavy with the stench of things burning, rotting—a smell like aged dragon vomit. I covered my mouth.

"Well, you aren't Queen Fiona."

I spun around to face the speaker.

The speaker had the form of a tall man, flawlessly perfect in face and body. He was pretty much an eidolon of masculine beauty—at least until you realized exactly how he was dressed. He wore robes of black leather whose dark color couldn't quite hide the shape of human faces whose mouths and eyelids had been sewn shut. That was bad enough, until I realized I could see eye movements behind the sewn eyelids. He reclined in a throne made of skulls bound together by strips of flesh and sinew.

"I've wondered what became of her the past few weeks."

"Who are you?"

"Frank. Frank. Frank. You know who I am." He laughed, and in the sound I could hear the screams of a million tortured souls.

He was right. I already had a pretty good idea.

"I am the Dark Lord Nâtlac, Prince of the Lower Depths, Father of a Thousand Sorrows, Keeper of the Blasphemous Rite of the Elder Gods Who Are Not Named . . . do I really need to go on?"

"I guess not."

He stood and stepped down off of the throne to slowly circle around me, as if he were sizing me up. With every step, the floor under his feet cried a little. The buzzing became louder as he approached me and I realized that the face he wore right now probably bore no resemblance to exactly what he was.

He raised a finger and traced it across my face, and his touch made my skin feel as if it had been flayed, burned, the flesh eaten away by carrion ants and replaced by ground glass. "You are a pleasant surprise. The queen has become too *pedestrian*. Temporal power. So obvious."

The ground glass under his touch turned into a million black spiders that scattered around the inside of my skin.

"So, Frank Blackthorne, what do you want in return for this virgin soul of yours?"

CHAPTER 27

"I'm not giving you my soul."

"You wear the ring and I grant you my power. But I must be paid in my chosen currency. You think I grant Queen Fiona her gifts because I enjoy her company?"

I tore the ring off my finger. My entire body, now the princess's again, still felt as if it were crawling with tiny burning spiders with legs made of slivers of broken glass. I knelt alone in the center of the circle consecrated to the Dark Lord. The moon hung above my head, heavy and pregnant and about to birth something horrifying.

Everyone had edged away from me, even the queen. Even Lucille.

"Must have been a bit of a show," I whispered with lips cracked and bleeding. "Sorry I missed it."

"Frank?"

An arrow flew from somewhere in the massed army.

"No!" Queen Fiona and Lucille screamed simultaneously.

*   *   *

"She really annoys you, doesn't she?"

"She could scourge the ground bare and rule half the world in darkness for a thousand years with the power I could grant her. But no, she kills her husband and spies on petty court intrigues."

The arrow slammed into my shoulder, throwing me into the ground with a force that felt like it broke bone. If my body weren't still crawling with the aftereffects of my contact with Lord Nâtlac, I might have screamed. Instead, I stared blankly up at a moon that seemed to stare back, and clutched the ring that now burned like a hot poker in the palm of my hand.

Somewhere I heard Queen Fiona screaming, "The thieving bitch can only die here by *my* hand!"

"She's about to invade Lendowyn. And where are the infernal beasts? The demon hordes made flesh? She should feast on the hearts of her enemies, and she buys off the opposing militia. There's half a chance she'll walk in and take over with no opposition at all. What kind of army of encroaching darkness is that?"

I glanced down at my shoulder. The arrow toppled over. At least the elf-king had done well by me in the clothing department. That arrow should have passed through decent chain mail, but the silvery-black elven leather had kept it from piercing my shoulder.

Didn't keep me from having one hell of a bruise, but I really wasn't in a position to complain.

The massed troops were eerily silent. Silent enough that I distinctly heard one set of footsteps crunching across the burned ground toward me.

"Why wouldn't she? You already have her soul, why hold back?"

"I don't have her soul."

The silence broke when I got to my feet. I'm sure I heard a gasp from here or there. I'm not sure how well I was seen in the moonlight, but I think the nonlethal nature of the arrow strike wasn't quite obvious back among the ranks that could see me.

"Frank! You're all right."

I drew on every fiber of my being to steady myself, and somewhere within me I finally found the wherewithal to project an intimidating royal voice from the princess's body.

"Do not approach me!" I said, staring at Queen Fiona, almost within arm's reach.

"You *dare* command me!"

"In the name of the dread Lord who owns your fealty, *I demand it!*"

She gave a laugh that was only half sincere. "You cannot call on the Dark Lord. You blaspheme his name."

"I'm afraid he told me different."

*   *   *

"How . . . just, how?"

"For one soul I only grant so much power. If you truly want the blessings of my dark grace upon you, you must take an offering to ground sacred to me, and take their life with a weapon consecrated in my name. Commit their souls unto me, and I shall grant desires wondrous and horrible."

"Does your army know what the ring I hold is?"

"You know nothing!"

"It is the conduit to the Dark Lord himself. It is what made you his priestess."

I heard mumbling in the ranks, and I allowed myself a smile. "No," said the queen, "She lies!"

"Tell them why you ordered them not to kill me."

"You are the pledged sacrifice—"

"And if you do not take the life by your own hand with a tool consecrated by your Lord, you'll gain no power from the death of a royal virgin. Offering that soul to the Dark Lord Nâtlac would confer great power, wouldn't it?"

She stared at me, eyes widening.

"That power, combined with the ring of the Dark Lord himself, would ensure there'd be no question who was the true will of Lord Nâtlac in the world of men."

She said nothing, and even in the pale moonlight I could see her face drain of color. Somewhere behind me, I heard Lucille's draconic voice near breaking, **"Oh, no. Frank, you didn't . . ."**

The queen echoed Lucille, whispering, "You didn't."

"How much more powerful is that soul when freely given unto him?"

"So how did she manage to avoid giving you her soul if that's the price of the ring?"

"I never said she did not give it to me. I said I did not have *it*."

"You are too late," I told the queen, "and you are no longer the High Priestess."

I was playing to the gallery, projecting my voice. By the noise level in the ranks, I could tell that it was having the intended effect. I don't know exactly what kind of show happened when I put on the ring, but there was *something*. I'd seen it just from the reactions of everyone when I came back to reality. The arrow bouncing off the elf armor was just a random bonus. I knew I had some credibility now with a good fraction of the troops in earshot.

Given human nature, a ruler with a reputation like Queen Fiona only commands loyalty in direct proportion to the number of her subjects who believe *everyone else* is loyal. Enough people break rank at once, and you lose all the drones who only fell into line because they thought *everyone* was a good soldier. I had just handed a lot of people a reason to break rank.

I held up the ring between my thumb and forefinger so everyone could see it. "I'm talking to him now, and I have a message for you." I took a step toward the queen, who couldn't take her eyes off the ring. "His Darkness says he's very disappointed in you."

Queen Fiona screamed in rage and jumped me.

Even though I'd been expecting it, it still knocked the breath out of me, especially when she slammed my bruised shoulder into the ground. My grunts of pain probably were enough to shatter my illusion of portraying a new Dark Queen of Nâtlac, but they were fortunately drowned out by sudden shouts from the ranks of the massed Grünwald army.

She wrestled the ring from my hand and sprang away, laughing manically. "No! You can't replace me! I am the hand of the Dark Lord moving in the world! And I will crush you, you little *bitch!*"

I got up and ran toward Lucille.

"What did you do?"

The sounds of chaos in the troops surrounding us became steadily worse, and I heard swords meet. "I improvised!" I ran up and hugged her forearm. "Fly!"

"Archers?"

"Busy. Fly!"

"You won't escape me that easy!" the queen screamed at us as she put on the ring.

So, yes, I sold my soul to the Dark Lord Nâtlac. It wasn't like I wanted to, but that was the price of taking possession of the ring. And I didn't exaggerate; in exchange for my particular soul, the Dark Lord was willing to offer me quite a lot. I really could have become the head of Queen Fiona's little cult, and—if I'd had it in me—I could have reigned in darkness for a thousand years, enslaving half the world to my will and burning the rest to ash.

I guess it's lucky for everyone that I didn't find that very appealing.

Compared to that, what I ended up trading my soul for was much smaller in scope, almost trivial. I just asked for a bit of a change in how the ring operated.

I had seen the way out of my dilemma the moment the Dark Lord Nâtlac said that the queen had sold her soul to him, but it was not currently in his possession. Clearly, the "rules" allowed you to exchange souls, all I needed to do to get mine back was to find some sacrifice of equal or greater value, take them to a site sacred to Nâtlac, and kill them with a weapon consecrated in his name.

Normally I'd object to that sort of behavior, but given the enormity of my situation, I had decided to make an exception. Especially since I already had two of the three things I needed back in the real world.

The princess's body already stood on a sacrificial spot and—while I might still count as a royal virgin on a technicality—Queen Fiona had spent a few decades pissing off the Dark Lord. It wasn't hard to figure which one he'd value more.

All I needed was a weapon consecrated in his name.

That, of course, was where the ring came in.

"Lucille! Now!" I screamed at her, hugging her scaly forearm with all my strength. I didn't know what was about to happen, but I suspected that it wasn't going to be pleasant.

Lucille brought her wings down and started lifting off into the air just as Queen Fiona screamed in triumph, the ring on her finger glowing black in the moonlight.

Her screaming didn't stop.

I glanced back as Lucille rose into the air. Queen Fiona had frozen in place, the hand bearing the ring outstretched toward us as if she meant to grab us out of the sky. The ring pulsed with an ebon blackness darker than the surrounding night.

Every muscle in her body was drawn tight, and the veins swelled and pulsed under her skin. The ring's dark glow swirled around her like a mist, burrowing into her eyes, ears, nose, mouth.

She screamed long past the point any air could have been left in her lungs.

The ground beneath her feet cracked, fissures racing from her feet outward toward the edges of the circle. The queen's knights, Sir Forsythe and the man carrying *Dracheslayer*, scrambled backward, staying ahead of the fissures.

"Faster!" I called to Lucille.

"I'm trying—"

Not all the archers were fixated by the queen's fate. Arrows found their way out of the growing chaos below us. I felt one slam a glancing blow off the back of my elven armor, knocking the breath out of me. Unfortunately, Lucille was a much bigger target, and I saw one cut a gash across the foreleg I held, another slam into her neck. Lucille's scream echoed the queen's.

We began losing altitude.

Below us, something moved, undulating within the fissures that radiated from where the queen still stood. I cast a panicked glance back toward her and wished I hadn't.

As I looked, ragged tendrils of pure black whipped out from the fissures around her feet, wrapping around her legs, arms, neck, barbed tendrils stabbing into her mouth, chest, abdomen . . .

The screams stopped just before the tendrils tore her apart.

I looked away, and down at the army. We dived toward it, and while several archers were still trying to shoot us down, the ground fissures had reached this far, and seemingly random soldiers were suffering the queen's fate.

I shut my eyes and told myself that I should have been more specific when I asked the Dark Lord to change the ring into something that would execute the queen.

I felt Lucille wince with another arrow impact and she screamed something very un-princesslike. I opened my eyes just as she belched forth a stream of fire into the faces of the remaining archers.

Then we hit the ground and I was thrown down a hillside with bone-numbing force. I tumbled, rolling to a stop against a pile of corpses. I pushed myself away from the dead soldiers, barely noting that they were dead by conventional violence, not fire or being torn apart.

I turned around and looked back up the hillside and saw Lucille silhouetted against the night sky, underlit by the flames of what I supposed were burning archers. I saw soldiers run at her, swords drawn, only to be batted aside or immolated.

"Die. You worthless evil bastards. Die!"

Everyone between me and her had either already been killed, or had retreated. Behind both of us, back toward where the queen had been, I heard screams being cut short by a sound like tearing fabric.

I ran up the hill. As scary as an enraged dragon might be, it couldn't compete with the anger of the Dark Lord Nâtlac.

"Lucille!" I called up at her. "We still have to get out of here!"

I heard a swordsman scream, and I saw his body tumble though the air above me.

"**Attack a country your own size!**"

As I ran up the hillside, I caught sight of a red glow behind her.

Dracheslayer.

"Lucille! Look out behind you!" I screamed, but she couldn't hear me.

The glowing red blade came down toward her unprotected neck.

CHAPTER 28

❧

"Lucille!" I screamed my throat raw.

Dracheslayer struck with a clang and a shower of red sparks.

Sparks?

I crested the hill in time to see that another sword had interposed itself between *Dracheslayer* and Lucille's neck. *Dracheslayer* was held by the knight in full plate who had flanked the queen opposite Sir Forsythe. His armor was the worse for wear, dented and stained with soot and blood. His left gauntlet was missing, and his visor hung half off his helmet. The other man wasn't in plate, but in black leather embossed with spikes and skulls, like the vast majority of the queen's rapidly diminishing army.

What set this newcomer apart was the fact that he was much larger than average.

The bearer of *Dracheslayer* stepped back and held it in an awkward defensive posture. "Fool. Step back so I can slay the dragon."

"No," said his large opponent. "Brock will save the princess."

Lucille turned, finally noticing what was happening. As she did, Brock rushed the other man. No. Rushed isn't the right word. Strode briskly might be better.

In any event, Brock moved in, and *Dracheslayer* rose in a shaky defense as Brock swung his own sword. Sparks flew, and they moved slowly away from Lucille. I looked up at her and saw her readying to breathe hell down on the pair.

Damn it, she doesn't know who Brock is.

I scrambled forward between her and the fighting men. "No, Lucille, the big guy is on our side."

"Frank, you're all right!"

I looked up at her and saw her side and leg peppered with arrows. Blood had slicked the ground beneath her. "You're not."

"Scratches. They aren't taking down this dragon so easily."

"We need to fly out of here."

"Oh . . . Maybe they took me down a little." She flapped a wing briefly, wincing. I saw a dozen arrows piercing it.

"You can't fly—"

I was interrupted by a clang and a bellow of pain that, for some reason, found the pit of my stomach and turned it inside out. I spun around to face the two swordfighters, but it seemed to take an eternity. The bellowed rage, the sound, was familiar enough to send shivering dread throughout my body.

"Frank!"

I knew what I was going to see, and I didn't want to.

I knew why the knight bearing *Dracheslayer* had sounded familiar. I knew why he held *Dracheslayer* so clumsily. I knew why his first impulse when the queen's plans fell apart wasn't to retreat, but to run across a battlefield to attack an enraged dragon.

Brock had scored a glancing blow, but it had been enough to knock his opponent's helmet completely off. His victim bellowed in rage as blood streamed down his face.

My face.

"As close as possible," said the elf-king. And he hadn't said he didn't *know* where the wizard was, the elf-king had said, "I can't say."

"Elhared," I whispered, staring at myself wearing full plate, holding *Dracheslayer* two-handed to deflect another one of Brock's swings.

"Brock will finish you." Brock proclaimed between swings. "This is Brock's destiny."

Of course it was Elhared. Of course he was working with the queen. And now Brock the Barbarian was destined to kill off my body, and not only couldn't I stop it from happening, but I couldn't tell if I should have stopped it if I could.

The whole chain of events was clear now. Elhared's plot—me, the dragon, the princess—it wasn't just a power grab on his part. It might not have even been his idea. He was working with—for—Queen Fiona. The elaborate con to put Elhared on the throne in my body was just a means to put a compliant ruler on the throne of Lendowyn.

Elhared hadn't chosen me at random from that dockside tavern. He had picked me because I was of interest to the queen, and possibly because wrapping my soul in the princess's body made a particularly attractive sacrifice.

Even the damn book he was using, the elf-king almost flat out said that the evil tome was from Nâtlac himself. Like the elf-king had said, "souls were his business." And where would the mediocre wizard Elhared get a signed first edition of the deep thoughts of the Dark Lord Nâtlac?

When the original plan went bad, about the time Elhared ran afoul of Prince Dudley, he must have returned to the queen's fold and the queen decided to switch to Plan B, plain old-fashioned invasion.

When Plan B fell apart around the queen, Elhared had decided to return to the original one; kill dragon, take princess, rule Lendowyn.

I hate intrigue.

"You can't kill him!"

I looked up at Lucille, "What . . ."

"Brock saves princess!" Brock swung hard against Elhared, knocking my body to its knees.

"That's Frank's body! We need it to fix this."

Elhared raised *Dracheslayer* to deflect a blow coming down on his head. Brock didn't seem to hear Lucille. He was grinning, and there was almost a euphoric expression on his face. I knew how he felt. The chance to be the hero of the story, however ill-suited you are to the task, can be intoxicating.

"He knows where the book is!"

Shouldn't I be the one yelling that?

In desperation, I fumbled out the elf-king's silver mirror. Technically we had Elhared, and he seemed to *love* technicalities. Maybe Brock wouldn't flat out kill the guy before I figured out how to work the thing.

Brock raised his sword for another crushing blow against the raised *Dracheslayer*.

"Brock save—" Brock's voice was cut short by a strangled gurgle.

"I know," Elhared said, pulling a bloody dagger from Brock's gut with his off hand. "'Brock saves princess.' 'Brock saves princess.'" Elhared slammed the dagger home into Brock again, and the large barbarian let his sword slip from his fingers. "Brock will now shut the hell up."

"No!"

"Yes!" Elhared said, slamming the dagger home one last time, and letting Brock topple slowly like a felled tree. Brock said nothing, but I saw tears on his cheek, glinting in the moonlight as he fell.

I held up the mirror, and watched as the last few pieces of the shattered glass fell out of the silver frame.

Elhared got to his feet. "Well, that was an annoying distraction."

"You bastard, he was trying to save me!"

"There's a lot of that going around. I think Lendowyn needs a better class of heroes."

I dropped the useless mirror, drew my dagger, and ran at him while he faced Lucille. It was foolhardy, but I was relying somewhat on his reluctance to kill his ticket to royalty.

He saw me coming and knocked the dagger out of my hand with the back of his gauntlet. As my only weapon tumbled away into the darkness, he slammed my face with the pommel of *Dracheslayer*, dropping me to the ground next to Brock.

Elhared hooked a finger at me. "Best you stay there, unless you forgot, there's a throne in this for you as well."

Lucille took the opportunity to swing at Elhared. Given the way she'd been decimating trained soldiers, the blow should have sent Elhared flying.

But he spun, *Dracheslayer* almost moving of its own accord to block Lucille's swing. He did so clumsily and with the flat of the blade. But even so, just contact with the blade resulted in a sizzling impact that caused Lucille to pull her arm away with a scream, a fresh wound burned into her flesh.

Elhared laughed. "Surprised? Did you think I hadn't planned for this? You think I just *wasted* my years with that conniving bitch?" He swung *Dracheslayer* and Lucille dodged, whipping her tail around to slam Elhared in the back. He stumbled from the impact. And Lucille brought her wounded forearm down to slam Elhared facedown into the ground.

"Drop the sword, you traitor! You're going to undo this cursed spell!"

"Like hell, you spoiled brat," Elhared's voice came muffled from beneath her taloned hand.

I almost smiled. Lucille seemed to handle things pretty well by herself.

Then I noticed her grimacing. The muscles in her forearm trembled. For the few moments when nothing moved, I could see how badly wounded she really was. There didn't seem to be a square inch of her body that didn't glisten with blood. Steam came from between the fingers that held down Elhared.

She glanced in my direction and said, **"I tried."** Hearing that voice crack was like the ground itself caving in under my feet. **"I'm sorry, Frank."** Her words distorted into a scream of rage and pain as she pulled her hand up, clutching Elhared and tossing him away down the hillside. The inside of her hand was a smoking bloody wound.

Elhared got up from where he'd fallen. The bastard was laughing. *Dracheslayer* seemed to be glowing even brighter in his hands. "The more of your blood it tastes, the stronger it becomes." He started walking up the hill toward her.

She was going to need help.

I started to push myself up, and I felt something grabbing my leg. I looked down and saw Brock clutching my ankle. "Great," I told him. "Glad you're still alive. I need to help Lucille."

Elhared was halfway up the hillside. "The next taste it has will finish you."

"No, it won't!" she screamed down the hillside at him. She opened her mouth wide and vomited a pillar of brimstone and fire completely enveloping Elhared and *Dracheslayer*. The scalding wind from the blast knocked me back to the ground from twenty feet away. The ground where Elhared stood exploded upward in a cloud of embers and steam.

"My body," I whispered.

Not that I blamed her.

Brock groaned.

"Take it easy," I told him. "I think it's over."

She didn't stop. She expelled roaring flame for a full thirty seconds, smoke boiling up in front of her. The air between us was turning near opaque from smoke, haze, and heat shimmer.

As the inferno continued, and molten fury poured down the hillside, I had the time to realize how wrong this seemed. If Elhared was truly being reduced to ash in front of us, it showed a rather glaring oversight in a plan that otherwise had a sort of twisted elegance.

Would Elhared have gone head-to-head with a dragon and *not* expect to be toasted?

No, something was very, *very*, wrong with this.

Lucille finally ran out of flame. She collapsed, shaking the ground. I could barely see her through my watering eyes, a humped unmoving shadow through the smoke.

"Lucille!" I called out. "Are you all right?"

"Frank?" She groaned. **"That. Took a lot out of me. I'm sorry. About your body."** I heard a wheezing exhale, then nothing.

"Lucille?"

No answer.

"Lucille!"

Instead of her voice, I heard my own voice chuckling. "No apologies necessary, Your Highness."

I saw a glint of red though the smoke, moving toward the unmoving dragon. The fact that I'd seen this coming didn't lessen the sinking in my gut. Of course if those blind dwarves from wherever had enchanted a dragon-slaying weapon they just *might* have anticipated the possibility of a little fire damage and acted accordingly.

"No." I moved to run, to stop Elhared, but Brock still had a death grip on my ankle. "Let go!"

I looked down as I tried to kick myself free, and Brock stared up at me. In his free hand he held up a bloody dagger, hilt toward me. He spoke in a wet whisper. "Brock. Save. Princess." He coughed up a gob of bloody phlegm. "Save . . . Princess . . ."

As I took the dagger, he let me go.

Elhared wasn't paying any attention to me. He was moving toward Lucille at an unhurried pace now that the dragon was unconscious. "Enough distractions."

Since a frontal assault worked so well last time, I ran around behind him, silently as I could.

Elhared continued addressing the unconscious dragon. "I am going to salvage this situation for once and for all. You should be happy that your throne will finally be occupied by someone worthy of it."

Between the smoke and his continued talking, I was able to easily slip behind him. Bringing the dagger up to his neck was a little more difficult because of the size difference. I had to strain to reach, but it had the desired effect, and he stopped a stride short of Lucille's neck.

"Elhared," I said, "have I mentioned that you are an incredible asshole?"

"Occupational hazard, Francis. You don't get to be a wizard, especially an *old* wizard, by being all warm and fuzzy."

"Drop the sword. I won't let you kill her."

"Please! You're a two-bit thief who's never thought an inch beyond your own skin. I actually admire that about you. And if I were you, and I am, I would start thinking about who's got that skin right now."

"I mean it. Drop the sword!"

"Francis, stop the pretense, you aren't going to kill your own body." *Dracheslayer* rose to deliver the fatal blow to Lucille's neck.

"Don't call me Francis!" I screamed at him as I shoved the blade up under his jaw, right above the gorget. He went stiff, and *Dracheslayer* slipped from his hands, thudding to the ground between us and Lucille.

I dodged backward as he spun around to swing wildly at me. His other hand clutched the right side of his throat, where I'd buried the blade to the hilt. He stared at me with wide eyes as he staggered in my direction. He coughed up blood and managed to gurgle something that sounded like, "Wha?"

"You're surprised?" I yelled at him. "You arrogant condescending dimwit! You're actually *surprised?!*"

He took another swipe at me as he stumbled forward.

"You can't imagine for a moment that you might be wrong about something?"

Elhared fell to his knees in front of me, bleeding my blood from my mouth. He clutched the hilt of the dagger and yanked it out of his neck.

"Blug," he said.

"Of course I wasn't going to let you kill her! But you couldn't just drop the damn sword!"

He waved the dagger vaguely in my direction,

clutching the open wound with his other hand as blood drenched his armor. "Glup," he said, his lips foaming blood. "Thlop."

"You idiot!" I slapped the dagger out of his hand. "You moron! *Why'd you force me to do this?!*"

He toppled face first into the ground at my feet. I kicked him, not caring about stubbing my toes on the plate mail. "Why did you try and kill her? Why did you pull something so stupid when someone had a knife to your neck?"

He might have groaned.

"Are you happy now? You got my damned body! Are you happy?" I kept kicking, leaving bloody boot prints on the armor. "Answer me, you sponge-brained conniving little prick!"

I don't know how long I berated the wizard, but eventually Lucille groaned and belched out a small rolling cloud of sulfur smoke. I stopped and looked up at her. She regarded me with a half-lidded eye and said, **"I think he's dead."**

"But I'm not finished kicking him!"

I think she may have laughed at me.

"Thank you." She groaned and closed her eyes. **"You not only saved me, but you saved my kingdom."**

"You're welcome."

"You're still a lowlife lying thief."

I sighed. "I never said otherwise." From the sound of her breathing, she had already slipped back into unconsciousness.

I stared at my corpse and said, "Damn it."

A voice called out from behind me. "My Lady, please step away from that abominable creature."

There was no possible way that could be who I thought it was. The universe just couldn't be that cruel.

I turned around to face the speaker.

The universe *was* that cruel.

Running up the hillside, sword bared, was the ill-named Sir Forsythe the Good.

CHAPTER 29

I scrambled to get *Dracheslayer* even as I felt dread growing in the pit of my stomach. I was under no illusions about my ability in combat, even when I was still me. I had only won my confrontation with Elhared because the man had been pathologically overconfident. I had no hope against Sir Forsythe, who I had personally witnessed clear out a bar full of ruffians, each of whom was my better when it came to the whole fighting prowess thing. Having a real magic sword might have given me some advantage, but I strongly suspected I still needed to know how to wield it.

I held up *Dracheslayer* and did the one thing I could do.

I bluffed.

I leveled *Dracheslayer* in Sir Forsythe's direction and tried to summon the voice of command I had used on the queen. "Halt your approach, or I will cut you down where you stand."

And, in response, he stopped.

It was so unexpected that I almost dropped

Dracheslayer in shock. Somehow I retained my composure . . .

Up until the point Sir Forsythe dropped to one knee and bowed his head. "My sincerest apologies, My Liege."

The tip of *Dracheslayer* fell and buried itself in the ground by my feet. I tried to speak, but nothing came out. I stood there, open-mouthed, as paralyzed as if he'd run me through with his sword.

He reached up and removed his helmet, looked up at me and said, "The queen is dead. Long live the queen."

I shook my head.

"No. Just . . . No."

Ever have one of those moments when you suddenly realize that you have accidentally made yourself the nominal leader of one schism of a dark cult of evil?

Neither had I.

Apparently, in my improvised efforts to sow enough confusion for us to escape, I had said a few things that at least some of Queen Fiona's former followers had taken to heart. At this point I barely remembered saying anything, but whatever it was had made an impression on Sir Forsythe. I supposed the Dark Lord tearing apart the ex-queen had granted me some credibility.

"I await your command, Your Highness."

I took one hand off the hilt of *Dracheslayer* to rub my temple. "Just get up."

Sir Forsythe stood.

"First thing, no one hurts my dragon. Got that?"

"Yes, Your Highness."

"Second, if you want to serve your Dark Queen, get some healers over here."

After that, things got a little complicated.

By dawn I had some good news. Both Brock and Lucille survived their injuries. Brock just had too much gut for a simple dagger to strike deep enough to hit anything vital. Once they stopped the bleeding he was all right.

When he woke up he blinked up at me and asked, "Did Brock save the princess?"

I thought of the dagger he'd handed me and smiled, a little weakly. "Yes. Princess Lucille wouldn't be alive if it hadn't been for you."

"Good." He leaned back and smiled.

"Can I ask you a question?"

"Yes?"

"I see that you hooked up with the queen's army after we split up."

He looked a little sheepish. "Brock didn't join officially. Found some armor during escape, but Brock then pressed into service."

"Thought it was something like that."

"Brock does not serve the Dark Lord."

"Oh, like I'd hold that against anyone at this point. But I do have another question."

"What?"

"Where'd those mares come from?"

It turned out that no one had actually had the bad sense to bring a bunch of in-season mares around a bunch of warhorses. Brock had helped the mares along. He spouted a long list of herbs and other ingredients, some of which he could only name in his native tongue, that when combined with a mare's piss created a nearly irresistible equine aphrodisiac. Apparently all the ingredients were either in the supply tents or growing wild.

"Brock spent a lot of time with the women in the village. Brock learned much herbal lore."

"I think I've said before, Brock is a surprising man."

As for Lucille, dragons are notoriously hard to kill.

I watched the new day break from sitting on a rock next to Lucille. I still carried *Dracheslayer* because I didn't trust anyone else with it around her. I'd shoved the point into the ground, and I rested my chin on the backs of my hands, folded over the hilt. I hadn't sheathed it, and I knew it was a rotten way to treat a sword, but I had trouble summoning the energy to care.

Besides, it seemed I had an image to maintain if I wanted to keep control of the situation, and holding a glowing magic sword while seated next to a dragon was maintaining that image with the least amount of effort on my part.

Around the hillside below us, a small army had gathered, maybe a third of the troops' original number. Most bore wounds that they'd sustained in their fight against the old queen's faithful servants. I didn't know how much of the original Grünwald army was left. I supposed it depended how many had been too close to the fissures that still radiated from the wrecked ritual space where Queen Fiona had met her messy end. However many there were, the remaining Grünwald faithful had retreated, probably to gather reinforcements.

"What a mess."

"Don't be hard on yourself."

"Lucille, I promise I'll hunt down Elhared's book. We'll get you back into your own body."

"Um."

"Um? What?"

"I . . . I'm sort of enjoying being a dragon."

"You—what?"

"I know, I was terrified at first. It was all so strange. But, Frank, I can fly! I took on an army all by myself!"

"I see."

"I never had . . . Oh, Frank. I'm sorry. Your body. I didn't mean . . ."

"No, don't apologize. I'm the one who killed Elhared."

"To save me."

"I wasn't going to let you die like that."

"I'd give this up if it would get you back to normal."

"I know."

"It is a mess, isn't it?"

Sir Forsythe approached us and bowed, and I marveled at how he had somehow come through the night with his plate mail polished and gleaming. "All the followers of the True Queen have been gathered and await your word. Your army is prepared to march on the False Prince at your command."

I had no doubt about it.

There was some attraction to the idea. After all, Prince Dudley was still out there, and the royal bastard did try and kill me. However, it was appealing only in the abstract. Once I imagined the particulars—the bone-cleaving and bloodletting particulars—it lost most of its appeal. Not to mention, I didn't think Prince Dudley ranked anywhere near the top fifteen things I cared about right now.

Then there were the practical problems with that idea. I really doubted that the whole Grünwald army had been present for the queen's ritual. The whole cult of Nâtlac thing might have been an open secret, but it wasn't *that* open. I didn't know about it until it was too late. The queen had brought only the initiates here. The main body of the regular army was probably still out there and massing as we spoke.

Not to mention the Lendowyn militia Prince Dudley had hired away. Those troops weren't motivated by religion. Swaying them required assets I didn't have.

No. Attacking Grünwald with the queen's own troops, while emotionally satisfying, would probably be suicide. And considering we still stood on Grünwald soil, the same could be said of staying here.

So, we only really had one option.

"Are you sure about this?" I asked Lucille.

"Just because I'm a dragon doesn't mean I want to abandon my home and family."

The words may have been upbeat, but I was beginning to understand the subtleties of her speech, and in the booming draconic voice I heard some of the same uncertainty I felt. Not that there was much we could do about it. Lucille was still injured, and while most of it was superficial, she wasn't going to fly anywhere until her wings healed.

So, we walked across the border into Lendowyn.

Or, more precisely, Lucille walked and I rode on her back. Appearances again. If I was going to lead an invading army of evil into another country, riding the back of a dragon and holding a glowing red-and-black sword helped offset the fact that I was a petite young woman. It offered some clarity about who was in charge here.

Behind us, Brock and Sir Forsythe led two ragged columns of armed servants of the Dark Lord Nâtlac who had pledged to follow me. As we marched across the countryside, panic followed. I felt bad about that, farmers and shepherds abandoning their fields and flocks, but I really didn't have much time to dawdle and reassure everyone. The army that followed me had only the provisions they'd carried out of Grünwald, and if I took too long to do what I'd come for, they'd start raping and pillaging the countryside just out of hunger and boredom.

Fortunately, the lack of any Lendowyn militia meant we could make good time. We were able to camp that night within sight of the lair where I had first met Lucille, less than a day's march from Lendowyn Castle.

That night she asked me, **"What about you? Are you sure about this?"**

I'd been half asleep, lying in the crook of her forearm, resting my head against the side of her neck, which was more comfortable than it sounds. "Of course I am."

"It's asking a lot of you."

"Not really. Besides, you pointed out that I'm legally you now. You said you didn't want to abandon your home and family."

She sighed.

I patted her neck. "It won't be any weirder than anything else we've been through. With the added bonus that I don't *think* anyone will try to kill us."

We had marched within sight of the castle before a contingent of Lendowyn's defenses finally rode out to meet us. They were the king's royal guard, so they were obliged to make a show of blocking our progress, but since there were only half a dozen of them, there was only so much they could do.

They made a brave stand, the lead man astride a white charger, a crimson cape blowing in the wind. He held up a hand as his mount came to a stop on the road ahead of us. "In the name of King Alfred of Lendowyn, halt."

I probably surprised the guy by calling for my small army to stop.

I looked at the six men blocking our progress and decided that the Lendowyn treasury wasn't *that* empty. The remainder of the royal guard was either setting up an ambush from cover, or had run away.

I slid off of Lucille's back and walked toward the men blocking our path. Sir Forsythe and Brock started to follow me, but I held up my hand so they stayed back by Lucille.

I walked up to the guardsmen. The leader was

the only man who had raised the visor on his helmet, so I could watch as his eyes widened in recognition.

"You've been looking for a princess," I said. "And I think the king may want to talk to us."

CHAPTER 30

The fact that I wore Princess Lucille's body meant I easily got an audience with King Alfred the Strident and his royal court. The fact that I was backed by an army of a few hundred men meant that it was only slightly harder to include Lucille in that audience. King Alfred and his retainers received us in the courtyard of Lendowyn Castle, where Lucille and I explained exactly what had happened.

It was easier to convince them than I had expected. It helped that we still had *Dracheslayer* and that there were corroborating stories from all over the kingdom. No to mention that everyone admitted to being a bit creeped out by Elhared, and even the king mentioned in passing that "the sour old bastard was probably capable of anything."

Of course, once the details had sorted themselves out, and everyone understood what had happened, the Lendowyn legal system reared its ugly head.

"Yes," said King Alfred, "of course we must find another wizard to switch you back."

"Your Highness," I said, "I killed my body saving your daughter."

"Hmm, yes, right. But legally we can't have you being my daughter now, can we?"

"Father?"

"Not now," Alfred said, "Father's thinking. We can swap you into the dragon? Would that work? Or maybe the elves could sell us the wizard's body—"

"I *want* to be a dragon!"

"You don't know what you're saying." Alfred turned to one of his advisors. "We'll set up a reward. The wizard who returns my daughter to her body will get her hand in marriage—"

"Daddy!" Her frustrated scream shook the walls of the surrounding castle as she reached out and scooped the king up to hold him in front of her smoldering maw. **"Shut up! I am not some all-purpose stipend to award to anyone you can't afford to pay real money. Are you trying to be known as King Alfred the Pimp?"**

"Honey, you're a *dragon*."

Smoke curled from her nostrils and I thought I saw the hint of a smile touch her face. **"And I suggest you don't forget that."**

"Besides," I told him. "I understand that you've already promised 'my' hand in marriage."

King Alfred looked down at me as Lucille gently placed him down on the ground. "What are you talking about?"

"Your daughter's hand to whoever brings you the princess along with the head of the dragon." She reached out and touched a talon gently on top of my head. "Princess." She removed the talon and reached up to place it against her cheek. "Dragon's head."

The king sputtered, his face turning shades of purple that were not normally found in nature. "You can't be serious."

Unfortunately for the sanity of King Alfred, we were.

When she had first broached the subject, I'll admit to being as incredulous as the king, if not in such a spectacularly flustered fashion. But her brainstorm made a perverse sort of sense. As she had said, she had made peace with, and probably preferred, being a dragon.

That didn't mean there weren't some practical problems with that lifestyle choice. The primary one being that she would become an enemy of the state, and a target for would-be dragon slayers. Also, she didn't want to abandon her home and family, and it seemed that sticking to life as a giant fire-breathing lizard would probably break those ties.

So, her reasoning went, to avoid those consequences she had to reclaim her identity as a member of the royal family *as* a dragon. And, since overturning centuries of Lendowyn legal precedent was probably impossible at this point, there was only one way to do that.

As much as the king might hyperventilate and plead with his advisors, his prior declaration—the one that enticed me into this whole mess—awarded his daughter's hand in marriage to whomever brought her and the dragon's head back to Lendowyn. No provision had been made for the case of the dragon's head still being attached to the dragon. More to the point, nothing in the wording of the declaration prevented the dragon itself bringing the princess back for the offered reward.

The king and his ministers put up a valiant fight. However, in this case, the law was clearer than it had a right to be. There was even a precedent for royal interspecies weddings. Lucille's great uncle Charles the Unbalanced had taken a unicorn as his royal consort. When he died from hoof-and-mouth disease, Queen Starmane reigned for about forty-eight hours before abdicating by escaping from the royal pasture and running off into the countryside.

Lucille told me that she was still remembered as the least objectionable monarch Lendowyn ever had.

So, despite the king's best efforts, under Lendowyn law, I had just been betrothed to a dragon.

So by the end of the month, Lucille was telling me, **"You look adorable in my grandmother's gown."**

"Yeah."

"Cheer up! It's your wedding day."

"Funny, I never pictured it like this." I leaned on the sill of the window in my royal chambers, waiting for the ceremony to start. Lucille, being fifty feet long and weighing several tons, perched on the battlements outside, sunning herself as she talked to me.

I really shouldn't have been complaining. The streets of the capital were hung with ribbons, and the population had spent the last week celebrating the upcoming nuptials. If anything, the people of Lendowyn seemed to not only accept the unusual nature of the new royal, but seemed to be taking it as a point of pride.

I guess it made a good story, for once having the princess capture a dragon.

My problem was, I was nowhere near as settled with the change in my identity as Lucille was with hers. And while she was one of the only people in the world who could understand what I felt, she had been so happy since coming home that I couldn't bring myself to tell her that I still didn't want to be a princess.

"Lucille?"

"Frank?"

"Can I ask you a personal question?"

"As your future husband, I don't see why not."

"I've just been assuming . . . That is a *male* dragon's body, right?"

"Wha—you're not worried we have to con-
summate the—"

"No!" I held up my hands. I didn't want to start
thinking how that might even be physically possible. "Just. I didn't know for sure, and I didn't
want this whole marriage thing to get hung up on
a technicality."

Lucille laughed. **"Frank, you're royal and this
is a political marriage. Normal rules don't apply.
You could be betrothed to a hay wagon and it
would all be legal. There might be a bias toward
procreative unions, but since I'm a dragon—"**

"It doesn't mean anything."

"Nope."

I didn't know how I felt about that. "Hey, you
didn't answer my question."

**"Yes, my dear. I'm very much a boy dragon.
Want to see?"**

"No thanks."

"Suit yourself."

I closed my eyes as it sunk in that I was going
to be married to a dragon in the most extravagant
ceremony Lendowyn could afford—meaning a
hell of a lot of people, but little in the way of alcohol. And all I could think of at the moment was
that I would have to go through the thing stone
cold sober.

There was a knock on the chamber door and I
was grateful for the interruption of what was rapidly becoming an uncomfortable conversation.

"I'll be right back," I told Lucille.

I walked across the chamber and pulled open the door. The hinges squeaked, then groaned, then became the low cry of millions of tortured souls. The daylight in the chamber became suddenly dim, red, and cloaked everything beyond ten paces in impenetrable darkness. The open door let in the smells of fire, rancid fat, and rotting meat.

I faced the Dark Lord Nâtlac in my doorway, and he greeted me with a bow.

Oh, crap.

"What are you doing here?"

There was some loophole, some flaw in the way I dispatched Queen Fiona. He was here to collect me—

"I am here to offer my respects, my thanks for dismissing an annoyance, and to present you with a wedding gift." He held up an ornately carved wooden box. His smile made me think of the wails of dying children.

"Is it a good idea to take a gift from you?"

"Is it a good idea to refuse one?"

"You have a point."

The Dark Lord held out the box, and reluctantly I took it.

"My dear confused Francis, I know your heart's desire on this day. It is beyond even my powers to return you to your old body. It has been consigned to the clay from which it came. I can, however, present you with this small token."

I opened the box, and inside glittered a small crystal pendant on a silver chain.

"Should you wear that, you can again live life in a male form, if only temporarily."

I looked down into the box. "Really?"

"Lies are one sin I do not indulge in."

"Does it require blood sacrifices or something like that?" I asked, but the lighting was back to normal and Lord Nâtlac was gone.

"Oh, pretty, what's that?"

I looked over to the window. It was filled by the side of Lucille's face, one eye blinking at me.

I closed the box and placed it on a table by the bed. "Wedding present," I told her. It was something I'd deal with later. It came from the Dark Lord, which meant there had to be some sort of catch.

The one that came to mind when I looked at Lucille is that Lord Nâtlac had not specified what *kind* of male form I'd be wearing.

"Who's it from?"

"Ah—" I was interrupted by the sound of trumpets announcing the start of the official ceremony.

"Oh, I need to get down into the courtyard."

"Yeah."

She turned her head away, then she turned back, **"If I haven't said so recently, thank you for going through this for me."**

"You're welcome," I told her. I watched her fly off the battlements.

"What else would I do?" I whispered to myself. I walked over to the table by the bed and placed my hand on Lord Nâtlac's wooden box.

What else?

Another knock came on my chamber door and I paused for a few moments as I glanced up at a mirror in the corner of the room. It wasn't Frank Blackthorne looking back. Instead I saw an attractive young woman, hair done in elaborate braids, poured into a white dress of silk and lace that did its best to emphasize the femaleness of the body inside. My hand clutched into a fist on top of the box.

I straightened up and looked the princess in the eyes.

"I'm doing this for you," I whispered.

The knock repeated and I strode out of the princess's chambers to go marry a dragon.